WOLFEAX

A Medieval Romance

By Kathryn Le Veque

Part of the de Wolfe Pack Generations Series

KATHRYN LE VEQUE
NOVELS

De Wolfe Motto: *Fortis in arduis*

Strength in times of trouble

Magnus de Wolfe, who takes after his Viking forefathers, has his story told in a unique and powerful way.

The story of a love nearly lost… but for an angel.

Paternal grandson of England's greatest knight, son of the man known as "Nighthawk," and grandson on his mother's side of a Norse king, Magnus de Wolfe has the blood of elite and royal warriors flowing through his veins. With older brothers who are much accomplished, Magnus needs his time to shine.

But his moment in the sun could potentially burn him.

Delaina de Courant is a courtesan. That's putting it kindly. A beautiful, intelligent, and accomplished woman, and that beauty was noticed by a nobleman when she was young and he took her as his mistress. Through the nobleman, she was educated and taught the finest skills and manners, so the result is the most sought-after courtesan in all of England. Delaina is very selective on the men she keeps, and she is wealthier than God himself because of the gifts of monetary tribute given to her by hopeful suitors.

Until Magnus comes along.

When the chaste knight from a powerful, noble family falls for a woman his parents would not approve of, Magnus finds himself caught in a maelstrom of emotion—duty versus his heart. His family's reputation against Delaina's known profession. It's a horrific battle until Delaina realizes that the love she's always wanted—and the knight she's always hoped for—is simply out of her grasp.

Or is it?

Help—and redemption—come from an unexpected source in this turbulent de Wolfe Pack Generations novel.

AUTHOR'S NOTE

Welcome to Magnus' story!

This is going to be a VERY unique tale—unlike most others I've told—so settle down for a sweet and poignant story.

WolfeAx centers on Magnus de Wolfe, Patrick de Wolfe's (*Nighthawk*) third son. *WolfeAx* is part of the de Wolfe Pack Generations series, which is a series about the grandsons of William de Wolfe (the Wolfe). Magnus' older brothers, Markus and Cassius, already have their stories told in *WolfeHeart* and *WolfeSword*, respectively.

Now, it's Magnus' turn.

In the epilogue of *WolfeSword*, we are told that his brother, Magnus, becomes lord protector once Cassius marries. Cassius became the Duke of Doncaster through his heiress wife, Dacia. I will point out that there were no dukes in England until the fourteenth century, when Edward III created the Duke of Cornwall in 1337. Being well aware of that, I used creative license to give Cassius a dukedom about twenty-five years earlier. The title of marquess, interestingly enough, wasn't created until later in the century by Richard II, so both titles came into being during the fourteenth century.

Back to Magnus. Now, he's a fully fledged knight in his own right as Edward II's lord commander. Leave it to a de Wolfe to have a prestigious title. In *WolfeHeart*, it is mentioned that not even the taller de Wolfe brothers would "mess" with Magnus because of how powerful and deadly he was, so we know that Magnus is one of those men that even the most skilled knights don't want to go up against.

I've got another "bird crumb" for you in this book—a de Winter has made his way into the de Wolfe bunch. Denys de Winter, the third son of Davyss and Deveraux de Winter (*Lespada*), now serves with Magnus. If you've read the de Winter series, then you know that the House of de Winter always serves the Crown. Without fail, they are the strong arm of the kings of England (no matter who sits on the throne), and Denys has been elevated to a secondary lead in this novel. Davyss is the Earl of Thetford these days—very cool, since the de Winters have been more military servants than peers in other books.

Now, this book has Edward II as a secondary character. There are many references to his father, Edward I, but he is referred to as "Longshanks," his nickname, so we can differentiate the two in conversation. I don't usually use nicknames like "Longshanks" or "Lionheart," or whatever, because unless they were referred to by that nickname by their contemporaries, I don't use it. In Edward I's case, however, to differentiate him from aaaall of the Edwards, I did so.

Something interesting to note: the city of London, all the way back to the twelfth century, had two elected sheriffs every year. According to a charter from Henry I, the liverymen of London elected two sheriffs every year to keep the peace. In this novel, the sheriff mentioned was actually one of the two for the year in which the novel is set. Liverymen, if you're wondering, were basically businessmen, forming trade guilds in the city.

Lastly, you're going to see Titus de Wolfe, the youngest son of Patrick and Bridey, and Magnus' younger brother, in this tale. Titus had a nice role in *WolfeShield* (Ronan de Wolfe's story), and he makes another appearance in this book. Titus will have his own tale told in *WolfeBorn,* slated for a 2024 release.

The usual pronunciation guide:

Denys—Dennis (just an alternate spelling)
Delaina—De-LANE-uh

And with that, you're off to the adventure of Magnus and Delaina. Keep an open mind—as you must with my novels—because anything can happen. And it usually does!

Hugs and Happy Reading!

DE WOLFE PACK GENERATIONS

The grandsons of William de Wolfe are referred to as "the de Wolfe Cubs." There are more than forty of them, both biological and adopted, and each young man is sworn to his powerful and rich legacy. When each grandson comes of age and is knighted, he tattoos the de Wolfe standard onto some part of his body. It is a rite of passage, and it is that mark that links these young men together more than blood.

More than brotherhood.

It is the de Wolfe birthright.

The de Wolfe Pack standard is meant to be worn with honor, with pride, and with resilience, for there is no more recognizable standard in Medieval England. To shame the Pack is to have the tattoo removed, never to be regained.

This is their world.

Welcome to the Cub Generation.

PROLOGUE

Year of Our Lord 1354
Raechester Castle, Northumberland

"A ND YOU DO not wish for my grandson to marry her because—*why?*"

"Because her sister… The woman has a reputation, Papa. And that is all I'll say about it."

The fire in the hearth snapped softly in the dim chamber. It was late on a winter's eve, and there was a thin layer of frost on the ground as the soldiers on the wall walk, bundled up against the chill, kept vigilant for the night. They could hear the men calling to one another, echoing through the torch-lit bailey of Raechester Castle, ensuring the safety of the castle.

But inside the solar, there was an air of uncertainty.

Magnus knew that. He could feel it. Gazing at his eldest son, his pride and his joy, he could hear the disdain in Padraig's voice when he spoke of the woman his son and heir wanted to marry. Valerian de Wolfe, or Val as he was known to the family, took after his Northmen forefathers in that he was enormous and blond. He looked as if he'd just stepped off a longship. His great-grandfather, Magnus Haakonsson, had been King of the Northmen about one hundred years ago, and Val's grandfather, Magnus de Wolfe, was named for him.

Powerful blood ran through the de Wolfe lines.

But so did powerful tempers.

Magnus' gaze shifted to Val, and he could see the rage rolling in the young man's eyes. He was in love and very much wished to marry the daughter of a local lord who evidently had a sister with a less-than-desirable reputation, and his father had issue with it.

Magnus had to be the peacemaker.

"It is the de Wallington family, is it not?" he asked evenly.

Padraig nodded. "It is," he said. "A good family for the most part, but every family has their oddities."

"You mean the sister."

"I do."

"What is so odd about her?"

Before Padraig could answer, Val spoke. "Last year, she fell in love with a de Gare knight who was passing north," he said, frustration in his tone. "The knight made it easy for her. He told her what she wanted to hear, if you get my meaning."

"Charmed her, did he?" Magnus asked.

Val nodded. "He was the flame and she was the moth," he said. "But you must remember that Edmund de Wallington keeps his daughters so confined that they are practically cloistered. Rosemary was so sheltered that when the knight showed her attention…"

"She fell for him."

Val nodded again, sighing sharply. "I have known Phoebe de Wallington for a few years, and she is a good and kind lass," he said. "She is not the fool her sister is."

"And Phoebe is who you wish to marry?"

Val's angry eyes took on a flicker of desperation. "Aye, Amag," he said softly, calling Magnus by the name that all his grandchildren called him—*Amag*. Something Val himself had come up with as a toddler because the name Magnus was too challenging. "She is my everything. She has been for six months. Papa seems to think that I am somehow sullying myself by wanting to marry her, but that is simply not the case. It is not fair that he should think so."

Magnus could hear the strains of longing in his grandson's voice, and he turned to his son, who was standing rigidly. He was a big man, with the de Wolfe dark hair in strong contrast to his son's fairness. But they looked alike for the most part, and they certainly acted alike. They were both stubborn and strong-willed.

Therein lay the problem.

"Paddy," he said softly. "May I ask you a question?"

Padraig looked at his father, perhaps already realizing he was about to be defeated in this situation and was unhappy for it.

"What it is?" he asked.

Paddy. Padraig was named for Magnus' father, Patrick de Wolfe, a man that the family had called Atty. It had been a childhood nickname that Patrick, a small boy with a speech impediment, had given himself. He'd outgrown the impediment but not the name. Every time Magnus looked at Padraig, he saw his father. He saw the man's strength and wisdom. At least, usually there was wisdom.

But tonight, Padraig was having a difficult time drawing on that.

"Do you recall when you meet Amelie?" Magnus asked.

He was referring to Padraig's wife, and the man nodded stiffly. "Of course I do," he said. "Why?"

Magnus cocked a knowing eyebrow. "You knew when you met her that her grandfather was a pirate," he said. "He had been known to engage in some fairly brutal tactics. He robbed, he burned, he killed. Do you recall?"

Padraig sighed and looked away. "That is different."

Magnus cast him a long look. "Is it?" he said. "Aidric de Berck scoured the coast from the Hague to the Friesian Islands looting, and God only knows what else, well into your marriage to his granddaughter. Half of the wealth in your coffers is because he gave it to you. Ill-gotten gains, I might add."

Padraig still wouldn't look at him. "What do you want me to say to that?"

Magnus pointed to Val. "That your son is the grandson of a pirate," he said. "The point is that you cannot choose which offenses to tolerate and which to reject when it comes to a family's character. No family is perfect."

"The de Wolfe family is."

Magnus looked at his son in disbelief. "You are mad if you think so," he said. "Paddy, I realize you want the best for your son, but you have already had your chance to arrange a marriage that would provide him with a prestigious bride, and you couldn't find one that you approved of. No one met your standards. Now, he's chosen his own bride and he wants to marry for love. You did. Why shouldn't he?"

Padraig sighed again, this time with great annoyance. "Piracy is different," he said, though he knew it was a futile argument. "The de Wolfe family is different. Our family was built on war and blood, but it is the way of the world. It is more acceptable than the sister of a woman who gave herself over to another man without the benefit of marriage."

"Now you choose to categorize what sins are more egregious than others?"

Padraig rolled his eyes. "While Phoebe is a sweet and obedient girl, her sister has ruined the reputation of all the girls in the family by allowing the de Gare knight to seduce her."

"She is not the only woman who has ever been seduced."

"She bore the man's child!"

"And that makes her a terrible person?"

"It makes her a whore."

Val flinched in his father's direction, but Magnus threw out an arm, stopping whatever Val was planning. Magnus wasn't sure what he had in mind, but he didn't like it. He pointed a finger at his grandson.

"Lift a hand to your father in anger and face my wrath," he growled. "Do you understand me, Val?"

Val's jaw was twitching furiously as he glared at his father. "I will not allow him to speak so about Phoebe's sister," he said. "It was *not* her fault. She was seduced by a bastard who knew exactly what he was doing. She was powerless against him, and I'll not have my father saying otherwise."

Magnus let his gaze linger on his hotheaded grandson for a moment before turning to Padraig. He could see that his son was regretful of having spoken before he could stop himself, but an apology was out of the question. Padraig never apologized for anything.

But he'd mentioned a very interesting point.

She allowed the de Gare knight to seduce her.

Magnus debated how to proceed at that point. He debated about how involved he should become in this argument between father and son, but unless he wanted Val to physically attack his father, perhaps he needed to become more involved than he already was. Perhaps he needed to explain his perspective on the subject of a man seducing a woman in a little more depth. For certain, he had more to say on the subject.

Personal experience, as it were.

Long ago, he'd experienced something that he swore he'd never tell his children. His wife knew because she had been directly involved, but the story of their courtship had been one of half-truths and generalized answers, at least to their children and grandchildren. All anyone knew was that Magnus had met Delaina when he was serving the king. Delaina had been a courtier and Magnus had been the king's very own captain of the guard.

But that wasn't exactly the truth.

It was part of it, anyway.

Now, Magnus could see that he was going to have to elaborate on something he swore he never would. He and Delaina had a pact about that, facts they kept buried. Magnus' father had known, as had his brothers and even his grandmother, but that was where it ended. His children never knew, but there was a reason for that. The honorable third son of the Earl of Berwick, a man known as the Ax in his younger years, had a hell of a past.

And so did his wife.

But perhaps it was time his son, and grandson, knew about it.

"Sit down, both of you," he said after a moment. "Val, you will sit out of arm's length from your father. If I see your hands wrapping around his throat, I will cut them off, so it is better if you are not tempted."

Val eyed his grandfather but wouldn't test him. Magnus

would very much do what he said he was going to do.

"As you wish," Val muttered. "I have no desire to have stumps where my hands used to be."

"That is wise."

"But I also do not feel like sitting down."

"Sit down or I will cut your legs off."

Val sat.

Magnus cast his grandson a long look before turning his attention to Padraig, who had yet to sit. But when Padraig saw his father looking at him, he found the nearest chair. He didn't want his legs cut off, either.

"That's better," Magnus said once Padraig settled down. "Now, I am going to tell you a story because I believe it is important to you both, as it relates to this situation. You will each glean something different from it, so do not interrupt me. Let me talk because I am an old man and have nothing to lose should you anger me by being rude. Is this clear?"

Val and Padraig nodded. Magnus sat back in his chair and collected a small cup of wine he'd been nursing, only half-full. His wife wouldn't let him have much wine these days because it upset his belly, so he savored the cups he was permitted to consume. Wrapping his big hands around it, he sat back in the chair.

"Now," he said. "This is about your mother, Padraig."

"What about my mother?"

"Shut up and I shall tell you."

Padraig didn't say another word as Magnus took a sip of his wine, his mind going back many years to the days of his youth. The cobwebs of time blew away gently as he envisioned the time in his life when he was young and strong and in a position of great power. Those were the days that brought him great comfort.

They were also the days when he first met his wife.

Indeed, it was time to tell the tale.

CHAPTER ONE

Year of Our Lord 1310
The Month of September
Westminster Palace, London

THE EVENING WAS full of wine, women, and song.

Not that he was able to participate in any of it. For certain, the captain of the king's guard didn't participate in the usual festivities. Those were reserved for the king's allies, and even enemies who pretended to be allies, and the king allowed it because he needed their wealth. Or armies or social position, or any number of advantages from the young king's perspective.

Edward II was now in control.

He had been for six years. Six years of the reign of Piers Gaveston, for the most part, under the guise of counselor of the king. A counselor that Edward's father had hated so much that he'd exiled the man, but once Edward I was dead, Piers had returned with great fanfare and many promises to the warlords of England.

Promises that were never kept.

But something major had happened. Parliament had convened several months earlier and, under much pressure from the warlords of England, the king had been forced to accept many new rules and ordinances that essentially limited his power. Promises made could now never be broken. Gaveston was once again banished and England, hopefully, was beginning to settle down after the turmoil of Gaveston and wars with Scotland.

Wars and turmoil that the captain of the guard had personally participated in.

Truth be told, he was looking forward to a little peace.

And this night was the start of it, or so he hoped.

As a gesture of goodwill toward the warlords who had essentially bullied him into accepting their ordinances, the king threw a lavish feast at Westminster Palace. The structure, newly renovated in light of the new king's coronation a few years earlier, was blazing with light and music and the heady smells of the dozens of roasted animals that Edward had ordered. Beef, mutton, pheasant, peacock, pork, and more filled the tables. The king wanted to show there were no hard feelings for being strong-armed into agreement.

But the captain of the guard knew differently.

Sir Magnus de Wolfe was that captain. He'd been with the king since the days of his father, Edward I, when he came to London with his brother, Cassius, who had been Edward's lord protector. But Cassius married and became the Duke of Doncaster, no longer a simple knight but now a peer. It had been Magnus who had taken over Cassius' position as lord protector, but when the king died and his son, Edward II, came to power, the new king decided he no longer needed a personal bodyguard, and Magnus was given the responsibility of managing the entire royal knight corps.

These days, he was lord commander.

To tell the truth, he didn't mind. He liked being in command of an elite group of knights and not simply a king's minder. That was really what the position as lord protector boiled down to—protecting the king in all situations, sometimes even from himself, and being focused only on one man.

Magnus wasn't cut out for something like that in the long term.

Lord commander was much more his style. He led armies into battle, fought enemies with an ax his Norse grandfather had given him, arranged protection for the king's movements, and the like. As the son and grandson of an earl on his father's side and the grandson of the King of the Northmen on his mother's side, his bloodlines were far more elite than most. *WolfeAx*, he was referred to in military circles. But as a de Wolfe knight, he was a legend, from a legendary family that had been instrumental in forging England as a country since the days of the Duke of Normandy.

It was this legendary knight who watched groups of lords and ladies head into the great hall of Westminster. It was a cool night, and the light from within the hall glowed from the big lancet windows, creating a halo of sorts and a beacon for all to flock to. Clad in full regalia befitting the commander of the king's knights, Magnus was moving from post to post, checking on his men and also making sure there were men inside the hall should the need for order arise. When there was a gathering the size of this one, chaos was always waiting to be unleashed.

But not on Magnus' watch.

"This evening ought to prove interesting."

A voice came from the darkness, and Magnus turned to see his second-in-command approaching. Sir Denys de Winter, from the great military family of de Winter, was not only one of the most capable commanders that Magnus had ever seen, he also happened to be Magnus' best friend. He was positively enormous, tall like Magnus' father and brothers, with a shaggy crown of fair hair and big dark eyes. He had a ready laugh and a booming voice, enough to scare the wits from some of the younger knights, and Magnus smiled at his comment.

"I believe that is a great understatement," he said. "Have you been watching the warlords entering the grounds?"

Denys nodded. "I've been on the wall," he said. "I was at the gatehouse when Arundel and Lancaster entered. Who did I miss?"

Magnus shrugged dramatically. "Gloucester, Worcester, Pembroke," he said. "At this point, we are awaiting Warwick. Aye, laddie, the true kings of England have arrived as guests of the man who officially holds the title, and I cannot imagine that this evening is going to be one of great peace and love. It is going to be a power struggle before our very eyes."

"We'll be lucky if there isn't an execution by midnight."

"Exactly."

They looked at each other knowingly, silent words of concern and some amusement passing between them. There were soldiers about, and a few knights at their posts, and they didn't want to start gossiping like women at what may, or may not, occur this evening.

All they knew was that it was going to be a fragile peace.

"Daventry just arrived," Denys commented. "My father should be here soon, also."

Magnus glanced at him. "Thetford is one of the most important warlords in England," he said. "I should think your father has a good deal to say about all of this, considering he was the one who made sure Gaveston took the cog across to Calais."

Denys grinned. "You can stake your life on the fact that he held his sword to the man's back until he boarded that boat," he said. "What about your father? Will he come?"

Magnus shook his head. "Nay," he said. "You know the trouble with the Scots right now. He will not leave Berwick, nor will my uncles leave their castles along the border. I'm afraid this gathering is going to have to get along without the earls of Berwick, Warenton, and Northumbria. They are shoring up the north while the king makes peace with his warlords in the south. But my uncle Edward will be present, though I've not seen him arrive yet."

"What about the mighty Duke of Doncaster?"

Magnus grinned. "My brother, Cassius?" he said. "He refuses to attend due to the fact that his wife should be delivering another child any day now, and he will not leave her. You know those two were sewn together with silk ties on the day they were married. He will not leave her side and she will not leave his. It is appalling, truthfully."

Denys snorted. "I have a pair of brothers who are the same way with their wives."

"Drake and Devon?"

Denys rolled his eyes. "Those two make me sick," he said. "They're so disgustingly sweet with their wives that I feel as if I need to bathe every time I'm around them simply to wash off the cloying stickiness that covers them like a spider's web. It bleeds all over me, and I hate it. Love turns a man into a fool, Magnus."

"You think so, do you?"

"And you do not?"

A shout came from the direction of the gatehouse, interrupting their conversation, and they turned to see a small party entering with an escort of torch-wielding soldiers. With all of the light emanating from the hall, it was a simple thing to see the radiant red and gold standards.

"There's Daventry," Denys said. "I'm surprised to see him tonight."

"Why?"

"Because I cannot believe that old boar is still alive. Shouldn't he be dead already?"

Magnus struggled not to laugh. "Sir Simon de Staverton is a well-respected and extremely wealthy man," he said. "But I will admit he is as old as dirt and does, in fact, resemble a boar."

"True."

"He's one of the only warlords with any common sense, so let us hope he does not die anytime soon."

Denys could see the party drawing closer to the hall entry. "I hear he has a reason to stay alive these days."

Magnus looked at him. "What reason?"

Denys lifted his blond eyebrows. "He has the Ruby."

Magnus frowned. "What Ruby?"

"*The* Ruby," Denys repeated, but realized Magnus didn't understand what he was telling him. "The Ruby that once belonged to Bristol. Before Bristol, it was Lord Falmouth. Before Falmouth, rumor has it that none other than Longshanks had the Ruby. That most beautiful of jewels, Magnus, the one that everyone wants and the one that is sold from earl to earl, to the highest bidder. *That* Ruby."

Now, Magnus understood. "Ah," he said. "Aye, *that* Ruby. She's with Daventry now?"

Denys nodded. "So I've heard," he said. "Truthfully, I've

never actually seen her. The lords who have kept her have been very greedy about not sharing her with the world. I heard that Falmouth actually locked her up in a chamber that was lined with silk on the walls and had a golden bed."

Magnus thought on the woman everyone called the Ruby, so spectacular in beauty, poise, and grace that the great lords of England passed her between them. A woman that beautiful wasn't meant for only one man, they said, and she was part of a group called the Seven Jewels of London—courtesans of the highest order, the most beautiful and coveted women in the inner circles of England's nobility. There was a Diamond, a Ruby, a Pearl, an Emerald, a Sapphire, an Amethyst, and a Garnet, all named for precious gems. They were women who had kept company with kings and princes, so cultured and educated that even the wives of those men who kept them did not oppose their presence. But, like most jewels, they were protected and kept from public view.

Such beauty wasn't meant for the masses.

"I have not seen any of them," Magnus admitted. "Although my brother, Cassius, saw the Ruby when she was with Longshanks."

"Oh?" Denys was interested. "What did he say about her?"

Magnus shrugged. "Beauty beyond compare, but very young," he said. "I seem to remember hearing him say that someone gave her over to the king in payment for a debt of some kind. She was supposed to be a hostage, but he took her as his mistress. He gave her over to Margit Barkwith for training."

Denys' features registered surprise. "I had not heard that," he said. "You mean the woman that owns the…?"

"The stew over on Farnham Street in Southwark, aye," Magnus finished for him, using the common term for a brothel in "stew." "I've heard that Margit has trained all of the Jewels in courtly manners and techniques for the bedchamber. Enough to please kings, anyway."

That gave Denys something new to think over as he turned to watch Daventry's party draw closer to the gaily lit hall. "Mayhap not enough," he said. "Longshanks sent her to Falmouth."

Magnus shook his head. "The man had little time for a woman like that," he said. "Or mayhap his wife made him send her away. In any case, let us put aside talk like that, because we sound like a pair of fishwives. I shall head over to the hall and make sure nothing untoward is happening. In fact, gather a dozen of the other knights and join me. The king is due to arrive momentarily, and a heavy presence of royal knights might be enough to deter any of the warlords from becoming too aggressive."

Nodding smartly, Denys headed off into the night to find the requested men while Magnus headed for the enormous hall in the distance. Truly, it was a lovely sight on a night like this, but sights could be deceiving. Not that he was a man of superstition, but something told him to be on his guard tonight.

It was just a hunch he had.

CHAPTER TWO

S HE DIDN'T USUALLY get invited out.

Like a bird in a gilded cage, Lady Delaina de Courant was, under normal circumstances, kept away from the light and life that was part of England's social whirl. But the very kind Lord Daventry had insisted she attend the king's grand feast at Westminster and had even commissioned a gown for her for this very event. It was a gown of layers of sheer white fabric, called gossamer, with gold embroidery through it. Quite literally, she looked like an ethereal shower of gold when she walked. Everything glistened.

But she was nervous. She wasn't used to being around crowds of people like this. At most, she entertained in the hall of the lord she happened to belong to at any given time, and she was very good at entertaining men in general, but women… that was where she had issue.

Or, more correctly, they had issue with her.

But Lord Daventry didn't seem to think any of it was an issue. He sat next to her in the fine carriage his family had commissioned forty years ago, made from iron and silk, painted the gold and red of Daventry's standards. He'd been talking a blue streak on the entire journey from his town home of Haydon Square. The man was full of life, happy to be out and about, thrilled at the prospect of attending a kingly feast.

Delaina had listened without speaking the entire way.

But that was usual with this relationship. She'd been with Lord Daventry for several months now, and it had been one of her better positions because she wasn't expected to do anything other than listen and look pretty. There was no affection involved, no duties that relegated her to the bedchamber. She was something lovely to behold, a comfort to both sight and spirit, and that was all Lord Daventry expected of her—although he did like his feet rubbed, and she'd done that a few times. Nothing sexual about it. It was simply because he was a round, old man with swollen feet.

Still, it was better than some of the positions she'd held.

And far more lucrative.

The life of a courtesan was a luxurious one, but not always easy. She was chattel, and she had long accepted that. She didn't mind being property as long as she was kindly treated, and she'd been fortunate, for the men she'd belonged to had all treated her well. They'd given her money and jewels, horses and finery. Daventry had even given her a home of her very own, a smaller manse at one of the many bends of the Thames, called Swan's Landing.

But she'd only been there twice. Lord Daventry liked to keep her close.

As the old man prattled on, she'd dreamed of that house. It was of waddle and daub construction, but it had a big brick façade with dark beams running through it. It was three stories, with the second and third stories built wider than the first floor. The big chamber on the second level took up half of the floor, with enormous windows that overlooked the river. The whole house was spartanly decorated, but Lord Daventry assured her that she could spend whatever she wanted to in order to make it to her liking. She tried not to have big plans about it because plans could change, but it was delightful dreaming about it.

The carriage passed through the streets of London, arriving at Westminster to great fanfare. Torches and servants lined the drive, finely clad men in silk hose approaching the carriage as it came to a halt. Lord Daventry exited first, resplendent in his green brocade tunic with gold tassels, followed by Delaina in her white gossamer gown.

All anyone could do was stare at her.

It was uncomfortable. Having been kept so closely and very nearly isolated for so long, being in the open with dozens upon dozens of people looking at her was unsettling.

Delaina took Lord Daventry's arm when he extended it to her, gathering her skirt a little so it wouldn't drag in the dust. Behind her, her lady's maid, who had followed in another carriage along with Lord Daventry's knight and personal attendant, fell in behind her. Delaina didn't like having a lady's maid, but Lord Daventry had insisted, so the severe-looking woman with the hawklike nose followed primly.

"Sir Simon!" another lord called to him, lifting his hand in greeting. "How good to see you again!"

Lord Daventry could see the man several yards ahead, dressed in fine leather and silk, with a rather large retinue following him. He lifted a swollen, reddish hand in response.

"Lavenham," he called. "My dear lad, I have missed you. You are here tonight, also?"

Jonathan de Lambert, Lord Lavenham, broke away from the herd of retainers following him and rushed to Lord Daventry, taking the man's hand in greeting. For a moment, they simply beamed at one another.

"My dearest fellow," Lavenham said, still holding his hand. "How long has it been?"

Lord Daventry grinned. "Months," he said. "Years. Centuries. Who can count? All I know is that it has been a very long time, and I am delighted to see you again."

"As I am delighted to see you, my old friend," Lavenham said. But Delaina was on Lord Daventry's arm, and his gaze inevitably drifted to her. "And you have brought… someone quite beautiful with you. My lady, it is an honor."

Lord Daventry gestured to Delaina. "It is for you, indeed," he said. "This goddess is Lady Delaina de Courant. A more spectacular beauty you will never see. Go ahead and worship her, but only from afar. She belongs to me, and I do not share."

Lavenham reached out and took Delaina's free hand, giving it a genteel kiss. "My lady," he said. "He is absolutely correct. You are a goddess. We are in awe of your company this night."

Delaina forced a smile. "You are too kind, my lord," she said. "The honor is mine."

She had a smooth, lower-pitched voice that flowed like liquid silk. It did something to a man's ears, like the song of a siren.

Lavenham lifted an eyebrow. "De Courant?" he repeated. "I've heard the name. Where are you from?"

"Cornwall, my lord."

Lavenham cocked his head curiously as he thought a moment. "Is your father Callum?"

"Aye, my lord."

Lavenham's eyes lit up. "I know your father," he said. "He fought in Longshank's armies, did he not?"

Delaina nodded. "He did, my lord."

"How is the man?"

"Dead, I'm afraid."

The excited look faded from Lavenham's features. "I see," he said. "I am very sorry. When did this happen?"

"Five years ago, my lord."

Before Lavenham could reply, Lord Daventry held up a hand in a silencing gesture. "Come now," he said, pushing past his old friend. "An entire feast is waiting for us, and we are wasting time here. Let us move into the hall and claim our seats. You may ask all the questions you wish once I am comfortable and with a drink in my hand."

Delaina was pulled along as Lord Daventry began to walk. He was a big man, so people naturally stood back as he moved. Lavenham's attention was on Delaina, however. He'd just experienced something that nearly every man who met her experienced—once the voice hypnotized, her appearance locked in a man's attention. It was a combination of attributes that could hold a man's focus like nothing else.

Bewitching was the appropriate term.

And Lavenham was bewitched. He gathered his horde of followers and pursued Lord Daventry and the goddess into the great hall, where a wide world of pageantry, food, and wine opened up before them. The world of England's king and his wealth was on full display.

But so was the wealth of his warlords.

It was no secret that the king coveted the wealth of the men who both supported and opposed him, men who stood in the way of absolute rule. They wore their golden-hilted swords and daggers, with gold medallions hanging from their belts, and any number of jewels in strategic places. The wives were even more lavish, displaying their rubies and sapphires in gaudy fashion.

Delaina had seen it all. She'd attended functions like this before, though they were a rarity, and she knew that these events were essentially beasts on parade.

As Lord Daventry led her into the vast hall that smelled of roasting meat, smoke, and perfume, she restrained herself from looking about too much because she didn't want to come across as if she was gawking. Which she was. But she didn't want anyone to think that she was. More than that, a position like hers wasn't… secretive. Gossip was the blood in the veins of most English nobility, so she was fairly certain that some of them knew who she was.

"Sit here, my dear," Lord Daventry said, showing her to a cushioned seat at a long feasting table. "Sit and be comfortable. *Drink!*"

He bellowed for wine so loudly that Delaina winced because he'd hurt her ears. Finely clad servants rushed to do his bidding, bringing cups known as *mazers*. These were specific drinking vessels with no handles, no knobs, made from polished wood with a metal band around the lip. They were expensive to produce because each one was labor-intensive, but it was another example of the king's wealth because every guest had a mazer. Delaina had one with a silver band around the top, giving the wine a slightly metallic taste when she drank.

But it was delicious.

"There you are!" Lavenham suddenly appeared across the table, taking a seat and collecting his own cup of wine. "I thought I had lost you in the crowds of people. God's Bones, I do not think I've ever seen so many warlords in one place. If someone were to burn this building down, they would destroy most of the great lords in England. Ha! If I had known this, I'd have sold the information to the French!"

He was jesting. Sort of. Lavenham's loyalty had been based on his financial situation at times.

As he laughed at his own joke, Delaina found herself looking at a lovely woman several chairs down. She was wearing a dark blue silk gown and had a caul on her head, essentially a silk skull cap, that was sewn with tiny pearls. It was quite lovely, and as Delaina admired it, the woman caught her stare and turned her nose up at her.

That told Delaina all she needed to know.

But she was used to it.

"Careful with your treasonous talk, Lavenham," Lord Daventry responded to his friend's comment. "If someone hears you and does not know better, you will find yourself in the Tower of London."

Lavenham waved him off. "There is no sense of humor in the upper echelons of the English nobility," he said, looking around the crowded hall. "But, I will admit, they are a handsome bunch to behold. Speaking of handsome, I am missing your wife. How is Lady Daventry?"

Lord Daventry wasn't quite sure how he felt about the question, given his mistress was sitting right next to him. "At home in Norton," he said steadily "How is Lady Lavenham?"

"The same. Cold and irrational."

"Then I am sorry for you," Lord Daventry said, but he didn't mean it. He set his cup down and turned to Delaina. "My dear, shall we take a turn about the room and see my old friends?"

Delaina smiled at the old man and began to stand up, but Lavenham stopped them. "I am sorry," he said. "I did not mean to offend with my question about... Well, with my question.

Please do not leave on my account."

Lord Daventry eyed him, having reached his fill of Lavenham's tactless behavior. He hadn't seen the man in so long that he'd forgotten what a buffoon he could be. "Then mayhap you should take a turn about the hall and see your old friends," he said. "Surely you do not wish to speak to me for the entire evening."

Lavenham smiled and lifted his cup. "The evening is young," he said. "Shall we speak of how you have been since we last met? I seem to remember hearing you had been ill."

With a sigh, Lord Daventry planted his bulk back in his chair. "It was nothing," he said. "Indigestion only."

"I am sorry to hear that. Are you still feeling poorly?"

"On occasion," Lord Daventry said. Then he turned to Delaina and leaned into her. "I will chase him away, my dear. Be patient."

Delaina forced a smile. "Not to worry, my lord," she said. "Speak to him as long as you wish. Surely you do not want to spend all of your time conversing with me."

"And why not?"

"Because we converse all the time."

He grinned, flashing dingy teeth. "But I like speaking to you," he said. "You are gentle and intelligent. You are a most congenial companion."

Delaina smiled modestly. "You are kind, my lord."

"Are you going to keep her all to yourself?" Lavenham called across the table, interrupting their quiet conversation. "I, too, would like to speak to this glorious creature. I had no idea Jerome de Courant even had a daughter. I am very sorry to hear of his passing, my lady."

Lord Daventry sighed heavily at the intrusion, turning to

look at him. "You are touching on a difficult subject, lad," he said. "She does not wish to speak on her father."

That wasn't exactly true. Delaina had no love for a father who sold her off in exchange for a debt and started this life she led. But she knew that Lord Daventry was trying to get rid of a man who couldn't take a hint, so she didn't say a word while Lavenham appeared contrite.

"My apologies," he said. It was finally beginning to occur to him that he wasn't wanted, so he drained his cup and slammed it back to the tabletop as he stood up. "I think that I will find some old friends to speak with. Farewell, my friends."

With that, he slipped away, and his entourage, who had been back against the wall, flitted after him. As he vanished into the smoky, crowded hall, Lord Daventry shook his head.

"I thought he would never get the hint," he said. "He is a nice man, but he runs off at the mouth."

A smile played on Delaina's lips. "But he is a valuable ally."

"He is."

"Does he have a big army?"

Lord Daventry lifted his eyebrows in resignation. "Big? Aye," he said. "Big and well equipped. You would not believe it, but Lavenham is an excellent warrior. He comes from a family of knights."

Delaina nodded with interest just as several royal knights entered the hall through the main doors. They were dressed to the hilt in mail and weapons, their tunics proudly proclaiming their royal link. Her attention was diverted from Lavenham to the group of fairly massive warriors who had just made an appearance, a group of men she'd been familiar with, once.

A long time ago.

She leaned toward Lord Daventry. "The royal knights have

arrived," she said. "The king's appearance must be imminent."

Lord Daventry was in the process of accepting a second cup of wine from a nearby servant. He glanced at the group, knowing who they were, knowing what they were capable of.

Everyone in the room did.

"Indeed," he said after a moment. "They herald his arrival more than trumpets ever could. Do you recognize any of them?"

Delaina was fixated on the heavily armed men. "Nay," she said. "The men I knew those years ago are long gone. Do you know any of them?"

Lord Daventry had commented on Lavenham's prowess as a warrior, but the truth was that Lord Daventry had quite a military background as well. He, too, came from a family of knights and warriors, and the Daventry army was large and well trained. In his youth, Lord Daventry had been an excellent knight and a strong fighter, but that was before age and ill health had slowed him down. Still, he knew the fighting men of England and the powerful houses. He knew the players. He found himself studying the knights who, although they were wearing royal standards, had elements of their houses or families on their bodies.

And he knew some of them on sight.

"Aye," he said after a moment, his gaze lingering on a tall knight with chin-length blond hair. "I've seen them before, most recently at the meeting of Parliament."

"Who are they?"

Lord Daventry was still looking at the knight. He pointed. "That tall man," he said, "is Sir Denys de Winter. His father is Davyss de Winter, the Earl of Thetford. I met Denys many years ago at his father's side, as he was newly knighted then. But, clearly, he has gained much experience if he is in the king's hall. Surely you have heard the name of de Winter, my dear?"

A woman in Delaina's position was usually quite astute about the families of England because of the company she kept. She knew who they were and their histories. The Jewels were always educated on the powerful players in England's hierarchy, so she knew the name and more.

Being a courtesan meant she knew as much, or more, than the man she was with.

"I have," she said. "They command most of Norfolk. The de Winter war machine is well known."

Lord Daventry nodded. "Indeed, they are," he said. "De Winter had four sons, as I recall, but one was killed not long ago. One married the heiress of the earldom of East Anglia and the other commands Norwich Castle. Well-placed family, I must say."

Delaina nodded, watching as a knight with the broadest shoulders she'd ever seen began directing the others to move. "Who is the one in command?" she asked.

Lord Daventry caught sight of who she meant and lifted his eyebrows. "Ah," he said knowingly. "That one. That is a de Wolfe."

She looked at him. "You know him?"

Lord Daventry nodded. "I have seen him," he said. "He is from the most powerful family in Northumberland. That man is the son and grandson of earls. The de Wolfes control most of the border with Scotland. They have more elite knights than any family in England, save just a few. The knight you speak of is Sir Magnus de Wolfe, lord commander of the king's knights."

Delaina nodded in understanding. "A very important man."

"A *very* important man."

Her gaze lingered on the knight with the light brown hair. He'd had his back to her, so she never caught a glimpse of his face, only grasped his sheer size. None of the knights were wearing helms, in fact, even if they were heavily armed, so the lack of a helm was somehow less intimidating to the guests. Given that it was a social situation, they weren't fully dressed.

But that didn't mean they weren't ready to fight.

"Very interesting," she said after a moment. "Do you recognize any others?"

Lord Daventry tried to get a good look at some of the other knights, but they were too far away and his eyesight wasn't what it once was.

"Not at the moment," he said. Then he shifted uncomfortably in his chair before rising unsteadily to his feet. "I will return in a moment, my dear. Please remain here."

Delaina knew where he was going. "Is the pain bad this time?" she asked quietly.

He patted her hand as he stood up and tried to belch. "Nay," he said, fist to his sternum. "I shall use the privy and return swiftly."

Lavenham had touched on something that had been going on with Lord Daventry since Delaina first came to know him. The man suffered from terrible gastric issues, from pain in his gut to terrible bodily function issues to pain and pressure in his chest. He was a big man, having gone to fat long ago, and he ate too much, too often. Delaina was fond of the old man and tried to help him eat more sensibly, but he wouldn't hear of it. The result was the awful gastric problems, which were more or less constant. He was about to rush off to the privy to either force his bowels to vacate or force himself to vomit.

She'd seen it before, many times.

"Shall I go with you?" she asked. "At least allow me to be within earshot should you need help."

He patted her affectionately on the head. "No need," he said. "I will be back before you know it. And if you see Lavenham, hide under the table until he goes away."

She grinned at him as he winked in return. But that smile faded as she watched him walk away, trying to burp the entire time.

He simply wasn't a healthy man.

As Lord Daventry disappeared into the crowd, Delaina's attention returned to the knights who were still lingering just inside the entry, but it was in some manner of formation.

She soon found out why.

Edward II made his way through the hall entry to great fanfare. Men began to cheer for him, or at least some did, and he waved to the crowd as he headed toward the dais at the other end of the hall. But he moved slowly, smiling and lifting his hands, acting as if this adoration was something he always enjoyed.

That was far from the truth.

Everyone was on their feet, and Delaina was forced to rise also. She didn't want to. She didn't like Edward and hadn't since her days with his father, who had been a genuinely kind man to her. But his son had been an odd one—humorous one moment, petulant and spoiled the next. He had been generous to those who served him and enjoyed pastimes that servants might enjoy, much to the displeasure of his father. Delaina might not have had any opinion at all about him, except he didn't like to see her around his father even if the man's wife, Margaret of France, didn't seem to mind.

My father's pet...

My father's concubine...

All things that Edward the son had called her.

But it hadn't been like that at all, her relationship with the king, and she intensely disliked the man who seemed to think she was only good enough to warm his father's bed. Other than speak dismissively of her, he hadn't paid much attention to her, mostly because his father made his displeasure at his son's behavior known.

But there was no father to deter him now.

Therefore, Delaina kept her head down, hoping he didn't look in her direction, hoping that there were so many other people in the hall that she would blend in with the crowd. She could hear the people around her calling to Edward, and she finally dared to glance up to note that he had passed by her table. He had quite an entourage following him, men with swords in addition to the royal knights, who were now heading toward the dais with him. There were other men in fine silks, with pointy-toed shoes and clothing that might have been better suited to a woman.

Knowing the king couldn't see her, Delaina inspected it all.

But eventually, the man did take his seat, along with his retainers, and the feast began in earnest. Almost immediately, gaily dressed servants began to bring out platters of lavishly decorated birds—roasted peacocks, swans, and geese with their feathers returned to the brown flesh to resemble the live bird. The smell of fowl was overwhelming. Everyone was taking their seats at this point, so the table around Delaina began to fill with men and women. Drink was brought forth, along with trenchers, water bowls for washing fingers, and more.

In fact, Delaina was so distracted with the food and other things, including a group of entertainers who had begun to sing and dance, that she failed to notice just how long Lord Daventry had been gone. She had more wine and even boiled fruit juice with rose petals in it presented to her, and across the table, where Lavenham had once sat, a young noble couple sat down, and the woman smiled openly at her. Delaina smiled in return, and soon a conversation was struck up, though it was over the noise of the hall. But Delaina felt rather good that a young woman hadn't snubbed her.

Clearly, she didn't know who she was… yet.

But the woman was quite friendly. Her name was Lillian, and her husband was the son of an earl or baron or something. Delaina couldn't quite hear her.

The food was being served in courses, with the first course being the fowl accompanied by baked egg dishes. Between the food and the conversation, the second course was beginning when Delaina finally became aware that Lord Daventry hadn't returned. He'd told her to stay at the table, but he'd also told her he would return shortly, and he hadn't.

Concern began to clutch at her.

She tried to leave her seat. She tried to leave twice. But both times, Lady Lillian engaged her in conversation, and Delaina ended up sitting down again, until she finally told the woman that her lord was missing and she intended to look for him. Lillian looked at her rather blankly before nodding, and Delaina quickly left her seat, heading in the direction she had seen Lord Daventry go. The man had been in search of the privy, so surely he hadn't gone far.

And then she heard something.

Lavenham was suddenly in her proximity. She could hear his voice. She had no idea what would happen if he caught her without Lord Daventry, so she whirled about, trying to find a place to hide. She hoped that Lord Daventry wouldn't be too angry with her for leaving their table, but she also hoped he would understand her concern when he had not returned promptly.

Those thoughts flitted through her head, along with panic at the sound of Lavenham's voice, as she took aim for one of the pillars in the hall to hide behind. With her beautiful dress shimmering like a shower of gold, she reached the pillar and slipped in behind it, only to run headlong into an enormous, solid body.

Startled, not to mention slightly in pain, she gasped as she stumbled back. Hands—enormous hands—reached out to steady her.

"My lady, my deepest apologies." The low, rumbling voice sounded full of concern. "Did I hurt you?"

She'd hit him with her left arm and hand because she'd been grabbing for the pillar, and her momentum had her left shoulder taking the brunt of their collision. When she blinked and cleared her vision, she found herself looking into eyes of a shockingly pale blue. The face was strong and angular, with a square jaw and prominent cheekbones. The hair on his head was cropped, but not too short, a shade of light brown with a good deal of gold in it. He had it cut in a way that had it standing up a little, feathering back.

She'd never seen such a handsome man in her entire life.

"I… I am not injured, my lord," she said. "It was my fault. I was not looking where I was going."

The blue eyes twinkled with some relief. "Nor was I, my lady," he admitted. "I had my head turned as I rounded the pillar and was not paying attention to what was in front of me. It was utterly my fault."

He still had his hands on her, the biggest hands she'd ever seen. His grip was like iron, but it wasn't uncomfortable or even intimidating. It was simply… strong.

She'd never felt such strength before.

"Mayhap we are both to blame, my lord," she said, looking over her shoulder to see if Lavenham was still in the vicinity. "I will not tell anyone if you will not."

He grinned, flashing big, straight teeth and deep dimples in both cheeks. In fact, something about that grin made Delaina's heart jump in a way she had never experienced before. Her heart was fluttering and pounding to the point where she thought she might actually become ill, yet it wasn't unpleasant.

Quite the contrary.

"I swear upon my oath that I will not tell anyone how clumsy I was, my lady," he said. "As long as you are uninjured, I am satisfied."

She smiled at him, reluctantly, but she simply couldn't help herself. His smile made her feel so very warm and giddy. "Be at ease, my lord," she said. "I am well enough. But I fear I am taking too much of your time, and I, too, must continue onward. I must…"

She stopped abruptly as Lavenham came into her line of sight. She must have looked startled, or frightened, because the enormous man turned to see what had her attention. Lavenham was close, speaking to someone else, and when he suddenly looked up and saw her, his features lit up.

"My lady!" he said happily. "I was hoping to find you. Where is Simon?"

She was clearly uncomfortable as she answered, "He is not with me, my lord."

"Are you alone?"

It was such a leading question, his intent clear by his mere tone. He'd dropped it about an octave, giving her a somewhat lascivious glance as he spoke those three words. As Delaina took a step back and choked on her reply, wanting to discourage him but not wanting to be rude, the massive man at her side put himself between her and Lavenham.

"She is *not* alone, my lord," he growled. "Unless you are blind. You must be, for you clearly did not see me standing here. Move along."

Lavenham looked at the man as if Lucifer himself had just made an appearance. He looked at Delaina, at the man, and then back again before slipping away without another word.

"God's Bones," Delaina said, exhaling heavily. "I did not know what to say to him. Your intervention was most appreciated."

The man turned to her again. "Is he harassing you, my lady?" he asked. "I am more than happy to toss him from the feast if he has been making a nuisance of himself."

Delaina looked at him, surprised at his declaration. She'd been so busy looking into that handsome face that she had completely failed to notice he was wearing the garb of a royal knight. In fact, when he put himself between her and Lavenham, she realized she had seen those shoulders before. Now she recognized him.

It was the man Lord Daventry had called de Wolfe.

"You are Magnus de Wolfe, are you not?" she finally asked.

His smile was back. "You have me at a disadvantage, my lady," he said. "You know my name but I do not know yours."

Oh, but that voice was smooth. Deep and smooth. She could listen to it all day.

"I am Delaina," she said. "And nay, the man you chased

away has not harassed me, but I have been avoiding him."

"Then allow me to escort you back to your seat, Lady Delaina," Magnus said. "I will protect you against feeble lords who smell of wine."

He meant Lavenham, who had imbibed too much drink already, and she giggled softly. "You speak of Lord Lavenham," she said. "I'm told he has a big army."

Magnus grunted. "So he does," he said. "But my army is bigger."

He said it somewhat comically, and she continued giggling. "I have little doubt," she said. "But it is always good to know whom you are insulting."

"Agreed," he said. His gaze lingered on her for a moment before he continued. "I must say that I should very much like to continue this conversation, but I fear that I have duties to attend to. Will you allow me to escort you to your seat?"

Delaina could feel the warmth from his gaze, friendly and curious. God, how she wanted to give in to it, perhaps even encourage it, but there was no way she possibly could.

And that was quite disappointing.

"Nay, but I thank you just the same," she said. "I am searching for my lord because he seems to have gone away and not returned."

"Oh?" Magnus said, looking around. "Who is your lord?"

"Lord Daventry."

"Daventry," Magnus repeated as the light of recognition flickered in his eyes. "Sir Simon de Staverton."

"The same."

"Where did he go?"

"To the privy," Delaina said. "He has not been well and has been gone a long time. I am concerned for his well-being."

"May I offer my assistance?"

There was a good deal of relief for Delaina in that question, because she honestly had no desire to wander the hall or grounds alone. Surely a knight would be trustworthy; at least, she hoped so. She didn't get the sense that he might be preying upon her, so she was willing to take the chance.

Moreover, she needed the help.

"You may, my lord," she said. "Thank you."

Magnus held out an elbow to her, inviting her to take it. "The privy, you said?"

Delaina eyed his arm a moment before slipping her hand into the crook of his elbow. She probably shouldn't have, but she found that she wanted to.

"Aye," she said. "Where is it?"

"I will show you."

He did. Magnus took her toward the entry, possibly noticing that almost every man he passed had to turn and look at Delaina as if they'd never seen anything so glorious before, but he didn't let on. He was focused straight ahead. Truth be told, however, he knew who she was. The moment she mentioned Daventry, he knew. He and Denys had only just been speaking on it.

The Ruby.

Christ, he could see why she was called that. He'd never seen any truth so clearly in his life. She had a sweet, oval face with creamy skin and a slender neck. Her nose was pert, her lips like a rosebud, but her eyes… they had to be seen to be believed. They were a shade of blue that was like the ocean when the water was crystal clear and one could see to the white sand below. He'd seen that kind of color before once, when his father took him south, to Dover. It was a vibrant, pale shade of bluish green. Her long lashes fanned out when she blinked, and her eyebrows arched delicately against her smooth brow.

But her hair was her crowning glory, the first thing one noticed about her. It was a pale shade of red, mixed with gold, and it glistened like liquid fire. Softly spun curls trailed to her buttocks, artfully arranged. Everything about the woman glistened.

She was far too beautiful for mortal men.

But she was a courtesan, a woman kept by men to please them. Had she been chaste and virginal, she would have been the most sought-after woman in all of England, and he found himself wondering why a woman of such glory should be relegated to the life of a concubine. That's exactly what she was. She was paid to please her lord—in this case, Lord Daventry. Magnus could hardly fathom that old, wheezing beast of a man bedding this ethereal creature. It just didn't seem right.

For her, anyway.

Magnus struggled to push thoughts of her from his mind as he took her out into the night, where the grounds of Westminster were still quite crowded even though the king had arrived at the feast. Men stood in groups outside, chatting, as royal soldiers milled about on the grounds and on the walls, although there were so many buildings and apartments at Westminster that the walls didn't necessarily have wall walks. The only places that had that kind of vantage point were the gatehouse and other areas next to the Thames.

Magnus led her away from the parade grounds, heading back toward the gardens and the buildings that ran alongside the river. The privies were back there, with waste running directly into the river. He was so preoccupied with trying not to think about Delaina and her occupation that he didn't realize until they were halfway to the river that he'd been taking enormous strides and she'd been struggling to keep up with him. He abruptly slowed down, looking at her sheepishly.

"My apologies, my lady," he said. "I tend to walk quickly everywhere I go. I swear to you that I was not attempting to make you rush forth with the speed of a newborn colt."

Delaina grinned. "I must admit that I am grateful you have eased your pace," she said, lifting her white gossamer skirt a little higher so it wouldn't drag through the dirt. "I had not planned on running tonight."

"No?"

"I did not bring the correct shoes for it."

He looked at the little foot she stuck out, clad in a delicate slipper of white silk. He nodded in understanding.

"Those will not hold up very well should you intend to do something strenuous," he said. "I will try not to lead a wild pace, I promise."

"You're doing very well now."

"Thank you."

He cast her a sideways glance, but there was a smile playing on his lips. "My pleasure," he said. He paused a moment before continuing. "As I recall, Daventry has a town home in London."

"He does."

"I hear it is an impressive place."

Delaina was concentrating on not dragging her skirt through the dirt, which was becoming muddy as they drew closer to the river. "He has spent a good deal of money on it, to be sure."

"Are you planning on staying in London long?"

"Through winter, I believe," she said. "He does not wish to winter in the country. He would rather be in the city where it does not snow as much. The cold affects his health."

Magnus understood. "Truthfully, I am not fond of the cold myself," he said. "I have often thought to go to more temperate climates like Marseilles or Rome and spend my winters there. It would be glorious to be warm in the wintertime."

She smiled. "I could not agree more," she said. "One year, I traveled to Valencia and spent the winter. It was indeed quite glorious."

"Valencia?" he repeated. "Near Aragon?"

"Aye."

"That was a long journey."

"It was," she said. "But very much worth the time."

He grunted. "I've been as far as Paris," he said. "I do not come from a family of travelers. We are rooted to Northumberland, and that is where we remain, but someday, I should like to see places like Marseilles or Rome or even Valencia. I envy you."

They were nearing the buildings that contained the privy, and Delaina was sorry. She'd very much liked conversing with Magnus, and she was coming to appreciate the fact that he was keeping the conversation from becoming too personal. No questions about where she was born or even why she was so concerned for Lord Daventry. That was the test of a truly noble and tactful man, in her opinion, and she was impressed. In fact, from what she'd seen so far, there was nothing about Magnus de Wolfe that wasn't impressive in general.

They finally reached the building that housed the privy. Just as they came to the door, a drunken man came stumbling out, nearly sprawling in the mud. He'd thrown out a hand to try to grab something on his way down, and that hand had come close to Magnus, who simply batted it away, and down the man went.

But he picked himself up and staggered off as Magnus watched with some disgust.

"'Tis is a bit early in the evening to be so drunk," he muttered. Then he removed Delaina's hand from the crook of his elbow and gently released it. "You will stay here. I'll go inside and see if I can find Lord Daventry. If you feel threatened or if someone approaches you, do not hesitate to scream. I will be at your side faster than you can blink."

Delaina smiled gratefully, and their gazes lingered on one another perhaps more than they should have, until Magnus disappeared inside. He had to, for it wasn't safe nor healthy for him to look at that woman in any way other than polite indifference.

They were at the corner of one of the walls, a tower with three stories to it, and Magnus trudged up the stone steps illuminated by torches every few feet. The privy was on the second floor, this one used only by the men, while the women had a separate, more nicely appointed privy at the opposite tower.

Reaching the second level, he proceeded into the chamber that had the privy, with wooden dividers between the holes where men sat to conduct their bodily business. There were five holes for this purpose, all of them lined up against the wall facing the river, and Magnus checked the first four holes only to find them empty. When he came to the last hole, there was indeed a big body seated upon it. The chamber was illuminated enough that he could see that it was Lord Daventry.

It took him a moment to see that he was also quite dead.

CHAPTER THREE

"H E DIED SITTING upon the shite hole," Magnus said in a low voice. "I've had a few soldiers remove his body and wrap it tightly in canvas, but he must be returned to Haydon Square, and it would be a gesture of goodwill on the part of the king to permit the use of one of his wagons for the transport."

He was speaking to a tall man with receding dark hair and a scar on his lip, but the man was one of Edward's premier advisors. In fact, the young king hardly made a move without advice, or approval, from Hugh Despenser the Elder, and that was why Magnus had come to him.

However, he was a man without a heart or a soul, as often reflected in his dark and mysterious eyes. Magnus didn't like or trust the man, but he was an unfortunate and necessary evil when it came to dealing with the king.

As Magnus reported on the death of a guest at the glorious feast, Despenser showed no compassion. All he could do was grunt unhappily.

"God's bleeding Bones," he muttered. "Daventry, you say?"

Magnus nodded. "He had a hemorrhage of some kind," he

said. "There was a good deal of blood everywhere, so he simply bled out with whatever it was. But I wish to keep this quiet and remove his body so no one at the feast is the wiser. Especially the king."

Hugh nodded firmly. "Agreed," he said. Then he waved a hand. "Get him out of here, de Wolfe. Where is his family?"

Magnus shook his head. "I do not know, my lord," he said. "He came with a companion."

Hugh frowned. "A companion?" he repeated. "A retainer?"

"Nay, my lord."

"Then who?" Hugh asked. "The man has a wife and son and, from what I've heard, a son who is not fond of his father."

Magnus nodded faintly. "I have heard that also."

Hugh continued. "The wife has some kind of disease that has turned her mind to waste," he said. "And I've heard the son has a gambling problem."

"We all have issues in our families, my lord."

Hugh gave him a half-grin. "Except for de Wolfe," he said. "You have no issues that I know of, and you make me sick because of it. How unfair."

He meant it as a jest, and Magnus smiled weakly. "We are power-hungry haters of the Scots, my lord," he said. "Have you not heard that about us?"

That actually made Hugh laugh, and he wasn't the laughing sort. "Thank God for the Crown of England that you are," he said. But his smile, an unnatural gesture, quickly faded. "You did not answer my question. *Who* is his companion?"

"A courtesan, my lord."

"Oh? Do you know her?"

"Delaina de Courant, my lord."

Hugh's eyes widened as he recognized the name. "*Her?*" he

said. "She is with Daventry now?"

"She accompanied him this evening, my lord."

Hugh's dark eyes began to glimmer. "God's Bones," he said, chuckling with delight. "So that is where she went? I had wondered."

"My lord?"

It was a question as to why Hugh should be concerned with something as minor as a courtesan, as if she were actually something important in the grand scheme of things.

Hugh nodded in response. "Surely you know she is one of the Seven Jewels of London," he said. "Those fine, well-educated, and overwhelmingly beautiful courtesans that find their way into the beds and purses of the wealthiest men in England. The Ruby used to be with the king's father, you know."

"I had heard, my lord," Magnus said. He hesitated before continuing. "But she seems terribly young to have been with him several years ago. She would have been a mere child."

Hugh nodded. "That is true," he said. "Have you not heard the story, from your brother Cassius, mayhap?"

"I have not, my lord."

Hugh rubbed his hands together gleefully. "The Seven Jewels of London, they say, were selected by none other than Edward himself," he said. "Before he married the fair Margaret, I mean. After Eleanor's death, he was eager to have more sons, so he began collecting the most beautiful daughters of noblemen that he could find. I suppose not for marriage, but a man can have a few bastards running about to remind him that he is still virile. But Delaina came to Edward in a unique way."

Magnus wasn't one to relish gossip, and Hugh was the king of the court gossips, but in this case, Magnus found himself interested about the magnificent lady he'd just spent time consoling in the wake of her lord's death. His curiosity about her was growing, so against his better judgment, he responded.

"How?" he asked.

Hugh snorted lewdly. "From what I remember, he took her in payment for a debt," he said. "From the Earl of Somersby, I think, but I'm not certain. In any case, the earl owed Longshanks some taxes that he'd tried to steal away from the man, and in payment for those taxes, Edward took Lady Delaina."

Magnus' brow furrowed in confusion. "He bartered with her?"

Hugh nodded. "Or so I have heard," he said. "Bartered and sold. Rumor has it that Edward sent her to Margit Barkwith because he saw the value in such a beautiful woman and wanted her to be… educated. Men pay well for such services, in fact. She's been used for her value more than once."

"What does that mean?"

"In exchange for a debt owed," Hugh said. "You know—if a man needs to pay a debt, he uses what value he has, and Lady Delaina is quite valuable. I've heard she has even been exchanged for property. As I recall, she was the most beautiful of the Jewels, with red hair and blue eyes. At least, she was a beauty when she was younger. Mayhap she is even more of a beauty now. But that brings about an important point… now that Daventry is gone, she has no lord and master. She could be of great use."

Magnus didn't like the sound of that at all. Not that he had any attachment to Delaina, but Hugh was an unscrupulous man, and that didn't sit well with Magnus when it came to a woman he'd just met. It was madness and he knew it, but he could see in Hugh's expression that he wanted to get his hands on one of the Seven Jewels of London.

The one Magnus happened to have met.

"I will see to Daventry's body, my lord," Magnus said, changing the subject because he was feeling unsteady with the way the conversation was going. "I will put de Winter in charge whilst I am seeing to this task."

He started to walk away, heading toward the perimeter of the hall that was full of sweaty, smelly bodies eating and drinking, but Hugh stopped him.

"Wait," he said. "Bring her to me. I would see this Jewel of London. It has been years since I saw the woman. She was a magnificent child then. I can only imagine what she has grown into."

That was an understatement. Magnus didn't have words for what she'd grown in to, but in the same breath, he knew he wasn't going to bring Lady Delaina to Despenser. If the man wanted her, he could find her. Magnus wasn't about to bring that delicate creature into the lion's den.

He didn't even acknowledge the command. He simply turned away and headed back the way he had come. He'd left Lady Delaina with one of his knights, a big, powerful, but painfully shy man with a speech impediment named Loring St. Aldwyn. He trusted Loring with the lady, mostly because he was positively terrified of women and would be disinclined to speak with her. He would simply guard her. And there was no better guard dog than Loring St. Aldwyn.

Even though Magnus skirted the hall to stay away from the festivities in the center of it, he still ran into pockets of men, drunk and fighting or laughing. He managed to move around them, finding his way out into the cool, dark evening. The path from the hall led across a manicured bailey, designed with patches of gardens, and toward the gatehouse where the Daventry carriage and escort was already waiting. Before he'd gone to seek Despenser, he'd ordered a wagon brought forth, and one was already waiting with a canvas-wrapped body atop it.

He went straight to the carriage.

Delaina was sitting there, wrapped in a heavy fur and brocade cloak to match the fine dress she was wearing. She had a hood pulled up over her head, and she'd been staring off into the bailey impassively as he approached. When she caught sight of him, she sat up a little, looking at him rather anxiously.

"Did you inform the king, my lord?" she asked.

Magnus nodded. "I informed Lord Despenser, and he will inform the king," he told her. "Lord Daventry is on the wagon behind the carriage. When you arrive at Haydon Square, are there servants who can bring him inside?"

She sat back against the carriage, and for the first time, Magnus could see defeat in her expression. "Aye, my lord," she said quietly. "There are servants to bring him inside."

"Good," Magnus said. "I am certain the king will wish to know the arrangements for his funeral. May I send word to you tomorrow once you've had time to speak to a priest?"

She looked at him strangely. "Send word if you wish, my lord," she said. "But I will not be there. You may send it in care of Lord Daventry's majordomo, a man named Eustace von Vechta. He will be able to give you any news."

His gaze lingered on her for a moment. "Where are you going?"

Somehow, the formalities seemed to drop in that question. Up until that point, he'd been completely professional with her.

Proper address was observed. But that all changed with that question because it was one of concern. He didn't know why he should be concerned, but he was.

In reply, she smiled thinly. "My lord is dead," she said. "I am no longer welcome in his home, so I will be departing this night."

"And go where?"

She hesitated. "You will forgive me, my lord, but that is not your concern."

She was right. He didn't even know why he asked the question, but something compelled him to. He had a feeling that when she left through the gates, it would be the last time he ever saw her, and that simply didn't sit well with him. More than that, she was without the protection of a man, and any woman without protection, be it a woman like Delaina or a lowly servant, was a vulnerable woman. He would be a poor knight indeed if he let her return to Daventry's home alone, knowing she was simply going to gather her things and depart.

But perhaps he was being a little *too* concerned. Perhaps she knew something he didn't.

"You are correct," he said after a moment. "It is not. But I will ask you one question, and you will do me the courtesy of answering honestly."

"What is it?"

"Are you going alone?"

She looked at him as if confused by the question. "Of course I am going alone," she said. "Lord Daventry is dead. I must go alone."

"Do you have a place to go?"

"I told you that was none of your—"

He cut her off. "I know what you told me," he said. "But if

you are thinking of traveling alone tonight, that is foolish and dangerous. I do not care where you go, but if you have a place to go and an escort, I will not trouble you any further. Do you— and *do* you?"

She was becoming increasingly guarded; he could see it. She was clearly debating what to tell him. Suddenly, she was climbing out of the carriage, with her resplendent cloak, and she motioned to him.

"Will you walk with me for a moment, please?" she asked.

Magnus didn't hesitate. He came alongside her, and they started to walk, off into the manicured bailey where torches burned brightly. There was plenty of light and very few people as she continued to walk.

"Sir Magnus," she said. "Let us not pretend any longer. You must be aware of who I am. Of *what* I am. So there will be no mistake, I will be plain."

So the truth was presented. Magnus admired a woman who would speak so bluntly. She may be petite and fragile-looking, but he suspected there was far more beneath the surface. It was just a feeling he had.

"You are one of the Jewels of London," he said quietly. "Aye, I know who you are."

She came to a halt and faced him. "How did you know?"

"Because it is well known that Daventry had a Jewel in his possession," he said, gazing steadily at her beneath the torch-light. "Men talk, my lady. London itself is a cesspool of rumors and lies. I know you are not Daventry's wife and he does not have a daughter. I am not as stupid as I must look."

"You do not look stupid, I assure you," she said. "But since we are being honest, I will tell you that I must move along tonight. With Daventry dead, there is no reason for me to remain at Haydon Square. In fact… in fact, it is best that I do not."

"Why not?"

"Because it is."

"I thought you were being honest with me."

She frowned. "I am," she said. "But there are things you need not know. They are not your concern. Suffice it to say that I will leave tonight because I must."

She was right: her business wasn't any of his concern, and he was being rather intrusive. He had no idea why. All he knew was that he didn't like the thought of this gorgeous creature fending for herself now that the man who provided for her was gone.

He scratched his head. "Forgive me for being ignorant, my lady," he said. "I do not know what the life of a concu… I mean, a… a companion such as yourself is like. I do not know the protocols involved when your lord passes on. Is there somewhere you must go now?"

A smile played on her lips. "You were correct when you called me a concubine," she said. "The kinder term is courtesan, and if you must know, there is no particular place that I must go, but I must leave Haydon immediately."

"You cannot stay even the night?"

She sighed sharply, sensing that he wasn't going to let up on his questions unless she gave him an answer he could understand. "I could, but I do not wish to," she said. "You see, Lord Daventry has a son who has made it plain that when his father passes on, he wishes to take me as his own… companion."

"And that is undesirable to you?"

"I will slit my own throat and jump into the river before I allow that beast anywhere near me."

Now the situation was beginning to clear up a little for Magnus. "So you want to leave before he receives word of his father's death and comes to claim the man's estate."

"Exactly."

"Where is his son?"

She shook her head. "I am not certain, but the last I heard, he was in London," she said. "So, you see, he is already here, somewhere. And I cannot let him claim me as his father's property."

Magnus thought on that for a moment, rubbing his hands together and cracking his knuckles, something he always did when he was tense or pensive or even bored. It helped him think.

"I understand," he said. "Then you do not have anywhere to go so much as you are simply fleeing for your own sake."

"Aye," she said. "Not knowing where Jerome de Staverton is making me… nervous."

Magnus could see that. "Can you return home, then?" he said. "Surely your parents would readily—"

She cut him off softly. "I have no parents," she said. "Even if I did, I would not return to them. I would not shame them so. Sir Magnus, you must understand that a woman in my position cannot simply go… *home*. I have prepared for this moment, at least as much as I can, and I have decided on a course of action."

"What will that be?"

"I keep telling you that none of this—"

"I know, it is none of my affair," he said. "But I am asking out of concern."

"Why?"

"Because if you did something desperate, I would feel responsible."

She sighed heavily, eyeing him as she debated what to tell him. But she quickly gave up, perhaps suspecting he wouldn't let the subject drop if he felt she might endanger herself.

"Very well," she said impatiently. "If you must know, I intend to join the cloisters."

He frowned. "You would become a nun?"

"I would rather belong to God than to one more man."

That was such a brutal but truthful way of putting it, and he could hardly dispute her. In fact, he felt a good deal of pity for her, an emotion that usually wasn't part of his repertoire. He had compassion when it was suitable, but pity... that was altogether different. He could feel himself slipping into behavior that was unplanned and probably unwelcome.

"My lady," he said quietly. "I cannot pretend to know how it feels to lead the life that you do, but I will tell you this: I have two sisters, young women whom I adore, and I would kill for them without hesitation. I would defend them to my last breath. Part of a knight's oath is to defend the weak, and, at this moment, you seem fairly weak to me. You seem quite alone, and when I look at you, I can imagine my sisters, should they be weak and defenseless, as you are. Because of this, I would like to offer my services. Let me escort you back to Haydon Square, where you may gather your things, and then I will take you anywhere you wish to go for the night so that you may arrive safely. Will you at least allow me to show some chivalry to you?"

Delaina was looking at him in shock. "You want to... to escort me?" she said. "But I am not your responsibility."

"Every woman's safety is a noble knight's responsibility, my lady."

She looked at him as if trying to figure out just how earnest he was. Perhaps he was trying to trick her somehow. But in the end, she simply shook her head.

"You are kind and generous, Sir Magnus," she said, perhaps a hint of sorrow in her tone. "But I will again say that I am not your responsibility. I will do this alone, but I thank you for your offer."

"You do not have to do it alone."

"Oh?" she said. "And how shall I pay you for this gracious offer? If you expect me to warm your bed, I will not do it. You may as well know now."

He took great offense but fought it. "I expect no payment," he said. "Payment was never suggested in any form. I am sorry that you are suspicious, my lady, but I suppose I do not blame you."

Delaina could see that he was insulted, and her firm stance wavered a little. "In my experience, men always want something," she said quietly. "My apologies if your offer was without reciprocation."

"It was and it is."

Her gaze lingered on him for a moment, and he swore he saw her weakening. It was in her expression, in her eyes, but just as quickly, he could see her stiffen. *She is not accustomed to someone who wants nothing from her,* he thought. *She's protecting herself.*

"Come," he said, indicating her carriage several yards away. "Return to Haydon Square with Lord Daventry. Should you decide to take me up on my offer, send word to me before you leave and I shall come to you. I will not insist, my lady. If you want my assistance, you may have it. If not, then I wish you well. I truly do."

She let him lead her back toward the carriage, all the while wondering if this was the right thing to do, if she shouldn't take him up on his offer. Since the moment of their acquaintance, Magnus had been nothing but kind and chivalrous, even when he knew who, and what, she was. She'd never gotten the sense that he was judging her in any way. In fact, quite the opposite.

But it'd made a bit of sense to her since he told her about his sisters. Men who had other women in their lives, like sisters or mothers or even aunts, could show a little sympathy when it came to the opposite sex. At least, that had been her experience. But that wasn't always the case. A good example of that was Jerome, who had once had a mother but who clearly had no sympathy or compassion when it came to women. It was true what she had told Magnus: she was indeed terrified of Lord Daventry's son. The man was vile and unpredictable, one who drank alcohol to excess and gambled until there was nothing left. Even though Delaina had known Lord Daventry for a relatively short amount of time, she'd been around long enough to see what his son had done to him.

And she wanted nothing to do with that son.

They walked in silence to the carriage, finally reaching it as Magnus reached out to open up the door. Delaina didn't enter right away; she stood there for a moment, looking at him, wondering if she should apologize for the fact that she didn't want his help. Perhaps that was something that she needed to do, simply so he wouldn't think she was entirely ungrateful.

"I would thank you for your assistance this evening, Sir Magnus," she said. "I do not know what I would have done had you not been so accommodating. And I want to assure you that your offer of continued assistance has been appreciated. I am sorry that I cannot accept it."

He lifted a dark eyebrow. "You can accept it, my lady," he said. "You simply choose not to."

That was true. Delaina wondered if she heard a bit of a rebuke in that statement. "For my own reasons, as I am certain you will understand," she said. "It is nothing personal against you, I assure you."

He shrugged. "It does not matter if it is or not," he said. "As you said, none of this is my concern, and you are correct. I'm simply sorry that you have been conditioned to believe that every man wants something from you. That must be a difficult burden to bear."

Delaina was fairly certain he was somehow insulting her. She had known too many men in her short lifetime, and she understood a man's pride. She understood that when men were refused their desires, they often became bitter or insulting, or sometimes both. Magnus had been denied his want to escort her home or protect her, as he had offered, and she had refused. Of course he was feeling insulted. But the more she thought about it, the more she began to feel some offence.

None of this was genuinely any of his business.

"My burdens are my own," she said. "You know nothing about me, Sir Magnus, and let us keep it that way. Although I am very grateful for your assistance, it ends here. I shall take Lord Daventry home and that will be the end of it. However, for your kindness to me in my moment of need, I wish you a good life and much happiness."

He simply looked at her before shaking his head as if truly feeling some pity for a woman who thought the entire world was out to gain something from her. She had no idea what a genuine offer of kindness was. As he'd seen from the start of their association, she was a prisoner of the wall of protection she'd built around herself.

Not that he blamed her.

But he did feel sorry for her.

Without another word, he indicated for her to climb into the carriage, and she did, with minimal help from him. A severe-looking servant tried to climb in with her, but Delaina chased the woman away. Once she was situated inside the carriage, alone, he shut the door and whistled loudly between his teeth, causing the horses to start. Waving an enormous arm, he indicated for the carriage, and wagon, to start moving, and they did, heading for the gatehouse as Magnus stood back and watched them go.

And feeling an odd sense of disappointment.

"I thought you were going with them?"

Denys was suddenly at his side. Magnus hadn't even heard him walk up. Distracted from his disappointment, he turned away from the party as it passed through the north gatehouse.

"Nay," he said. "She is adamant that she does not want a royal escort, but I have a feeling she simply doesn't want me around. I offered to escort her and Daventry back to Haydon Square, but she thinks I will expect something in return."

Denys looked at him curiously. "Expect what?"

Magnus cast him a long look. "She's a courtesan," he said. "What do you think she will give me in exchange for my services?"

Denys was dense a moment longer before his eyes widened and he realized what Magnus meant. "I see," he said. "But you do not expect *that*."

"Of course I don't.

"Would you like me to follow the escort to ensure they make it safely home?"

Magnus nodded. "Go ahead," he said. "But do not linger. Once they are securely at Haydon Square, return to me with all due haste. I will need you once these drunken warlords start departing the feast."

Nodding smartly, Denys headed off toward the royal stables, which were some distance away. Magnus returned to his duties, which were in the hall this night. There were hundreds of finely dressed lords and ladies, but all he could think about as he watched the festivities was one small, magnificent woman he'd had a chance encounter with. He'd had chance encounters with many people in his lifetime, but not like this. Never like this. Something about Delaina de Courant stayed with him, and he couldn't figure out why. All he knew was that as the evening deepened, so did his sense of disappointment.

The most exquisite creature he had ever seen was out of his life forever.

That was reason enough.

CHAPTER FOUR

WHAT HAVE I done?

Delaina kept asking herself that question as the carriage bumped and lurched down the quiet London streets, heading for Haydon Square. London was dark at this time of night, with an occasional light emitting from a window and voices now and again. The world was quiet and the night was still, and thoughts of Magnus de Wolfe wouldn't leave her. If her affairs were none of his business, then why did she feel as if she'd just done something terribly wrong? As if she'd just chased away someone who was, perhaps, legitimately honorable?

That was rare in her world. Honorable men were mostly a myth as far as she was concerned, though she knew some existed. Somewhere, they did. Perhaps she'd had one in front of her all along and failed to notice the air of nobility all around him. Perhaps she'd mistaken it for royal arrogance and knightly ambition. She knew that Magnus was from one of the finest families in England, a family with a long and respected history, but her natural defensiveness when it came to men had prevented her from accepting his generosity and the nature in which it was intended.

Try as she might to stave off regret, she couldn't seem to. She was beginning to bask in it.

So she travelled back to Haydon Square in brooding silence, her thoughts lingering on Magnus when she should have been focusing on what lay ahead. The moment she reached the Daventry town home, she would be compelled to report the death to Lord Daventry's majordomo, and the man would send out the necessary notifications, which would include Jerome de Staverton.

God, how she even hated to think that name.

Delaina knew the moment that Jerome received the notification, he would come flying back to Haydon Square with the air of a conquering hero. For a man who had spent the bulk of his adult life gambling and trying to squeeze money out of his father one way or the other, this would be a moment of triumph for him.

She did not want to be part of his spoils of war. Therefore, she had to get out as soon as possible. Given that she brought her wealth with her to any position, it was a complicated issue because her wealth was spread out. Coinage and jewels were kept with her closely, but things like horses and properties, of course, were mostly in other areas. Swan's Landing was no longer hers with Daventry's death, and she had kept her four fine horses there, but at the moment, she might have to sacrifice them simply to get away. She couldn't stay at Swan's Landing because that would be the first place Jerome looked, so that lovely home and those beautiful horses would have to be let go.

But the coinage and jewels would come with her.

She was lingering on just how to pack her valuables when Haydon Square came into view. It was an enormous, fortress-like home toward the Aldersgate of London's wall. It was situated on a corner, an intersection of two streets, and it stood out like the prow of a massive cog—big, square, and imposing. The moment she laid eyes upon the brick structure, her heart began to race.

She had to plan what she needed to do and how quickly she needed to do it.

As far as finding lodgings for the night, Delaina wasn't exactly aware of any because she hadn't spent any time in the ones around London, but she was confident she could find some. They would more than likely have space for her if she were to offer them a generous fee. She could pack her possessions on her own, but she would have to see if she could pay a couple of Daventry's men to help her transport her belongings. However, she rejected that idea almost as quickly as she considered it because she was afraid if they knew where she had gone, Jerome would be told. The last thing she wanted was for that bastard to know her whereabouts.

She could only take what she could carry.

The gatehouse of Haydon Square was a three-story monstrosity with living quarters over the gate itself. As the party approached, there was a good deal of shouting, and she could hear the sentries calling to the men in the escort. She heard the answers to their queries, including the news that Lord Daventry had been brought home as a corpse. That caused the gates, massive iron and wood panels, to crank open at an alarmingly fast rate.

Now, the moment she had been dreading was upon her.

As the party entered the gates, the entry to the manse opened and people begin spilling out into the darkened ward. This included the majordomo, a man born in Bremen whom

Lord Daventry had hired long ago. He was big and loud, and he spoke with a heavy accent, but he was quite efficient in running the household.

Delaina had no feeling toward the man one way or the other, however. He had never been cruel to her, but he had never been warm, either. Warmth simply wasn't in his nature. However, he was extremely protective of Lord Daventry, and there had been some shouting matches between him and Daventry's son from time to time, even in the short time she'd been with Lord Daventry. Delaina could only imagine what kind of shouting matches were going to take place tonight once Jerome arrived.

Whatever they were, she wasn't going to be here.

As her carriage lurched to a halt, she opened the door herself and climbed out before anybody could help her. She was halfway across the bailey when Eustace von Vechta came toward her, a shocked expression upon his face. Delaina could hardly look at the man, far more concerned with herself and her immediate future to spare him much time.

"What happened?" Von Vechta demanded in his heavy accent. "What happened to our lord?"

Delaina paused long enough to answer his question. "We were at the feast and he excused himself to the privy," she said steadily. "He was found not long after, dead. You will make the arrangements to bury him, von Vechta, for I will not. It has been a troubling evening, and I must… retire." She didn't want to tell him more than that for fear he might try to prevent her from leaving.

She rushed past him, and he stood there a moment, dumb-founded, before turning to the carriage with the body on it. He rushed toward it, forgetting all about Delaina as she made herself scarce.

Lord Daventry had a suite of rooms toward the back of the manse, massive chambers that took up the entire rear of the home. The windows overlooked a garden with a towering wall, but beyond the wall was more of the city. Delaina had never been fond of the view, with walls and other homes and the smoke that would hang heavily in the morning when the breeze from the Thames was still. She had a key to the door that opened the suite, the only person to have one other than Lord Daventry and von Vechta, but once she was inside, she threw the bolt and knew she was safe for the moment. Not even the big Germanic majordomo could break through that bolt.

Rushing into her chamber, she went to work.

The white gossamer clothing began to come off, carefully laid upon the bed that was covered in embroidered silk linens. Her chamber adjoined Lord Daventry's larger chamber, with a connecting door that she could lock on her side. Although she was the man's courtesan and, by the accepted rules of the day, he could do as he wished with her—and *when* he wished—Lord Daventry didn't insist that they share a bed. Sometimes, he would ask her to climb into bed with him when the nights were cold and his blood wasn't circulating, but even then she was no more than a glorified warming pan.

He'd never bedded her.

Not that he probably hadn't thought about it. Even Delaina knew that. But he'd never made demands of her, and as she passed the open door that led into his chamber, she paused a moment, regretting the death of the man. This position had been such an easy one for her because of the lack of expectations. The old man had simply wanted a companion. But as she'd told Magnus, this was the last position she would ever have as a courtesan, a companion, or a concubine, because any debt her father had used her for those years ago had long been paid. The man was dead, and she was no longer obligated to uphold any deal he'd ever made.

But time was of the essence. She couldn't stand there and reflect on memories—Von Vechta was probably already preparing to send word to Jerome—so she rushed to her wardrobe and began to carefully remove only the things she had brought with her when she had come into Lord Daventry's possession. She pulled out two rather large satchels, opened them up, and hurriedly shoved items into them. Shifts, robes, surcoats—everything she'd brought with her.

Unfortunately, she knew there wasn't going to be enough room in the satchels for everything, because when she came to Daventry, she'd also brought four big trunks. But she couldn't worry about that. She certainly couldn't send for them once she got settled, so she'd simply have to take what she could carry plus the box that contained her fortune. It was heavy with coinage, but that couldn't be helped.

Using a key she kept hidden in a wall niche under her bed, she opened the secret panel in the wardrobe and pulled forth the coin box. It went into one of the satchels, buried beneath her clothing.

In the midst of packing, she managed to pull on a woolen traveling dress. It was dark blue, with pockets built into it, and a matching cloak with rabbit lining. She wore two heavy shifts underneath it, plus the only pair of boots she owned, heavy things used when she was riding one of her horses or traveling. Her hair, which had been caught up in a gold net and lined with ribbons of gold, would simply have to remain as it was until she found safety and had the time to comb out the elaborate style.

Hurry!

A voice inside of her was pushing her; fear was like the cracking of a whip. She stuffed the satchels until they could hold no more, knowing she was leaving a good deal behind. *They're only possessions,* she told herself. Possessions could be replaced.

But her sanity, and well-being, couldn't if Jerome got his hands on her.

Fully dressed for travel in a short amount of time, she grabbed her satchels and realized that they were too heavy for her to carry very far. Resourceful as few women were, Delaina ran into Lord Daventry's chamber and found two large leather belts. Returning to her satchels, she strapped them together. It took a bit of twisting on her part, and some struggle, but she managed to sling them onto her back so that her shoulders and torso could bear the weight more ably than her arms could. With those two big bags strapped to her, she gave one final pass over the chamber, grabbed a purse that had her jewelry in it—nothing Lord Daventry had given her—and slipped from the chamber for good.

Delaina never looked back.

Escaping the house wasn't difficult, fortunately, because everyone was focused on the front yard and Lord Daventry's body, so she was able to move down the back stairs. They were narrow and treacherous, difficult with the two big bags strapped to her back, but she managed to make it down without breaking her neck. The stairs took her into a small corridor next to the majordomo's chamber and a few other housekeeping rooms. It was dark because of the late hour, and she could hear the talking and weeping toward the front of the house as Lord Daventry's body was brought inside. With the servants distracted, she bolted for the rear of the manse and to the door that led out into the yard.

There was a garden back here, the one she could see from Lord Daventry's chambers, and it was quite dark at this hour. She knew there was a postern toward the rear that led to the street beyond, a gate used by smithies and other trades when doing business with the manse. The key was kept in the buttery, of all places, only known by a few, and she was able to get the key and open the gate.

It creaked loudly as it was opened.

That was enough to panic her. Surely someone had heard her. Delaina pulled it closed after her, locked it from the outside, and took the key with her so they couldn't easily follow her—or better still, so they'd be unaware that she escaped through the postern even when the key turned up missing.

Now, she was on the run.

There was a certain exhilaration to that. There was also a certain fear. She knew she was heading northeast at this point because she'd been on this road before. Once, she'd been entertained by a lord out of Ipswich, so she was acquainted with the road. She also knew there was an inn about five miles out, outside of the walls of London, situated in a small village called Ratcliff. Beyond that, a few miles away, was another small village along the Thames where she might be able to catch a cog or a ferry and go anywhere she wished to go.

Anywhere to get away from the life she'd been leading.

It was dark and late by the time she reached Aldersgate. Usually, the gates were closed at nightfall, and this was no exception. As she drew closer to the gates, she could see that they were shut and bolted. She thought that perhaps a coin might open them, and she could make it to Ratcliff and its inn,

The Greyhound and the Mouse. She tried not to think about what would happen if they wouldn't let her through the gate, so she moved forward with the belief that a coin would get her anything.

"My lady?"

A voice came from the darkness, and, startled, she turned to see a heavily armed knight standing a few feet away. He was leading a horse, a muscular beast, and as he took a step toward her, she took a step back.

"What do you want?" she demanded, frightened. "You will leave me in peace or I will scream louder than anything you've ever heard. I'm warning you."

He stopped moving when he realized she was backing away from him and held up a hand to ease her. Then he pulled his helm off.

"My name is Denys de Winter," he said, making sure she could see his face in the dim light. "I am a royal knight. Please do not be afraid. Magnus asked me to follow your escort to ensure that you did not come to harm. I was just about to leave when I saw you come from the postern and run in this direction. I swear to you that I mean you no harm, my lady, but where are you going?"

Denys de Winter. Delaina recognized the name. Lord Daventry had spoken of the man that very evening.

"De Winter," she said, looking him over. "Your father is the Earl of Thetford."

Denys nodded. "He is, my lady," he said. "May… may I assist you wherever it is you are going?"

She looked off toward the enormous gate. "You could ask those men guarding the gate to open it for me."

"Alas, I cannot."

She looked back at him. "Why not?"

"Because it is not safe for you outside of those gates," he said quietly. "In fact, it is not safe for you standing here all alone. Surely you realize how vulnerable you are, my lady."

Delaina knew that. She wasn't stupid. But she was determined.

"I can take care of myself," she said. "If you will not ask those men to open the gates, I will. I will pay them for their trouble."

Denys sighed faintly, realizing quickly that he was matching up with a stubborn young woman. He knew how she had reacted to Magnus' offer to help her, and he suspected she was going to react the same way to him. But, unlike Magnus, he didn't have much tact. And foolish young women annoyed him.

"Let me tell you what is going to happen to you if you continue along this path," he said. "You are wandering alone in a town where men will kill you without a thought, or worse, they will molest you in such a way that you will wish you were dead. You have lived a life of relative luxury and protection, but that ends now if you continue what you are doing. If you go outside of these gates, know that there are a plethora of outlaws out there who will happily slit your throat, steal your possessions, and leave you to die on the side of the road. They do not care if you were a finely dressed courtesan. They do not care that you are a woman. They will steal from you and murder you just the same, and your dreams of whatever life you seem to be fleeing toward will be finished. Is that how you wish for your life to end?"

By the time he was finished, she was looking at him with a mixture of outrage and fear. Great fear. "You're simply saying that to frighten me," she said, though her voice was starting to tremble. "You're very cruel to do that."

"I'm realistic," he said, forgoing the polite demeanor he'd had earlier. "I am a man of the world. I know what men are capable of. Do you?"

She stiffened. "Mayhap more than you do," she said. "You shall not discourage me from my intentions, Sir Denys."

"I am not trying to discourage you," he said. "I am trying to help you. But what you're doing is stupid. Magnus offered to escort you, to take you anywhere you wanted to go, and without any thought of recompense. In gratitude for his offer, you insulted him. He sent me here to help you, and you have insulted me, too, with your stubbornness. If you truly think you can make it wherever you're going without an escort, then I will let you go. But when those outlaws catch you and rip off your clothing, remember that we tried to help you and you only have yourself to blame for your fate."

With that, he gathered his reins and turned for his horse, preparing to mount as Delaina stood there and tried not to feel the fear he'd been trying to instill in her. But the truth was that he was right—and she knew he was right. It went against every cell in her body to agree with him, but deep down, her common sense told her that he was completely right about everything.

She wasn't stupid. Delaina was highly intelligent and educated. Her lords had seen to that. She knew what lay in wait beyond those walls and even within them, but her desire to flee was stronger than her common sense at that moment. If Sir Denys left her standing here, she knew in her heart of hearts that he would be leaving her for the wolves, the wolves she'd tried so hard to ignore and pretend as if they would not bother her.

But they would.

She didn't want to die on her first night of freedom.

"Very well," she said just as he mounted his horse. When he looked down at her, she took a few steps toward him. "I know you are correct. It is dangerous out there. But I must get to the safety of an inn, somewhere. Will you help me?"

There was a hint of vulnerability in her question, and Denys nodded slowly. "I said that I would," he said. "Where do you wish to go?"

Delaina sighed faintly, looking around, trying to think of a tavern that would be far away from Haydon Square. "I am not entirely sure," she admitted. "Do you know of any places where I will be safe for the night?"

Denys dismounted. Silently, he went over to her, close enough to remove the satchels she was carrying on her back. Once he removed them completely, he nearly staggered with the weight.

"God's Bones," he muttered. "What do you have in here? Rocks?"

Delaina wasn't comfortable enough with him to tell him what, exactly, she was carrying, so she simply nodded. "Nearly," she said. "Where will you take me?"

Slinging her satchels over one big shoulder and indicating his horse with an extended arm, he began to move toward his steed. "Come, my lady," he said, returning to a polite demeanor now that she was acting in kind. "I know of a place."

Delaina looked at him. "Where?"

He showed her.

☙

"YOU DID *WHAT*?" Magnus said, shocked.

"I took her to The Pox," Denys said.

Magnus' jaw dropped. "The Pox?" he repeated, aghast. "You took her to that sordid place?"

Denys nodded. "Thing about it, Magnus," he said. "She could not be safer anyplace else. All of the doors to the chambers that are rented are reinforced with iron, with great big bolts on them. An army of barbarians could not break through those doors if they tried. It seemed to me that it would be the safest place for her if she is running from Daventry's son. That's the last place he'll look."

Magnus had to admit there was some sound logic there. He wouldn't have picked The Pox, the seediest, most questionable tavern in London, but Denys did have a point. Because of the clientele it had, the rented chambers were like prison cells. Even the walls were reinforced, or so he'd heard. The owner of the place had grown weary of constantly replacing doors and walls, so he'd had them built with oak and iron to keep paying patrons safe.

But it was still no place for a lady.

"I suppose there is some wisdom in your decision," he said after a moment, raking his fingers through his hair. "But that place…"

"I know."

"And how long does she intend to remain?"

Denys shook his head. "I do not know," he said. "She was not even going to accept my help until I told her she was being stupid about it. She seemed… panicked."

Magnus frowned. "Panicked, indeed," he said. "She seems to think Daventry's son will be after her now that the father is gone."

Denys shrugged. "Whatever her fear, it was enough to drive her out into the night with two satchels strapped to her back."

Magnus looked at him in disbelief. "Truly?"

"Truly. Heavy ones, too."

That was the measure of the lady's fear. Not that Magnus had discounted it, but perhaps he hadn't given enough credit to her terror. Clearly, Denys had seen the proof.

Another interesting event in a long and eventful night.

Magnus had been reflecting on their conversation since Delaina departed Westminster. Somehow, someway, he was certain that he must have given her the wrong impression of his intentions, and, if so, the burden of the bad behavior was on him. He couldn't imagine what he'd done, but hearing that Denys had called her stupid for her stubborn behavior somehow gave him hope that he might be able to smooth things over with her and genuinely be of some assistance. If she'd allowed Denys to escort her to The Pox, then perhaps there was reason to be optimistic that Magnus could help the woman somehow.

She seemed badly in need of it.

"I should have put more stock in the fear she tried to relay to me," Magnus said after a moment. "She seemed nervous, but not reckless. The truth is that women like Lady Delaina are property. A possession and nothing more. I do not blame her for wanting to leave that life, but I admit that I'm curious to know how she fell into it at all."

Denys shrugged. "Who knows?" he said. "I will say that I've never seen a woman quite as beautiful as her. She has something over a mere mortal woman."

Magnus grunted in agreement. "True," he said. Then he glanced back at the hall, hearing the distant sounds of the feast, the music and the laughter. "Speaking of mortals, they're going to be there all night. Mayhap I'll slip over to The Pox to see if the lady needs further assistance."

"Why?" Denys asked. "She did not ask for any further help from me. She's not keen to have us around, you know."

"I know," Magnus said. "But she's a helpless woman. We would be remiss to dump her at The Pox and simply leave her there to fend for herself. A woman of that beauty? It's pure madness to leave her alone."

Denys' gaze lingered on him a moment. "Magnus," he said. "Forgive me for overstepping, but why the insistence on helping her? We've known other women to suffer some measure of discomfort or tragedy during our service, but you seem to be going out of your way for Lady Delaina. Why?"

Magnus paused, considering the question. "I don't know," he said. "There's something about her that makes me feel a good deal of pity for her, I suppose. As a knight, we are sworn to protect the weak."

"She's not weak."

"She's a lone woman."

"She's not your duty."

"I am well aware," Magnus said, starting to become annoyed. "Are you wondering if I am attracted to her? I would have to be dead not to feel some kind of attraction toward her, but it will go no further. She's a courtesan, Denys. Do you know what my mother would do to me if I came home with a courtesan on my arm?"

Denys grinned. "Probably the same thing my mother would do to me."

"Exactly."

A faint roar of laughter came from the hall again, causing both knights to turn to see if they could isolate the cause of the revelry. But there was nothing obvious. After a moment, Denys turned back to Magnus.

"If you are going to go to The Pox, then you'd better hurry," he said. "I'll need your help with the drunken warlords when they want to go home."

Those were essentially the same words Magnus had spoken to Denys when the man had departed to follow Lady Delaina, and Magnus grinned, dipping his head in acknowledgement before rushing off into the darkness, toward the stables across the road.

Denys watched him go, the smile fading from his face. Magnus seemed awfully concerned for a woman he'd just met, which wasn't like him. The Magnus he knew didn't notice women. They certainly noticed him, but he simply didn't have time for them.

Except one.

Apparently, he had time for the one he shouldn't make time for at all.

And that wasn't a good thing.

CHAPTER FIVE

S HE COULD HEAR the fighting from her chamber.

She had a big one, looking over the entrance of the fine establishment known as The Pox and facing the River Thames. When Denys brought her to this rather enormous hovel sheltering the dregs of humanity, she had been resistant. She'd almost run off. But Denys had assured her these were safe, clean chambers in spite of the clientele, and, being exhausted and having no idea where else she could go, she agreed. But only for the night. Denys took her inside and procured her the best room they had, and here she was, overlooking the half-moon as the cold light from it danced upon the river.

Had the fighting not been so loud, it would have been a lovely night.

It was quite a place she found herself in.

In fact, Denys hadn't been wrong. The door of her chamber was reinforced with iron, and there was an enormous bolt to keep it secure. She felt as if she was in prison, but along with that cell-like feeling, she also felt very safe. No one could break down the door, including Daventry's son. Not that he'd find her here. He wouldn't even think to look for her in a place like this.

Perhaps more of Denys' brilliance in bringing her here.

The chamber was surprisingly clean, with a big bed and a hearth that was burning warmly. There was a table with a couple of chairs, a chamber pot under the bed, and even a wardrobe cabinet that wasn't in terrible shape. In fact, the entire room was in shockingly good shape, considering the establishment.

But she'd paid a fine price for it.

Not that she cared. For safety and comfort on this night, she would gladly pay. Before he left, Denys had ordered her a bath and food, which had already been brought. Denys didn't leave until the bath was put into her chamber and the food placed upon the table. He told her not to open the door for anyone, not until she was ready to leave, and she would listen to him. He didn't say anything about sending word to him or to Magnus when she was ready to move on, taking them up on their offer of an escort, but that was to be expected, considering she'd made it clear that she didn't need, or want, their help.

But that wasn't exactly true.

Now that she'd had their assistance, she realized just how foolish she had been behaving. Shock at the situation and an overwhelming fear for her future had seen to that. She knew that now. But she didn't go so far as to tell Denys to apologize to Magnus for her, though she had thanked him profusely for his help. Maybe that was enough. Maybe not. All she knew was that for the first time in her adult life, she was free and alone. No lord, no expectations, and she wasn't anyone's property. Not anymore.

She could hardly believe it.

Lost in the thought of an unexpected future, Delaina took a leisurely bath in the small copper pot that had been brought for that purpose. She'd brought expensive soap and oils with her, the very finest because Lord Daventry liked her skin to be soft, and she washed all of the gold leaf out of her hair and scrubbed her skin with lavender-scented soap until it was rosy and clean. She remained seated in the pot until the water grew tepid and she was forced to get out, but she felt clean and calm. After donning an expensive night shift with long, flowing sleeves, she brought her food over to the hearth and ate it as she combed out her damp hair by the fire.

As she ate the simple but plentiful fare of bread, cheese, boiled eggs, and boiled beef, she began to think on her future. This moment was so unexpected that she was still overwhelmed by it. It had never occurred to her that Lord Daventry would die anytime soon, but now that the moment had come, her entire future was laid out before her. She'd told Magnus that she would rather join the cloister than continue the life of a courtesan, but that wasn't entirely true. She knew how nuns lived, and she wasn't keen on woolen underwear and gaining nourishment from the word of God. But she'd rather do that then be used by a man who would eventually tire of her and pass her to the next one.

That was no life for any woman.

A knock at the door startled her from her thoughts. Fear clutched at her as she stood up, comb in hand, and hesitantly moved toward the door. But she didn't answer; she simply listened. Listened for a hint of who was on the other side.

The knock came again.

"My lady?" The voice was muffled. "It is Magnus. Will you open the door?"

Filled with a good deal of relief, but also a good deal of curiosity, Delaina threw the bolt and yanked the heavy door open. True enough, Magnus was on the other side, standing in the darkened corridor. When their eyes met, he smiled timidly.

"Denys told me that he'd brought you here," he said. "I came to make sure you were taken care of and did not require anything further."

Delaina looked at him with surprise. "You came all the way over here from Westminster?"

"I did, my lady."

"Just to see if I needed anything further?"

"I did, my lady."

There was something comically chivalrous in the declaration, and Delaina wasn't as resistant to him as she had been before. The man was going to be of service whether or not she wanted him to be.

With a chuckle, she opened the door wider. "Come in," she said. "Come in before that constant fight down in the common room makes its way up the stairs and somehow involves you. I would not wish for you to be injured whilst on your errand of service."

Magnus' smile turned genuine as he came into the warm, moist chamber. He stood just inside the door as she closed it and locked it, then threw the bolt again for good measure.

He snorted softly. "The security of this place is stronger than Westminster itself," he said. "But I suppose they have good reason."

Delaina made her way back over to the fire. "I suppose they do," she said. "I should be offended that Sir Denys would bring me to such a place, but I must say that he was right about one thing."

"What's that?"

"It's quite safe," she said, pointing to the iron door. "No one can break through that."

Magnus looked at the secure door. "True enough," he said. "I can see that you are well protected."

She nodded, lowering herself back to the stool she'd been sitting on. "I am," she said. "Thanks to you."

"Denys brought you here."

"But *you* sent him to make sure I did not do anything foolish," she pointed out. "He called me stupid. Did he tell you that?"

Magnus nodded. "He did."

She looked at him to see if he had any reaction to that declaration one way or the other, but his expression remained impassive.

She finally broke out in a grin and averted her gaze, resuming the combing of her hair. "I suppose I was," she said. "I realize that now. But you must understand that I was desperate to get away from Haydon Square."

"Even at the cost of your safety?"

"Even at the cost of my safety," she agreed softly. "In fact, I was just sitting here, thinking about the events of the day and where I now find myself."

Magnus came away from the door, just a couple of steps, just enough to pull a chair out from the table and lower his bulk onto it. The mood between them seemed calm and conversational. She hadn't asked him to leave, so he wasn't going to. He was intensely curious about this glorious creature and intended to satisfy that curiosity.

"And where do you find yourself, my lady?" he asked. "What conclusion have you come to?"

She was staring into the fire, combing her hair absently. "That I have an uncertain future," she muttered. "I've never been in this position before."

There was wine on the table and one cup. Magnus took the liberty of pouring himself some of the wine then taking a long and deep drink.

"What position is that?" he asked.

She stopped combing. "Free," she said. "Do you have any idea what that feels like? I am *free*. For someone who has been kept as property, as one would keep a stallion or a dog, I thought freedom was something I would never know, yet here I am. The thought is overwhelming."

Magnus watched her as she spoke. "You do understand that a woman has no true freedom, my lady," he said quietly. "You do not have a lord or a husband, but you are not free. You must have a place to live, a source of income, things of that nature. You cannot achieve those on your own."

She looked at him then. "I thought so too," she said. "But I have my money with me. I can go anywhere I wish and pay for my passage. Mayhap I can go to France and assume a new life there. I will tell people that I am a widow. That would be respectable. I could purchase a home, mayhap have an income."

"By doing what?"

She had to think on that. "I can sew," she said. "I can make things. Fine things. I can do sums. I can read."

"How can those make you money?"

She shrugged. "Mayhap I can be a tutor," she said. "I can teach children. I could be a nurse to the children of a fine lord."

He nodded. "You could," he said. "But what about the cloister? You told me that was where you were bound."

She eyed him somewhat sheepishly. "I fear that I spoke too soon," she said. "I do not think I am the type of person they would be looking for, and, frankly, I am not entirely sure I could endure the life. That means I must make my own way in life, somehow. But it is a position I never thought I would be in, not ever."

Magnus finished off the cup of wine and poured himself another. "But here you are," he said. "May I make an observation, my lady?"

"I suppose so."

He lifted an eyebrow. "You are not the sort who would be a nurse to children and wipe their dirty noses," he said. "A woman like you… you should be the lady of the finest house in England. You are educated and talented. Why would you waste yourself as a nursemaid?"

She lowered her gaze. "Because a woman like me does not marry a fine man, Sir Magnus," she said. "That would be most frowned upon."

He shook his head in bewilderment. "You should be the most sought-after bride in England with your beauty and education," he said. "It is a travesty that you are not. I do not understand how your father could not see this for himself. Did he truly use you as barter?"

That was the wine talking, loosening his tongue, and he was sorry as soon as he said it. He held up a hand to apologize, but she shook her head.

"I do not mind the question," she said. "Since you have tried your best to assist me, mayhap you should know whom, exactly, you are trying to help. You should know how unworthy I am of your gesture. May I explain?"

He nodded, somewhat hesitantly. "If you wish to, then I would be very interested to hear."

She went back to combing her nearly dry hair; the liquid fire of the strands glistened in the light of the hearth. When she spoke, it was pensively.

"My parents were from fine Cornwall families," she said quietly. "My mother was a d'Vant, of St. Austell Castle. My father's family practically owns all of Penzance. It was a much-anticipated marriage, joining two great families. Unfortunately, it was a disaster."

"How so?" he asked.

Delaina took on a distant look, remembering the history that was part of her fabric. It had brought her to this point in her own life.

"My mother was in love with another man when my parents were betrothed," she said. "My father refused to release her from the betrothal."

"Was the betrothal longstanding?"

"Aye," Delaina said. "They had been betrothed as children and grew up knowing one another, knowing they would be wed, but there was no love between them. They did not even like each other. My mother loved someone else she very much wished to marry, but my father wanted the d'Vant dowry. They're very rich, you know. He married my mother, took the money and consummated the marriage, and sent her back to her family. I was born exactly nine months later."

"Did your birth bring your parents back together?"

She shook her head. "Nay," she said. "My mother died in childbirth. I lived with my mother's parents, the d'Vants, and enjoyed a wonderful childhood. When I was old enough, I went to foster at Okehampton Castle. All the while, my father simply stayed away. He served the Earl of Somersby, as a knight, but I never saw him. I never even heard from him until one day when he simply showed up at Okehampton. He came to take me away."

"Away where?"

She sighed faintly, regretfully. "I had just become a woman," she said. "He took me to the earl's castle of Midthorpe. I did not know why until we got there and then he told me—I was to marry the earl's son. I spent a couple of days speaking to the young man, who was barely my age, and he was a nice boy. I liked him. But his widowed father, the earl, decided he would rather have me for himself, so a wedding was set."

Magnus' brow furrowed slightly. "Somersby is dead," he said. "I do not remember when, but I do remember hearing he had died."

She nodded. "He did," she said. "He killed himself."

Magnus' features registered surprise and disgust. "I see," he said. "Did you end up marrying him?"

Delaina shook her head. "This is where everything becomes quite complicated," she said. "My father was a gambler, you see. I learned that he owed Somersby a good deal of money. In fact, my father died in a fight whilst gambling in Exeter. Before Somersby could marry me, he was forced to surrender me to King Edward because he owed the man a good deal of taxes he did not have the funds to pay. As it turned out, Somersby liked to gamble as well, and he used money meant for the king. That is how I ended up with Longshanks."

Magnus was listening intently. "You are correct," he said. "Your situation *is* very complicated."

"It is."

"And it seems that there was much gambling going on at Okehampton."

She nodded. "I suppose there's not much to do in the wilds of Devon," she said. "But in answer to your question, I never married Somersby. But I became his mistress."

Magnus knew what that meant. That sweet, beautiful woman had become a whore to a widower. When she should have married a fine knight or a noble lord, she was relegated to the concubine of a selfish old man.

Jaw twitching faintly, he shook his head in sorrow. "You did not deserve that," he said. "I am sorry he did that to you."

She forced a smile, mostly because she'd never heard anyone apologize to her for what life had brought her. "You needn't be troubled," she said. "I've long learned not to be. At first, I was devastated, of course. The moment he took my innocence, I knew I would never be suitable for a decent man, and that was difficult for me. I have always hoped for a husband and children, for a fine marriage, like any girl. But Somersby ruined that for me. And then I went to Edward."

Magnus was feeling increasingly sorry for her. "How long ago was this?"

"It was the year before he married Margaret of France," she said. "He took me in trade for the taxes Somersby owed him, but he never paid much attention to me. I did not become his mistress. He simply added me to the group of women he'd collected. The Seven Jewels of London, we were called. Have you heard of us?"

Magnus nodded. "You are the Ruby."

"I am," she said, her gaze riveted to him for a moment. "Then you've heard of the Jewels."

"Most men in London have, at least men who know anything about politics and the king."

She accepted that answer. "Do you know why he collected us?" she said. "Why he sent us to be trained in the most exclusive brothel in London? Why we learned to please a man but also why we learned to speak different languages, play instruments, sing, massage a man's cares away, and run his household?"

Magnus slowly shook his head. "I do not," he said. "Why?"

She looked at him as if the answer was obvious. "Because we were the most valuable prizes he had," she said. "To reward an ally or to lure an enemy, we commanded the highest price. Longshanks presented his Jewels to men he wanted to impress, men with whom he wanted an allegiance, or men he wanted to control. The Diamond went to Humphrey de Bohun when the man was set to turn against the king. The Pearl went to Roger Bigod, much to the distress of his wife, but Bigod kept the Pearl in spite of her protests. And me… I went to the Earl of Bristol, Henry de Dunstanville. Edward needed his harbor and his ships for his war with Scotland. He wanted de Dunstanville's loyalty badly."

Everything she said was making a great deal of sense. Politics reached into every dark corner of the nobility of England and into private houses, private lives. Magnus remembered being surprised she had been used for actual barter, but he didn't know why he was. He'd seen it before, just not with so fine and educated a woman.

"So you went with Bristol," he said. "How did he treat you?"

She snorted. "Like a mare," she said. "I was kept in a chamber morning, noon, and night so that he always knew where I was and could come to me when he chose to. I was expected to be ready for him, always. I was bathed regularly, oiled, massaged, fed the finest food, and given the most beautiful clothing, and all I had to do was be ready for him when he came to call."

Somehow, knowing the life of a courtesan and actually hearing about it were two different things. Magnus was a man of the world; he knew how these things worked. But looking at

Delaina and hearing what she had been subject to was making him sick to his stomach.

"I am sorry," he said, not knowing what more to say. "That is no life for you."

"Nay, it wasn't," she agreed, her manner bordering on agitation. "Bristol is a younger man, you know. He's virile. He would come to me twice a day at times, always demanding that I pleasure him. He didn't seem to want more, but he used me quite a bit. There were days when I prayed for death. I did not want to have to see him one more time, not one more bloody time. If I did not pleasure him fast enough or well enough, he wasn't beyond slapping me. Then he would become angry because my face swelled."

Magnus closed his eyes to ward off the horrors of a man who would show such brutality to such a lovely creature. "The man is a bastard," he muttered. "A bastard who must prove his manliness by striking a woman. That is no man at all."

Delaina shrugged weakly. "Fortunately, he grew tired of me quickly when his wife returned from her trip to France," she said. "He gave me to his friend, Lord Falmouth, who locked me in a chamber and kept me surrounded by silks and luxury. He was afraid to let me out, afraid to join me. I was locked in that chamber, alone, for months until Lord Daventry came to visit. He and Falmouth are old friends. Lord Daventry took one look at me and tried to purchase me. When that did not work, he got Falmouth drunk and won me in a game of chance. And that is how I came to Lord Daventry, who was a genuinely kind man."

Her voice trailed off after that, leaving Magnus struggling not to look appalled by the whole thing. She was staring at her lap at that point, comb still in her hand, her glorious hair almost completely dry in the warmth of the fire. Now he was beginning to see the human cost of someone being labeled a courtesan, the price paid by a woman with no control over her destiny or her life. The price of being a pawn, used like a servant, treated like a whore. Less than human.

Less than a woman.

God, she didn't deserve that.

"You do not have to tell me any more than you already have," he said softly. "I can see that you have been treated horrifically, so you do not need to speak on your past anymore. I will spare you that pain. But just know that I have come to help you, Lady Delaina. Now that you are free of your prison, I will help you do what you wish to do. And I will not expect anything for it. Is that clear?"

She lifted her head, looking at him with those sea-colored eyes. "Nay," she whispered. "You do not understand. I *want* to speak of this. No one has ever told me they were interested in my life. You are the only one who has ever shown enough compassion to ask."

There was a plea in that, a hint of desperation. The wall of self-protection she'd kept around herself was crumbling, and all Magnus could see was the vulnerability. Therefore, he slid off the chair and ended up on his buttocks in front of her, both of them sitting in front of the fire, facing one another in the glow of the flames.

"Then tell me," he muttered. "Tell me everything you wish to tell me. You have suffered terribly, and as a man of honor, when I see suffering, I am inclined to help. But I do not know if I can help you, and that is troubling to me."

She smiled faintly, reaching out to put a soft hand on his arm. "You already have," she said. "Do you not understand that? It all started when Sir Denys called me stupid. No one has ever called me stupid before. But he did it out of concern. I have become so accustomed to men showing a lack of concern toward me that I almost didn't recognize it."

Her hand was searing his flesh like a branding iron. He was afraid to look at it where it touched his skin, afraid he'd see smoke. Smoke and something more. Something more that was causing his heart to race.

He'd never experienced anything like it in his entire life.

"Then tell me how I can help you," he said. "Tell me, and if I can do it, I will. But you should know that Hugh Despenser knows of Daventry's death, and he further knows that you, the Ruby, were in Daventry's possession. He has asked me to bring you to him, but I will not do it. God only knows what he wants to do with you."

A ripple of fear crossed her face, but she settled down quickly. She was, if nothing else, a strong woman. She was a survivor. She was also resigned to her lot in life, no matter how much she wanted to be free.

"I am certain he wants to use me to bribe another lord to do his bidding," she said softly. "But you must not disobey him. He is a powerful man."

Magnus cocked an eyebrow. "And I know *how* he came into power," he said. "I would be doing England a favor if I turned him over to the warlords who hate him, so he will not tangle with me. My loyalty is to Edward, not to Hugh. He knows that."

"But I still do not wish for you to be punished because of me."

"No one will punish me," he said. "I am the one who does the punishing, so no one will touch me. But the fact remains that Despenser knows you are no longer with a lord. That means you must leave London as soon as you can until

Despenser forgets about you and moves on. Based on this conversation, the cloister is not a choice any longer?"

Delaina didn't respond right away. She took her hand off his arm and simply sat there, gaze averted.

"It is not," she finally said. "But mayhap I should reconsider."

"Why?"

She shrugged. "Because I will never marry," she said. "Soon, I will be too old to be the Ruby. Men do not want courtesans or mistresses who are too used. I've already had five lords. Let us be honest, my lord—I can speak of freedom and of going to France to earn my own way, but is that really the best choice for me? I do not know. England is my home, and I do not particularly want to leave it. If I remain, then what is left for me? If I do not go to the cloister and, eventually, no man will want me, my only alternative would be to return to Margit."

So what Cassius and Hugh had told him was true. Training, or at least some sort of guidance, had come from Margit Barkwith, the London proprietress of the most famous brothel in town. But hearing she might return to Margit because no lord would want her didn't sit well with him. She was a Jewel— she was a woman who should be prized above all others. He couldn't imagine her returning to a brothel.

Nay, that didn't sit well with him at all.

"What about marriage?" he said. "Certainly you would be able to find a husband, as the dowager Countess of Somersby."

Delaina looked at him then, a weak smile on her lips. "There was no marriage."

"No one needs to know that."

She laughed softly. "So I should lie about it?" she said. "Lying about being a countess on top of my unmentionable past would not be a good way to start a marriage. Moreover, I'm far too old."

He frowned. "I do not believe that," he said. "How old are you?"

"I have seen twenty and eight summers."

He was surprised to hear that. She looked ethereal and ageless, not a mark or a line on her exquisite face. "I would have believed you had you told me you had only seen eighteen," he said. "You are ageless, my lady."

The smile faded from her face, but it was because she was awed by his words. And touched. "Thank you," she said sincerely. "That is very kind of you."

"It is the truth," he said. "And I say that without guile because there is nothing I want from you. I do not resort to flattery. I only speak the truth."

Her smile returned, modestly. "Again, you are very kind," she said. But her smile soon faded. "I do not know what I did to warrant attention from such a noble knight. I had forgotten such men existed in the world, my lord. Thank you for showing me that men with good hearts still live."

It was his turn to fight off a modest smile. "We do," he said. "There are many of us, believe it or not."

"I was fortunate enough to find one in you, my lord."

"And you will call me Magnus. We have become friends, and friends are not so formal with one another."

Her grin blossomed. "I do appreciate that we have become friends," she said. "You have been kind to me from the beginning, and I thank you for that. Even though you knew who I was, you were still kind. That is a quality I do not see much of."

Magnus found himself staring into her eyes. Her cheeks

were pink from the warmth of the fire, giving her an incredibly alluring look. But he didn't dare let his attraction to her show because it would damage the trust they were building. He'd told her he wanted nothing from her, and that was the truth, but if she realized he found her beautiful… and there was infatuation there… it would ruin everything.

And he didn't want to ruin it.

"It has been my pleasure, my lady," he said, rising from the floor and returning to his seat because he was beginning to sweat. "Now, plans must be made. You cannot stay at The Pox for the rest of your life, so you must decide where you want to go and what you want to do."

Delaina stood up too, swamped by the beautiful, flowing sleeping shift she was wearing. "I know," she said. "We have spoken about a great deal this evening. May I at least have the night to think about it?"

"Of course," he said, picking up the pitcher of wine only to realize that it was empty. He set it down. "Sleep on it. See how you feel come the morning. I will return at some point and we will discuss the situation."

She nodded, putting her comb back into one of the satchels. "Sir Magnus," she said, then realized she'd agreed to drop the formalities. "*Magnus.* I realize you may have no answer to this question, but I have no one else to ask. May I?"

"Of course."

"What would you do in my situation? Do you think it wise to go to France and try to start a new life?"

Because the wine was gone and he was still feeling flushed being in her proximity, Magnus began leaning toward the door. "I do not know," he said honestly. "This is a new situation for me, also. If you would like me to give you my honest opinion, then I must think on it, as you must."

"I would very much like your opinion," she said. "Truly, I have no one else to ask. I have no friends, no family to speak of. Being a Jewel… it is a very lonely profession in so many ways."

He made it to the door, his hand on the latch. But his gaze never left her face. "I cannot imagine," he said quietly. "You have endured much in your life."

She headed in his direction. "And that is hopefully behind me now," she said. "But you must have many friends and family. You have probably not known a lonely moment in your life."

He smiled weakly. "I have three brothers and two sisters," he said. "My mother, my father, a grandmother, a grandfather, grand-uncles, five additional uncles, two aunts, and their families. There are dozens and dozens of us. Nay, I've never been alone in my life, and I like it that way."

"Are you the eldest son?"

He shook his head. "Nay," he said. "I am the third-born son. I have two older brothers, one younger brother, and two younger sisters."

She stopped her approach when she came to within a foot or so of him. "You mentioned that you have sisters," she said. "Are they married?"

He laughed softly. "Those two?" he said. "God help the men who marry them. They are as annoying as vermin, and there are times when I would like to swat them, but my mother will not let me."

He meant it as a jest, because she could see the twinkle of warmth in his eyes. It was quite endearing.

"But you love them anyway," she said.

"I do."

She was smiling because he was. "That tells me a good deal about you," she said. "*Il cuore è fedele alla famiglia.*"

He cocked his head. "What does that mean?"

"The heart is true to family."

"What language is it?"

"The language of Rome," she said. "One of the few I speak. But it means that a man's heart is true if he loves his family. And you love yours, which means you are a good man."

His smile waned. "I hope I am always considered a good man," he said quietly. "On that thought, I shall leave you now, but I will return on the morrow. I will make sure they send you food in the morning so you do not have to leave your chamber. Stay here and do not wander."

"I won't."

"Good," he said, throwing the big bolt and lifting the latch. For a moment, their eyes locked and something passed between them. At least, Magnus thought so. Something warm and shocking that filled his veins with liquid fire. "Good sleep, my lady. Lock the door behind me."

Delaina nodded, smiling at him as he quit the chamber. Throwing the bolt, she leaned against the door, visions of his handsome face lingering in her head.

She had felt something warm and shocking, too.

CHAPTER SIX

"Magnus? Are you awake?"

Magnus was, though barely. He'd been awake all night and into the morning, making sure the guests from the feast made it to their carriages safely. What happened once they left Westminster was none of his concern, but making sure they left in one piece was.

So far, everyone had.

"I am," he said, sitting up on his bed as Denys pushed the door open. He wiped a weary hand over his face, looking at the sunlight in the chamber and squinting. "How long did I sleep?"

"A few hours," Denys said. "I just rose myself."

Magnus yawned. "What time is it?"

"Midafternoon," Denys said. He came into the chamber and shut the door behind him. "I came to tell you that Despenser has summoned you."

Magnus stopped yawning and looked at him. "When?"

"Just now."

"After last night, he's awake?"

Denys shrugged. "Evidently," he said. "But I would wager to say that Edward isn't."

Magnus stood up, still exhausted, and staggered over to a basin of cold water. He splashed it vigorously on his face. "The man won't be awake for two days after last night's orgy," he said. "That means Despenser thinks he is in command."

Denys sighed. "Of course he does," he muttered. "He thinks he is in command every time Edward sleeps or gets drunk. Whenever he's not in his right mind, there is Hugh, trying to gain control of a kingdom."

"Did he say what he wanted with me?"

"Nay."

Magnus paused a moment before turning to look at Denys with a degree of suspicion on his face. "I would wager to say I know."

"What?"

"He wants to know about Lady Delaina."

Denys frowned in confusion. "Why should he want to know about her?"

Now Hugh's summons was starting to make some sense, and Magnus picked up a towel to dry his face and hands. "When I went to tell him about Daventry's death, her name entered the conversation," he said. "I did not tell you this, but Despenser wanted me to bring Lady Delaina to him. I did not, and I am certain he wants to know where she is."

Denys was still frowning. "Why should he want her?" he asked. "He does not need a woman."

"Not for himself," Magnus said, looking at Denys as he wiped off his chin. "To use her as Longshanks used her. She is a powerful prize for the right man. Lady Delaina told me that Longshanks gathered the most beautiful women he could and turned them into courtesans to suit his politics. I am certain that is what Despenser wishes, also."

The light of recognition went on in Denys' eyes. "Ah," he said. "What are you going to tell him?"

Magnus headed for his trunk where he kept his clean clothing. "I do not know," he said, pulling forth a clean tunic. "I spoke with her at length last night, and she has quite a story to tell. It seems that she has been used as a pawn ever since her father sold her off in payment of a gambling debt."

Denys grunted softly. "Humiliating," he muttered. "I never did agree with men who view women as property. I've seen it too many times."

"As have we all," Magnus said. "My grandfather always treated my mother as if she were the most important thing in the world, the most precious treasure, but he never treated her like property. My father never treated my mother that way, nor any of my sisters. We do not view women that way in my family, so I take issue with men who do."

"But many men do," Denys said. "Like Despenser. Whatever he wants her for cannot be good."

With his tunic pulled over his head, Magnus began to pull on his mail coat and other things that comprised his usual attire as lord commander. "Not him," he said. "You are the only other person who knows where she is, so do not tell anyone. Do not divulge it, no matter what."

"I won't," Denys said. "But I'm serious, Magnus—what are you going to tell him when he asks? If, in fact, that is why he wishes to see you?"

Magnus shook the mail coat down on his body, moving it into place. "Firstly, she is nothing to him," he said. "She does not belong to him. She does not belong to the Crown. She belongs to Daventry, who is dead, so in truth she would belong to Daventry's heir, his son, whom she detests. Despenser has no claim over her."

"Is that what you're going to tell him?"

Magnus thought on that a moment. "I am going to tell him that she went to Haydon Square," he said. "She did. She went there. He does not need to know that she fled. If he wants her, he can summon those at Haydon Square and ask them. They will report that she has disappeared."

Denys nodded. "That is best," he said. "It is not as if you are lying to the man, for she did go there."

Magnus went for his boots. "She did," he said, grabbing the leather shoes. But then he paused, looking at Denys with a puzzled expression. "Why am I doing this? Why am I protecting a woman I do not even know? I've never done this before, Denys. Is it because I feel such pity for her?"

Denys' jaw twitched faintly. "It is because you are a man who knows right from wrong," he said. "You have sisters. I have a sister. But Lady Delaina has no one to protect her. You are a chivalrous man, Magnus. You feel pity for her, but you also know that she has been wronged. To tell Despenser where she is would only add to the wrongs committed against her, only this time, you would be complicit."

Magnus gazed at him for a moment before nodding. "Exactly," he said quietly. "I needed to hear you say it. I needed to understand it myself."

Denys slapped him on the shoulder. "What you did not hear me say is that you are doing this because you are attracted to her," he said softly. "And you must be very, very careful if that is truly the case, Magnus. That kind of attraction will cloud your judgment."

Magnus knew that. At least, he knew it in theory. He began to put his boots on.

"My mother will murder me if I take up with her," he muttered, almost under his breath. "But she is a d'Vant. Did she tell you that? Her mother was a d'Vant, one of the oldest families in Cornwall. Some say they descend from a tribe of warlocks who used to populate Cornwall, men bred from incubi and mortal women. Merlinus Ambrosius was one of these warlocks, you know. King Arthur's trusted prophet."

Denys shook his head. "I did not speak with her long enough to know she was a d'Vant," he said. "As for being magical… one only has to look at her to see that she is unearthly in her beauty. But if she has magic, I would be very careful, Magnus. Mayhap she has bewitched you. Mayhap that is why you feel as you do."

Magnus actually considered that for a brief moment before breaking down in a weak grin. "If I were not a man of logic, I might believe that," he said. "As it is, keep your female hysteria away from me."

Denys chuckled softly as he headed for the door. "I'll be at the gatehouse should you need me," he said. "Otherwise, I wish you well with Despenser. He usually gets what he wants."

The smile faded from Magnus' face.

"Not this time."

CHAPTER SEVEN

"**W**ORD OF DAVENTRY'S death spread like fire last eve," Hugh said angrily. "I thought we were to keep this quiet, de Wolfe. Well? What happened?"

Magnus had been listening to the ravings of a furious man for the past ten minutes, ever since he entered Despenser's lavish suite of chambers in the royal apartments at Westminster. Word had it that Despenser simply moved himself in without being invited, and Edward didn't stop him, so now he occupied rooms facing the Thames. The city center of London was to the northeast, easily seen from his chambers, and that included the waterfront where The Pox was located.

However, everything was too far away for Despenser or anyone from Westminster to actually see anything in detail, so Magnus knew that Delaina was safe. For the time being, anyway. Despenser seemed angrier that word of Daventry's death had reached the ears of the guests than the fact the Daventry's Jewel hadn't been brought to him.

Magnus hoped it would stay that way.

"The man died in a garderobe that others were using," he said steadily. "We had to remove his body, and it was seen. We put it on a wagon that followed Daventry's distinctive carriage from Westminster. I cannot gouge the eyes out of every man who saw him, my lord. It was inevitable that rumors came about."

Hugh sighed sharply. He knew that. But he was still angry about it. "The king evidently liked Daventry," he said. "He was upset the entire night about it. And what about the son?"

"What about him?"

That enraged Hugh all over again. "Did you speak with him?" he demanded. "Have you seen him at all?"

Magnus' brow furrowed. "Why would I?" he said. "I do not know him, and I do not want to. The Daventry escort left Westminster, and that was the last I saw of it."

Hugh wasn't satisfied. "What about the Jewel?" he said. "I told you to bring me the Ruby. Where is she?"

Magnus shrugged. "I cannot tell you," he said, which wasn't really a lie. He couldn't and wouldn't. "She left with the escort, although I did send one of my men after the escort to ensure it returned safely to Haydon Square. The Ruby was seen going into the house, but that is all I know."

Hugh was quickly growing irate with Magnus' answers. "I told you to bring her to me," he said. "Go to Haydon Square and retrieve her this morning. That is a command."

Magnus lifted an eyebrow at him. This was where the conversation went from businesslike to personal, as it did so often when it came to Hugh.

"I am the lord commander," he said, lowering his voice. "I do not take commands from you. My commands come directly from the king, so if the king wants me to fetch her, then I shall. But you do not command me, Despenser. I have told you that before. You have your own men to order about, so send them to

Haydon Square and make your demands. But I will tell you that Daventry has an heir, so the Ruby would belong to the heir. You will have to take this up with him. Or did you not think of that?"

Hugh turned red in the face. He didn't like it when those under the king's command didn't fall at his feet or rush to do his bidding. Magnus de Wolfe was one of them. The man was powerful, so powerful that he knew Hugh didn't have superiority over him. He was one of the rare few who did, and Hugh had to take it.

But he hated every minute of it.

"If the king gives you an order, you will obey it," he snarled. "I will make sure Edward knows you have been disagreeable to his minister."

"And I will make sure the king knows you have been trying to usurp his power."

"How dare you say such things!"

"How dare you *do* such things," Magnus returned evenly. When he saw that Hugh was gearing up for what would surely be a nasty retort, he lowered his voice further. "Do not tangle with me, Despenser, for you shall lose. I command more men than you could ever hope to. One word from me and the House of de Wolfe will turn against Edward, and he will lose the north. And I shall make sure Edward knows it is all your fault, so know your place. Polite requests from you will be honored to the best of my ability. Commands will be ignored. Is this in any way unclear?"

Hugh was so angry that he was twitching, but he didn't immediately reply. He knew that everything Magnus said was true. He was one of the only men unwilling to bend to Hugh's will, so it was a standoff at the moment.

But that didn't dampen Hugh's resolve.

"It does not matter," he said after a moment, trying desperately to regain the upper hand in the conversation. "I have my own men, as you have said. I will find her and I will not stop until I do."

Magnus believed him implicitly. "I would suggest you speak with Daventry's heir," he said. "The man is in need of money, so I've heard, so mayhap he will sell her to you for the right price."

Hugh shrugged, a little too casually. "Mayhap," he said. "If he does not, then I shall take her. In fact, I will tell Edward about her, and then he can issue an order to you to go and claim her. If an order from the king is what you need, then I shall have it."

"Make sure it comes from his own lips."

"You can be certain that I will."

"Is that all?"

Hugh looked him up and down, his gaze licking the man from top to bottom, as if sizing up what was becoming a very large blockage in his quest for power.

"For now," he said. "You may go, de Wolfe."

Without another word, Magnus did. But he knew this wasn't going to be the last he heard from Hugh Despenser on the subject of Lord Daventry's Jewel.

The stakes were raised.

CHAPTER EIGHT

S HE HAD GONE to sleep to the sounds of a fight, and she awoke to the same.

It seemed the fighting never stopped at this place.

Delaina had slept long and hard, awakening only when sounds from the common room directly below her roused her from dreams that had been quite pleasant. She had been running through a field of golden wheat, with the sun warm upon her shoulders and laughter filling the air. It was her laughter, but someone else was with her, and she could hear his laughter as well. She couldn't see his face, but she could feel his hands upon her, strong and warm. They were having a marvelous time, whatever they happened to be doing, and that was when sounds of furniture being broken had roused her.

An unhappy end to a happy dream.

It took Delaina a moment to orient herself once she opened her eyes. She was in the room at The Pox, the surprisingly clean room in the surprisingly squalid tavern that every criminal, rake, and trollop seemed to visit. She was quite certain every murderer and thief in London was down in the common room, because when she had passed through it the previous day, she saw sights she had never seen in her entire life. She'd never seen such dirty, frightening people.

It had been quite an experience.

But as she awoke that morning, once again she saw the wisdom of Denys' decision to bring her to this place. No one would look for her. No one would dare even enter the place looking for her. She was very safe to the point of her wondering if she shouldn't simply stay put until she figured out what to do. The price was right, and she certainly wasn't going to run out of money, but she may become a little restless boxed up in the room overlooking the river. Though it seemed a small price to pay for her safety.

Rising from the bed that had been shockingly comfortable, she went about washing up before dressing in a soft lamb's wool garment. She had washed in the old bathwater from the night before, using her lavender-scented soap, and then brushing out her hair and loosely braiding it. She remembered that Magnus had told her he would have food sent to her in the morning so she would not have to leave the room, so she waited patiently for her morning meal to make an appearance as she repacked her satchels. She had thrown her possessions into them so quickly that several of them were wadded up and wrinkled. She made a mental note to ask for hot water when they brought her food, because the steam could help smooth out her garments.

And she waited.

It wasn't until midmorning that the rap finally came on her door. She rushed to the panel but did not unlock it, instead asking who had knocked. The reply was garbled, but it was a female, so she figured that she was safe enough. She threw the bolt and unlocked the door, then opened it up to a serving wench bearing a tray of food.

The woman took the tray over to the table and set it down. She was an older woman, with a tattered but clean dress, an apron that had seen better days, and her red hair shoved up into a cap. She talked nonstop from the moment she entered the door, but she had a deformity on her mouth and her words were difficult to understand. In spite of that, Delaina thought she was quite friendly, and tried to listen closely as the woman spoke of the weather, of a ship full of men from Copenhagen that had just arrived, and then began to talk about her own daughter for some reason.

Delaina simply stood there and nodded.

As the woman chatted up a storm, she gathered the dishes from the previous night. She also mentioned something about returning to remove the tub. It was then that Delaina asked for hot water, but the woman said she would do one better. Delaina's hearth had a big iron arm that was made for hanging a pot over the flame, and she told Delaina that she would bring her an iron pot with water so that she could have hot water anytime she wished. Delaina thought that was quite generous.

Then there was another crash in the common room down below, and the woman suddenly fled and slammed the door behind her.

Delaina was appalled to think that a woman such as that might be expected to quell any fights, but she soon forgot her outrage in favor of her rumbling stomach. She was quite hungry, so she threw the bolt and went over to the table where the food waited. She removed the cloth covering the feast and was greeted by simple but plentiful fare of baked eggs swimming in a wine sauce and small pasties stuffed with some kind of meat. She stuck her finger in the wine sauce and found it quite delightful. There was also bread and butter and stewed apples. Sitting down, she picked up the wooden spoon that came with the meal and dived in.

Delaina ate until she could eat no more. The baked eggs were stuffed with breadcrumbs and mushrooms and were delicious. The little pasties were stuffed with roast pork and were also very good. The bread was fresh, as was the butter, so the entire meal was shockingly good. Meals at taverns could vary a great deal in quality, so she was pleased to see that The Pox had good food. That would make her stay much more pleasant.

Once her meal was finished, Delaina cleaned up the table and went to tidy up her bed. Noise from the river caught her attention, and she found herself wandering to the window, watching the activity outside. Her window was right over the front door of the tavern, so she stood back to make sure she wasn't seen by anyone outside, but she did have quite a good view and found herself interested in a world she had never really experienced before.

As she had told Magnus the night before, her early years had been spent in Cornwall, which wasn't exactly a metropolitan shire. There were cities in Cornwall, of course, but nothing like London. Okehampton Castle had been one of the remoter castles in England, so she'd led a rather sleepy life there, as well.

Her first taste of a more sophisticated existence had been when she went with her father to Somersby Castle. Somersby had been quite busy, with a standing army of a thousand men and more people in and out of the castle than she had ever seen in her life. But even then, Delaina had been kept like a bird in a gilded cage, forbidden from interacting with anyone other than the earl and her father and a few select others. Every lord she had been with had treated her the same way, keeping her hidden away, saved and protected like a precious jewel would have been.

But unlike a cold, hard jewel, Delaina had life and emotion, and the isolation had been difficult. That was one of the things she had regretted the most as a courtesan—being kept from people. Being forbidden to interact with anyone at all other than her master. In that sense, she had been kept like a prisoner. Perhaps that was why she had been so determined to flee when Daventry died. The prison had burned down, and she was suddenly free.

But freedom would mean nothing if she didn't have a plan in place.

Magnus had asked her to sleep on those plans. He had asked her to think about what she wanted to do, realistically, and then he would come and see her at some point today to help her do what she needed to do. The truth was that she wasn't sure what she wanted to do now that the shock of her abrupt freedom had worn off. She had her money with her, and clothes that she had purchased herself, but she had left so much behind.

Oddly enough, she didn't really care. The items she'd left behind were like golden chains keeping her tied down to a life that no woman should be forced to live. Now she was going to have to start all over again without those golden trappings, and she really didn't mind. For the first time in her life, she had her self-respect, but the fact remained—what *did* she want to do?

That was a very good question.

Delaina thought about everything they'd discussed last night, from the cloister to moving to France and pretending to be a rich widow. She thought about it most of the afternoon, and it was still rolling through her mind when someone knocked softly at her door just before sunset. Thinking it was the serving wench finally returning with the pot she'd promised, she went to the panel.

"Who comes?" she asked.

"Magnus."

Startled, and perhaps a bit excited that he'd finally made an appearance, she threw the bolt and yanked the door open. Magnus stood there, larger than life in full battle regalia, and she motioned him forward.

"Come in, please," she said.

He obeyed, coming into the chamber and filling it up with his size and strength. He had his helm on, the first time she'd seen him wearing it, but he removed it the moment he came inside. That was the mannerly thing to do. Delaina threw the bolt, but when she turned to look at him, with the light of day pouring through the window, she got a good look at just how handsome he really was.

For a moment, her breath caught in her throat.

"Good day to you, Magnus," she said, sputtering over her words a little as she tried to reclaim her composure. "You have returned."

She was stating the obvious, perhaps out of surprise, and he cocked an eyebrow. "I told you that I would," he said. "I apologize that it is so late, however. I was up all night as the feast dissolved and drunken warlords headed home, so I slept during the day."

She smiled. "You need not explain yourself," she said. "You are a very busy man. I realize that."

He shrugged. "Busy enough," he said, looking around and noting the remains of the meal on the table. "You've eaten, I see?"

Delaina looked at the crumbs and empty bowls. "Aye," she said. "But earlier today. I've not eaten since. Are you hungry? Shall I send for food?"

"I'll do it," he said, going to the door and unlocking it before calling out to a servant somewhere down the corridor. Satisfied his wishes had been adequately relayed, he shut the door again and turned to her. "I've not eaten today, so I will share a meal with you, if you don't mind."

Delaina went to the table and began piling the dirty cups and bowls together. "Not at all," she said. "I am happy for the company."

"Good," he said, going over to the table and sitting in one of the chairs, backward, so he was leaning forward on the back of the chair. "Did you sleep well? I cannot imagine this place was at all quiet."

She grinned. "I have learned many new curse words listening to the shouting in the common room," she said. "I am certain those will serve me well in my new life."

He fought off a smile. "Particularly if you go to the cloister."

"Undoubtedly."

She looked at him and snorted, which caused him to chuckle. They laughed at each other for a few moments in a surprisingly warm moment while she tucked all of the used dishes aside.

"I will admit that the nuns more than likely will not appreciate those new words," he said. "Mayhap it is best if you do not go to the cloister."

"Agreed."

"Have you decided what to do, then?"

Her smile faded as she sat down in a chair opposite him. "I think so," she said. "I have been thinking about it quite a lot today, and I've come to a conclusion."

"What's that?"

"That I do not want to leave England," she said. "It is my home, after all. I do not want to leave it, not even for a new life in France."

He nodded. "Understandable. What will you do?"

She cocked her head thoughtfully. "Well," she said slowly, "I thought a great deal about what you said, how a woman cannot simply live on her own and earn her own way. But I know that's not entirely true. There are women who have taken over for their husbands when they have died, with their trades."

Magnus nodded. "That is true," he said. "Women have become tavernkeeps and blacksmiths and the like when their husbands have passed on. But you do not have a husband who can pass on his trade."

"I know," she said quickly. "But I was wondering… hoping, actually… if I were to give you the money, would you be willing to purchase land for me? Mayhap you know of some lord who would like to sell a small portion of his land with a home upon it. A cottage would do. I could simply tell everyone that I am a widow and I could turn the land into a farm."

His eyebrows lifted. "Do you know about farming?"

She nodded. "I learned much living with my grandparents when I was young," she said. "And I learned much when I fostered at Okehampton. I learned to milk cows and goats. I learned how to make cheese. Magnus, truly, I am not a useless woman. I know how to do a great many things, but I have no one to ask to help me. You have helped me so much so far, and I thought I would ask if you would consider helping me in this way?"

He scratched his head. "Of course I would be willing, but

where do you wish to make this purchase?" he said. "If you do not wish to be discovered, it would have to be someplace remote."

"Like in the north? Where your family lives?"

Now he was onto her. "You mean that you wish for me to ask my father if he will sell you some land?" he said, watching her nod. It was a big request, and he puffed his cheeks out when he realized what she wanted. "I do not know, Delaina. My father is the Earl of Berwick, but those lands are treacherous. I do not want you buying land where the Scots could raid and take everything from you."

"I see," she said, the excitement on her face fading quickly. "I know it is much to ask, Magnus. You are free to decline my request. I will not be offended."

He shook his head. "It is not that," he said. "It is simply that I would ask my uncle, the Earl of Warenton, rather than my father. All of his lands are so volatile, but my uncle Scott has lands that are more peaceful to the south. However, I am fairly certain he would not sell to a woman."

"Why not?"

"Because a lone woman in the north would be foolish to live by herself."

Her shoulders slumped further. "Very well," she said glumly. "I understand. If that is not possible, then there is only one thing I can do."

"The cloister?"

She smiled weakly. "Nay," she said. "Mayhap I will return to Margit. She established a business, and when I went to her for training, she taught me a great deal. Mayhap she would have some ideas on what I could do."

The warm expression from his face vanished. "You would

return to her brothel?" he said, sounding irritated. "Would you truly do something like that?"

She had no idea why he was so annoyed. "I cannot stay here forever," she said. "I know that returning to her is not ideal, but as we have realized, I have very few options on where I can go. I do not have many choices for my life in general. Mayhap someone—she has many patrons who are rich—would offer me… something."

His jaw was twitching. "What *something*?"

She refused to look at him. "Marriage, I suppose," she said quietly. "I know I said that I was too old, but mayhap they would not expect too much from me. Truly, Magnus, what other choice do I have? I wanted my freedom, but the truth is that I cannot simply be free. As you have said, a woman without support is simply not done."

He was still sitting there, grinding his jaw, looking at her most unhappily. "So you would return to a brothel," he said, sounding disgusted. "I thought you did not want to belong to another man ever again."

"If he was my husband, it would be different."

"You do not want to be married to anyone who visits Margit's brothel, Delaina."

She sighed sharply and stood up. "Of course I do not," she hissed. "But what else is there for me? I have had the entire night to think on this, and I must face facts. I am a damaged woman. I have let men touch me and I have taken money and jewels and horses and property for it. A courtesan is a polite word for whore, so let us speak plainly. I know what I am and you do, also, so do not act as if I have better choices, for I do not. I have very little choice in any of this, and you know it."

He did, but he hated to admit it. In fact, Magnus was having a very difficult time with the conversation for reasons he couldn't fully understand. All he knew was that Delaina was a woman among women, so beautiful and bright that she outshone the sun. Even as he sat there and looked at her, all he could see was grace and magnificence, an elegant woman who found herself in a horrible situation. As he'd known from the beginning, she didn't deserve any of this. He couldn't stand the thought of her going back to a brothel.

He couldn't stand the thought of another man touching her.

God, he was in trouble.

So much trouble…

"Delaina," he said softly. "I want to propose something, and I want you to listen carefully before you respond. Will you do this?"

She had her back to him, her messy braid trailing to her buttocks. But she nodded, once, and he continued. God help him, he couldn't stop himself, and he had no idea why not.

Something shocking was about to come forth.

"You do have another choice," he said. "You have me."

She didn't say anything for a moment. But after several long seconds, her head lifted and she looked at him.

"What do you mean?" she said.

He took a deep breath. "I mean that you can marry me," he said. "Marry me and I'll send you north to live with my father and mother until I can come for you. That will keep you safe."

Her eyes widened in shock. "What on earth are you saying?"

"I am saying that I will marry you, if you will have me."

That only caused her eyes to widen even more. They very nearly popped from her skull. "Nay," she breathed. "You do not mean it."

"I do."

That was evidently not the answer she wanted. She practically screamed at him. "*Nay!*" she said. "Magnus de Wolfe, leave this chamber this instant. Do you hear me? Get out!"

He frowned, but he didn't move. "Why should I leave?" he said. "What is wrong with you?"

Delaina burst into tears. "Get out," she sobbed. "I will not let you ruin your life by marrying me, you silly fool. You are offering out of pity, and I'll not let you do it. Get out of here and never come back!"

"Delaina—"

"Stop it!" she said, nearly hysterical. "What is the matter with you that you would offer for the hand of a whore? How dare you attempt to ruin yourself in that way! You are the lord commander of the king's knights, and you deserve a fine wife from a fine family, not a concubine who has been passed around by old and disgusting warlords. Get out and do not return!"

She was serious. Magnus could see that. As he stood up, she grasped the knife that was on the table and wielded it at him in a threatening manner. Magnus eyed the knife, unmoved.

"Put that down before you hurt yourself," he said, scowling. "And I am not ruining my life. No one has to know who you are but me. If you are willing to leave your past behind, so am I."

Delaine was still weeping heavily. "I cannot leave my past behind," she said quietly. "It is part of me, and I can never leave it behind. We do not live in a pretend world where such things are possible, Magnus."

"We do if I say we do."

She wiped at her wet face. "It is not possible," she said. "I cannot let you do this to yourself, Magnus. You are a darling for offering and I shall never forget your kindness, but I cannot let you do it. Please go now. *Please*."

"I won't."

"I am begging you."

"Nay."

"Then if you will not, I will."

With that, the knife clattered to the floor and she bolted for the window overlooking the river. Had Magnus been any slower, he wouldn't have been able to catch her as she tried to propel herself through the open window. He managed to catch her around the waist, and partially by the hair, dragging her back in through the window as she fought him. He pulled her back toward the chair he'd been sitting on, but he stumbled over one of her satchels on the floor, and that pitched him right onto the bed.

Delaina fought him like a banshee.

"Let me go!" she howled. "If you will not leave, I will. I will not let you do this to yourself, do you hear?"

Magnus had her tightly, though she was giving a good struggle. He had both enormous arms around her body, holding her like a vise, but his head was next to hers.

"Stop fighting," he said evenly, his lips next to her ear. "Delaina, cease your struggles. I am not leaving, and neither are you. If you do not wish to marry me because you find me unattractive or unpleasant, then you only need say so. You do not need to make it seem as if I have done something wrong."

As he'd hoped, her struggling dramatically lessened. "Magnus, please let me go," she begged. "You are mad somehow. You know that you cannot marry someone like me."

"I can if no one knows who you are," he said, his lips next to her ear and her soft body in his grasp. "We shall come up with a different name and a different background. That is all my family need know."

Her fighting stopped altogether. "Oh… Magnus," she said, the resistance draining out of her. "You are completely mad to think so."

"Why?"

"What if I am recognized?" she said, starting to weep again. "There are men in England who know who I am."

"There are very few who know who you are," he said, thinking that her ear against his lips was quite erotic. "Just a select few. Daventry is dead. What about the others who knew you?"

She sniffled. "Falmouth is not dead, but I've heard he's not left his home in many months," she said. "But Daventry's son… Jerome… he knows what I look like."

Magnus grunted. "I will take care of him," he muttered. "Who else knows?"

"Edward."

"The king will never see you again," Magnus said. "I will send you north to my father and resign my post. We shall live at Berwick."

She didn't say anything for a moment. "God's Bones," she muttered unhappily. "Now you truly *are* mad. How can you say that you shall resign a prestigious post for a woman you've only known a few short hours?"

"Does this mean you accept?"

Her answer was to push herself from his arms and stand up. Magnus was sorry, too, for holding her against him had been one of the more enjoyable things he'd ever done. He sat up, looking at her pale face, but all he could read in her expression was sorrow.

"I have never known anyone as selfless as you," she said, her voice hoarse with emotion. "Magnus, you have made me an offer that is something I've waited for my entire life. But you've not thought it through. You've not thought on how it would affect you or your family. I know you say that we could change my name, but we would live in fear for the rest of our lives that someone would betray our secret. Your family would be shamed. *You* would be shamed. You are the kindest man I have ever known, and I could not do that to you."

He sat on the edge of the bed, watching her. "You must trust me enough to know that I do not make foolish decisions," he said. "I would not be where I am today if I did. Delaina… you do not deserve the life you have led. Let me give you the one that you do."

The sorrow on her features flickered with hope. "That is the sweetest thing anyone has ever said to me."

"Will you at least think about it?"

"Nay. I cannot think on it."

He stood up. "Is it because you do not wish to be married to me?" he said. "I realize that I am not worthy of someone of your beauty, but I would make a good husband, I swear it."

She sighed faintly, a ripple of longing crossing her features. "Of course I would be honored to be your wife," she said softly. "You are the worthiest man I have ever met, and it would be like a dream to me if we were married. You *are* a dream, Magnus. A perfect dream. But I could not damage that perfection with what I am."

He smiled faintly. "You are a goddess," he said softly. "I would be the most fortunate man in all of England to call you my wife. I realize I do not know that much about you other than what you have told me, but sometimes, instinct takes over where knowledge is lacking. I trust my instincts when it comes to you. What I do not know, I can learn. What I cannot learn, I can feel. Will you at least give me that opportunity?"

She closed her eyes for a brief moment, lowering her gaze. "You speak like a poet," she whispered. "You do not know how badly I want to agree."

"You do not have to, not at the moment," Magnus said. "But sleep on it. Think on it. I will be back in the morning, and we can speak again."

She simply nodded without looking up at him. She was looking at her feet. Magnus leaned over and kissed her on the top of her lowered head.

"I will go now," he said softly. "Bolt the door behind me."

With that, he was gone, shutting the panel quietly behind him. Overwrought and overcome, Delaina made it over to the door and threw the bolt. Then she sank to her buttocks and wept for the dream that would never come to fruition, for the fine young knight that would never be hers. It was all happening so fast, so blindingly fast, but she completely understood when Magnus said he was running on instinct. So was she. But she couldn't even dare to hope that he felt something for her.

A knock on the door startled her.

Thinking it was the serving wench, perhaps motivated by Magnus' command as he departed The Pox, she pushed herself up from the floor and wearily threw the bolt again, pulling the panel open before asking who it was. She was moving lethargically, like a woman with the weight of the world upon her shoulders. But once the panel opened, she found herself looking at Magnus again.

He hesitated before speaking.

"I cannot leave you like this," he said. "I got to the stairwell and realized I cannot leave you like this. I have upset you terribly, and that was not my intention. I swear to you that it was not. May I please stay until you are calm?"

She stood back from the doorway as he came in without her permission. He simply stepped inside and shut the door. He had to look away from her to lock it, but when his focus returned to her, his expression was full of uncertainty. He looked so sad, as if he'd done something terribly wrong, but Delaina knew he hadn't. He'd tried to do the most wonderful thing in the world, and she'd berated him for it.

She was a monster.

Before she realized what she was doing, Delaina rushed to Magnus and leapt on him, anchoring her arms around his neck as she claimed his lips. He was startled by her onslaught for about a half-second before wrapping his big arms around her and holding her fast as they feasted upon one another. It was that instinct Magnus had spoken of, and they had it for one another. Though it was the first time they'd tasted each other, it was as if they'd been doing it all their lives.

Impulse consumed them.

Suddenly, they were over on the bed and Magnus was stripping off his tunics, his weapons. He had to pull away from her to remove his mail coat, but Delaina boldly stepped in and yanked it off him as if she'd done it a thousand times before. Off it came, and it ended up on the floor. He fell on top of her, kissing her, touching her, listening to her gasp with pleasure.

But she had some pleasure of her own to give.

She moved to his breeches, untying them, sliding them down his hips before her soft hands moved to sensitive places. Magnus hissed as she grasped his rock-hard erection, stroking it, cupping his testicles and squeezing gently. She rolled him over onto his back and straddled him, pulling his boots and breeches off before settling between his legs and taking his erection into her mouth. Her tongue did wicked things to him as her fingers invaded the crack of his buttocks, touching a place that very nearly sent him over the edge.

God, what the woman could do to him.

But he didn't want her to pleasure him, not to the point of release. He wanted to pleasure her, to acquaint himself with her magnificent body, and he pulled the lamb's wool garment right over her head, leaving her nude in the fading light of sunset. He took a moment to simply look her over, her perfect breasts and slender waist. She was magnificent. *A courtesan,* he reminded himself. *She has shared this body with others.*

But he was going to be the last.

He was the only one worthy of her.

Delaina ended up on her back when he flipped her over, assuming the dominant position. She gasped when he suckled her, gently at first, and then with more force. Bolts of excitement ran throughout her body, and she had to make a conscious effort not to cry out in joy. But her heavy breathing told Magnus how much she liked what he was doing to her, the hands in his hair encouraging him. She held him to her breasts as he nursed hungrily, his tongue lapping at her soft flesh.

Delaina was lost in a haze of desire, feeling Magnus' hands all over her, his mouth in tender places. When he began to kiss her belly, she put a hand in her mouth to keep from screaming. Though she'd had a man do this to her before, she'd found it horrifying and revolting when she had to pretend she liked it. But this time, she wasn't pretending. It was the most amazing thing she had ever experienced.

It was Magnus.

He moved lower still, his mouth now on the mound of dark

curls. Delaina instinctively parted her legs for him, and he settled his big body in between them, his mouth loving her most private core. Delaina couldn't help the cries of passion then; his tongue was wicked, his mouth hot, and she had never before known this act to be pleasurable. Every lap of his tongue and she was ready to scream.

She was quickly reaching her climax; Magnus could feel her body beginning to twitch. Lifting himself up, he gazed into her eyes, his fingers on her lips. He was so overwhelmed that he couldn't even speak. All he wanted to do was look and touch and feel. Delaina gazed back at him as he put his massive manhood at her threshold. There was no fear, no hesitation in their expressions. As he slanted his lips over hers, Magnus drove deep into her slick folds.

Delaina's knees came up, her body arching to meet his thrust. Magnus groaned with sheer delight. She was tight and hot, and he withdrew before thrusting hard again and seating himself fully. Delaina's pelvis rocked up against him, and he lost his control then, feeling the animal instinct to mate with this woman. His thrusts were measured and deep, pelvis against pelvis as they matched each other move for move. Sweat began to glisten. Magnus lifted himself up on his arms just so he could watch her magnificent body in the weak light. It was like nothing he'd ever experienced before.

His thrusts grew deep, harder, as he felt his release approach. She met his thrusts, and he could feel her tightening her walls around him, something she'd been taught to do at Margit's brothel. It was a way to make a man climax more quickly. He couldn't stop to think how she'd practiced doing it because it didn't matter any longer. She was his, and she was his for life now. No past, only the future.

He fell back on top of her, gathering her against him, his face buried in the crook of her neck. He could hear someone whispering sweet words to her, and realized it was him.

You are mine, beautiful girl.

You belong to me.

When she nodded to his words, reaching down to touch him where their bodies joined, he thrust hard as his climax approached. But just as he was ready to release himself into her, she suddenly removed his manhood from her body and began to stroke it furiously. He ended up releasing on her belly as she stroked him with an expert hand, grinding his teeth so hard that he bit his tongue. But as his spasms died down, he looked at her in surprise.

"Why did you do that?" he asked, panting.

She opened her eyes, panting herself. "What?"

"Remove me."

She realized what he meant. "So there will be no child."

He knew that was what she'd been taught, but in this case, he didn't agree with her. "You are mine forever, my angel," he whispered, reaching down to gently remove her hand from his manhood. "If you want marriage and family, I am willing to give those to you. May I finish?"

She looked at him with uncertainty but so much hope. So very much hope. "You… you already have."

He leaned down, suckling her earlobe gently. "But you haven't."

With that, he plunged his semi-erection into her, grinding his pelvis against hers and stimulating her passion yet again. But Delaina was so highly aroused that in little time, she was climaxing around him. He could feel her tight walls drawing at him, demanding seed that had already been spilt, but he kept thrusting gently until her spasms died down, enjoying the moment with every fiber in his body until he opened his eyes and saw tears streaming down her temples.

Immediately, he stopped.

"What is it?" he whispered, concerned. "Did I hurt you?"

She shook her head, opening her eyes to look at him. A hand came up to his face, stroking his cheek.

"Not at all," she said. "It is simply that… *that* has never happened to me."

He wasn't sure what she meant. "What do you mean?"

She sobbed softly, but there was joy in her expression. "You have taken your pleasure," she said. "But I have never taken mine. What we have just done… it has always been something I have dreaded. To be touched like that or to touch like that… Magnus, I've never enjoyed it. This is the very first time."

Now he understood. A smile played on his lips as he leaned over and kissed her lips tenderly.

"It will not be the last," he murmured. "Tell me you'll marry me, Delaina. I swear to you that I will do everything I can to make you happy. Give me that chance. Please."

She wrapped her arms around his neck, pulling her to him, and their hot flesh melded. Delaina was in a haze of satisfaction such as she had never known. Magnus was all around her, his body still embedded within her. She never wanted to move from this state, holding him as tightly as he was holding her. In this position, they fell into a deep, satisfied, and dreamless sleep.

It was a night to remember.

CHAPTER NINE

Lonsdale House
London home of the Earl of Hereford and Worcester

A S THE HOME of generations of the well-known de Lohr family, Lonsdale House represented the Earls of Hereford and Worcester in London.

A big, three-storied manor home built out of somber gray granite, it was as strong and powerful as the earls who commanded more than half of the Welsh marches. The family had close ties to the House of de Wolfe, linked by marriage and service as well as a long and rock-solid friendship.

It was early morning as Magnus approached the enormous manse sitting on a bend of the River Thames, and he recalled the fond memories of spending time at the place as a small boy.

Perhaps he'd only spent a couple of summers there, but it was enough for him to remember the good times with the de Lohr children. There were as many of them as there were de Wolfe children, so games and contests were always evenly matched. He distinctly remembered playing with the older boys of the current earl, boys named Christopher and Ashdon, Bing, and Blake. The latter two were twins, evil to the bone, and he could still feel the sting from the projectiles they would launch at his head.

The memory made him chuckle.

But that was a long time ago. He had seen the de Lohr sons many times in his lifetime, considering the House of de Lohr was a great supporter of the Crown. He had served with the many sons of Morgen de Lohr, Earl of Hereford and Worcester, because the man had six of them. They were all excellent warriors, even the evil twins, who had grown into fine and responsible knights. The eldest and heir, yet another Christopher de Lohr in a family with several men named Christopher in its illustrious history, was a particularly adept commander and a tribute to his famous great-grandfather.

The relationship between the House of de Wolfe and the House of de Lohr went back to that famous great-grandsire, a man who had served Richard the Lionheart on crusade before returning home and assuming the role as Richard's champion. He had done battle against Richard's younger brother, John, in the days when chivalry was alive and political intrigue was as common as a sunrise. Magnus' great-grandfather had served Christopher de Lohr and had been an extremely close friend all of his life. There had never been any time in the history of England that the House of de Lohr and the House of de Wolfe were on opposite sides.

They were loyal to each other, even more than they were loyal to England itself.

Given that Magnus' family was so far to the north and, at the moment, he needed help and advice, it was natural that he should seek it from the Earl of Hereford and Worcester. There were several families that his family was close to, and several well-respected lords that his father was personally great friends with, but somehow Magnus only really felt comfortable coming to a man that was greatly respected by everyone in England.

Morgen de Lohr was that man.

As he traveled down the road that led toward Lonsdale house, he found himself thinking on his unexpected future. Two days ago, he would have never imagined himself a betrothed man, and, truth be told, he wasn't exactly sure he *was* betrothed. Delaina had never given him an answer. But after last night, he was going on the assumption that she was agreeable to his marriage proposal, and now her problems became his. His biggest problem, as he saw it, was that he needed to get her out of London before Despenser tracked her down. The man may be power-hungry and ridiculous, but he wasn't a fool. He had very capable men he paid well to serve him. Magnus was concerned that one of those men might actually locate Delaina, because if Hugh was serious about finding her, he would leave no stone unturned.

And that was why Magnus needed to get her out of London as quickly as he could.

The decision to seek Lonsdale had been a swift one, nearly the moment he woke up that morning with his arms wrapped around Delaina. The night had been magical, and he knew, as he watched her sleep, that he couldn't sit idle while her entire life was at stake. Whether or not she had agreed to marry him, he was going to help her.

He had a stake in this now, too.

Therefore, as Lonsdale House came into view through the trees, Magnus debated just how much he should tell the earl. The most important fact was of Delaina's identity—he had told her that no one would know of her past except him, but that wasn't entirely true. If he expected help, those he sought it from would have to know why. He would have to swear the earl to secrecy, because he didn't want her background getting around, but considering he was going to be asking for the man's help, Magnus thought it only right the man should know the truth.

His biggest fear was that de Lohr would refuse him.

There was only one way to find out.

Lonsdale House was surrounded by an enormous wall with a gatehouse two stories tall. It was a rather imposing sight, sitting squat and powerful on the banks of the Thames, and Magnus had always appreciated the strategic position of the home. The de Wolfes had their own London town home, which actually belonged to his uncle Edward, but Edward the diplomat was not in residence at this time, was instead in Scotland trying to broker a treaty between Edward and John Balliol. Edward had followed in the footsteps of his diplomatic grandfather as one of the king's greatest negotiators.

It had become a de Wolfe tradition.

Soon, the gatehouse loomed before Magnus, and he called to the sentries, identifying himself. When they saw the royal tunic and heard the name, the portcullis began to lurch, slowly lifting as men began to tug on the chains. When it was about halfway up, Magnus dismounted his horse and walked the animal through the gatehouse, emerging into a large bailey beyond.

He was met by a de Lohr knight.

"Greetings," the man said. "I am Marcellus de Shera. We have met before, though I doubt you would remember. There were a lot of men in the hall at the time."

Magnus peered at the man. "De Shera," he said. "I remember you. It was when Parliament convened last autumn, was it not?"

"It was."

"And you are Coventry?"

Marcellus nodded. "Aye," he said. "My father is Augustus de Shera, son of Maximus."

The light of recognition came to Magnus' eyes. "Of course," he said. "The Lords of Thunder. I remember my grandfather speaking fondly of them. Is your father well?"

Marcellus nodded. "He is," he said. "Thank you for asking."

"And your grandfather?"

"We lost him a few years ago, unfortunately, but he was strong until the end."

Magnus smiled faintly. "Men who fought with Simon de Montfort usually live forever, if only in legend," he said. Then he gestured to the manse. "Is Hereford in residence?"

Marcellus nodded, indicating for Magnus to follow him. "He is," he said. "He has been here for a few weeks because there was a great feast at Westminster he was expected to attend."

"I know," Magnus said. "It was last night, but I did not see him."

Marcellus glanced at him. "He has not been well," he said. "A pain in his belly that he has had before, but Lady de Lohr would not let him attend on the advice of the physic, and he is quite angry over it. If you were at the feast, then mayhap you can tell him what went on. That might soothe his anger."

Magnus grinned. "Nothing like a wife denying one's wants."

"I would not know. I am not married."

"Nor I. But we have all seen what a wife can do to even the strongest of men."

Marcellus bit off a smile as he ushered Magnus inside the

manse, which was cool and dark and smelled slightly of dampness from the river.

Magnus hadn't taken two steps when Marcellus suddenly put out a hand.

"Be prepared, my lord," he said. "You may have to defend yourself."

Magnus looked at the man, puzzled, when he was suddenly hit from behind. As he struggled with his balance, the entry seemed to come alive with small children, all of them rushing at him and Marcellus. Worse still, they were bearing sticks. As Marcellus began pushing them away, sounding the alarm, Magnus found himself utterly besieged by a gang of tiny ruffians. One child hit him behind the knees, trying to disable him, while others were grabbing at his belt, trying to find his purse.

It was the most comical thing Magnus had ever seen.

However, he was not without experience when it came to rough children. He had a host of nephews and cousins who were similar in their mode of attack. Sometimes, he had to fight his way into Berwick because of his older brothers' children, or even the children of his father's knights. He knew how to deal with such bandits.

He started walking, grabbing the little hands that were trying to strip him. He trapped several little hands and the boys attached to them, dragging them over to a stairwell that had an iron sconce mortared into the floor at the base of it. He shook the iron post and, realizing it was stable enough, grabbed the silk banister on the stairwell and yanked. The thing came free, and he started to tie the children up to the iron sconce, much to their displeasure. In fact, one of them tried to bite him, and he pulled the cap off the lad and shoved it in his mouth to both silence him and keep him from biting someone else.

Behind him, he could hear a deep male voice.

"Thank God someone has given these wild animals what they deserve," he said. "Magnus, is that you?"

With a lazy grin on his face, Magnus turned to see Morgen de Lohr, Earl of Hereford and Worcester, standing a few feet away. But he didn't stop tying up the children that had been trying to rob him.

"You recognized me in my natural state, my lord?" he said. "Torturing de Lohr children?"

Morgen, a large man with a crown of blond hair, laughed softly. "They deserve everything you are doing to them," he said. "Poor Marcellus must contend with this every time he enters the house, only he serves me and cannot fight back as you do."

"Why not?"

"Because my wife becomes angry with him."

Magnus finished off the tie, and the three boys he'd captured began to howl and beg for release. Magnus looked to Morgen for the command to set the boys free, but Morgen shook his head.

"Leave them for the dogs," he said. "It will teach them a lesson."

Magnus fought off a grin as the boys started weeping. The other children who had been part of the attack scattered back into the shadows, leaving Marcellus harried but untouched. His features were full of annoyance as he reattached dirks and straightened out his tunic.

"Magnus de Wolfe has arrived, my lord," he said with great irritation. "I was coming to announce him when we were set upon."

Morgen chuckled. "Poor Marcellus," he said. "One of these days, I shall give him permission to do what he must to end these attacks once and for all."

Magnus was trying very hard not to laugh at Marcellus, but that battle was lost when the man rolled his eyes and turned for the entry. They all knew that would never happen.

Magnus followed Morgen into the great solar that overlooked the Thames, a room full of the resplendence of the House of de Lohr. As soon as he stepped into the chamber, he paused, closed his eyes, and inhaled deeply through his nose.

"Ah," he said with satisfaction. "It smells just as I remember it. Like leather and smoke and greatness."

Morgen went to the table where he'd been working when he heard the commotion in the entry. "You mean it does not smell like disappointment, irritation, and shame?"

Magnus started laughing. "I have smelled that before, my lord," he said. "At Westminster, most recently, as I spoke to Hugh Despenser the Elder."

Morgen rolled his eyes as he sat down. "Christ," he muttered. "Not him again."

"Unfortunately, my lord."

"Something must be done about him."

"I've heard that something is, my lord."

Magnus meant the rumors surrounding the intended removal of Hugh along with several other advisors to the king that the warlords considered a threat to England. And there were many. Magnus knew it, as did every man who was loyal to England. That included Morgen, along with Magnus' father and uncles.

Morgen's gaze lingered on him for a moment. "Who did you hear that from?" he finally asked.

"My father, my lord," Magnus said. "The Earl of Berwick may be in the north, but his interests are everywhere when it comes to England and her safety."

Morgen grunted. "Atty is a great man," he said, calling Patrick de Wolfe by his familial nickname. "Wherever he leads, I will follow."

"He says the same of you, my lord."

Morgen smiled faintly in thanks before turning to his table. He had been reviewing dispatches when Magnus arrived, but he pushed them aside and indicated the chair across the table from him.

"Sit," he said. "It has been some time since you and I last spoke. I would assume you were at the feast last night?"

Magnus nodded. "I was, my lord."

"Anything to report?"

Magnus thought a moment. "There was no violence, fortunately," he said. "Everyone behaved themselves, though I must say that my men were on heightened alert. One wrong move and the entire hall would go up in blood and flames."

"True," Morgen said. "My wife would not let me attend, unfortunately."

"I heard, but you truthfully did not miss anything of note. It was all quite tame."

Morgen shrugged. "That is the best we can hope for during these turbulent times," he said. "What of Edward? Did he enjoy himself?"

Magnus nodded. "As far as I could tell," he said. "The man did not go to bed until the sun rose, so I suspect he had a pleasant evening."

Morgen stared at him a moment as if expecting far more, but realized he wasn't going to get it. Suspicion took over. "Is that why you've come to see me? To tell me that the king presented a boring feast?" He shook his head knowingly. "You may dispense with the pretexts, Magnus. Why are you *really* here?"

Magnus smiled weakly. There was no use in denying that he'd come with a purpose, because he had. He wanted something from Morgen, so he had to be careful about asking, but he couldn't lie to the man. He needed him.

"I've come for your help," he finally said.

"You have it," Morgen said without hesitation. "What can I do?"

Magnus sighed, averting his gaze. "I am not entirely sure where to start, so I will simply start from the beginning," he said. "Have you ever heard of the Seven Jewels of London?"

Again, Morgen nodded without hesitation. "I have," he said. "Those pretty young women that Longshanks used to gain favors. Courtesans of the highest order."

"Aye," Magnus said. "Those are the Jewels I refer to."

Morgen cocked his head thoughtfully, stroking his chin. "As I recall, they came into Longshanks' court about ten or twelve years ago," he said. "I remember that they were all quite young, from good families. Are they still around?"

Magnus nodded. "They are," he said. "That is why I need your help, with one in particular."

"Oh?" Morgen said, interested. "What do you need?"

"I want to hide her at Lonsdale."

Morgen hadn't expected to hear that. "Why?" he said. "What has happened that you must hide one of them?"

Magnus sighed heavily, raking his fingers through his hair in an unsteady gesture. "I am not explaining myself very well," he said. "Forgive me. This is awkward, and I am not sure how to tell you what I must. I do not wish for you to think me foolish."

"I would never think that, Magnus," Morgen said, leaning forward on the table, his sky-blue eyes full of both concern and interest. "Simply tell me what this is all about. I will not judge you, lad."

Magnus glanced at him, hoping that was true. "Very well," he said. "It all started last night. Lord Daventry arrived at the feast with a Jewel on his arm. It seems that she had been with him for several months, and he wanted her company at the feast. To make a long story short, Lord Daventry died last night. At the feast."

"He did?" Morgen said, shocked. "What happened?"

"Some kind of hemorrhage. The man bled out, everywhere."

"Christ," Morgen hissed. "How ghastly."

"It was," Magnus said. "But the Jewel… My lord, I must swear you to secrecy on this matter, because if it were known, if Hugh Despenser were told, there would be… trouble."

"I will take it to my grave. What has happened?"

Magnus leaned onto the table and lowered his voice. "When Daventry died, I arranged for his body to be sent back to his home, Haydon Square," he said. "But the Jewel… with Daventry dead, she was free. Or, at least, she wanted to be. Normally, I do not interfere in how a man lives his life or the women he lives it with, but in this case, the Jewel had nowhere to go, and she refused to remain at Haydon Square. But it was more than that—when Despenser heard of Daventry's death, he knew the man had a Jewel and asked me to bring the woman to him."

"Did you?"

Magnus shook his head. "Nay," he said. "I did not. She was taken to a safe place, away from Despenser, and he is angry about it."

"He knows that you did this?"

"He does not know, my lord," Magnus said. "That is the problem—he wants her, and I will not take her to him, nor will I tell her where she is. He does not know that I am aware of her whereabouts, but I fear that will change, because she is in London. Because I refused him, I would be willing to wager that Hugh has men looking for her even as we speak. That is why I want to bring her here for safekeeping."

Morgen was trying to piece this tale together because Magnus wasn't doing a very good job. He could see, almost instantly, that there was something more here than met the eye. Magnus was withholding something, and Morgen suspected it centered on the Jewel herself.

"Magnus," he said after a moment. "I will ask you a question, and you will be perfectly honest with me."

"Of course I will, my lord."

"What is this Jewel to you that you should risk your career so?"

A ripple of vulnerability crossed Magnus' features. "I do not know," he said, sounding weakened. "That is the truth, my lord. I do not know. All I know is that I spent a good deal of time with her, speaking to her, hearing her story, and I realized that she has been grossly mistreated most of her adult life. She is bright, educated, and blindingly beautiful. She does not deserve what has happened to her, and if Despenser gets his hands on her, she will go back to the life she is trying desperately to run away from."

"And you want to bring her here in the course of her running away from that life?"

Magnus nodded. "You should also be aware that I think I

may have feelings for her," he said, stumbling over the words. "If that is not clear, I will make it so. I do not want there to be any misunderstandings. I do not know how it happened, only that it has. I have offered to marry her and take her north to live with my family."

Morgen's eyebrows lifted in surprise. "A courtesan?" he said. "Married to a de Wolfe?"

Magnus knew how it sounded. "I am well aware of the un-suitability, my lord," he said. "Believe me, I am. The only way this will work is if we change her name and give her a proper background so that my family is unaware of who she really is. That is why I have sworn you to secrecy. You know what only Delaina and I know. You must not betray me."

Morgen knew a man in love when he saw one. Or, at least, a man who thought he was in love. He could hear it in his voice, see it in his body language. Magnus de Wolfe was a serious, career-minded knight, a man who had risen to the top of the royal troops to become lord commander of the king's knights. He had worked hard for it. He had an impeccable pedigree.

But he also, evidently, had an Achilles' heel.

"I would never betray you, Magnus," Morgen said seriously. "But you are certain about this?"

"Without a doubt, my lord."

Morgen thought on it a moment longer before nodding. "I told you that I would help you, and I will," he said. "Bring her here, but do not tell anyone who she is when she arrives. You'd better create her new name and background before you come here."

Magnus was so relieved that he nearly slithered to the floor with it. "Thank you," he muttered. "From the bottom of my heart, thank you."

"Where is she in London?"

"The Pox, my lord."

Morgen scowled. "In that horrible place?"

Magnus grinned weakly. "Hugh, most certainly, will not think to look for her there."

Morgen grunted in agreement. "That is the truth," he said. "But remove her from that place and bring her here immediately."

"I will, my lord."

"Do you require help? I can send Marcellus with you."

"The same knight who cannot fend off small children?"

Morgen laughed softly. "He is a de Shera," he said. "I trust him with my life. You may take him if you wish."

Magnus hesitated a moment before nodding. "I am grateful," he said. "The less I involve my own men in this, the better."

"Who else knows about this?"

"Denys de Winter."

Morgen nodded in recognition. "You do not want to jeopardize his position," he said. "Send Marcellus in here, and I will tell him that he is to go with you to retrieve the lady. I will have to tell him that we are protecting her from an enemy intent on doing her harm so he will not know the truth of who, and what, she is. He does not need to know."

The warmth in Magnus' eyes faded. "Nay, he does not."

Morgen sat back in his chair, mulling over the situation. "What happens if Despenser gets his hands on her?" he asked quietly. "What then?"

"Then I will do what I must to retrieve her," Magnus said, a deadly gleam in his eye. "Make no mistake, my lord. She will go with me or I will kill whoever tries to stop me."

Morgen knew he was serious. "I know," he said. "But before

you drag your father and me into a war against Edward and Despenser—because, clearly, we will have to defend you—let us see if we cannot move the lady to Lonsdale without incident, shall we?"

Magnus stood up. "I will not forget this, my lord," he said. "I will repay this kindness, I swear it."

Morgen stood up as well. "There are no debts between de Wolfe and de Lohr," he said. "Families such as ours do not keep track of such things. Your father would do it for my sons, I am certain. And I will do it for his."

A smile crossed Magnus' lips, one of gratitude. With a dip of his head, acknowledging the earl's great generosity toward him in this situation, he quit the solar and went in search of Marcellus. He was not attacked by the de Lohr wolf pack as he left the manse, but he couldn't even think on that.

All he could think about was getting to Delaina…

Before Hugh does.

CHAPTER TEN

Westminster Palace

"NO ONE HAD seen Magnus all night." A man in a royal tunic, heavily armed, stood in front of Hugh as the sun began to rise over the Thames. "You told us to follow him, but we couldn't find him, so I sent a few men into London to look for him."

Hugh was seated upon a cushioned chair while a servant combed his hair with a gilded comb. He had a cup of warmed, watered wine in his hand, and eyed the soldier who had come to report on the movements of Magnus de Wolfe. Oddly enough, the man had been gone all night from his post.

That was damn curious.

"So he wasn't at Westminster last night," Hugh said thoughtfully. "Odd for a man sworn to command the royal knights, don't you think? Where could he have gone?"

The soldier, a big, shaggy man missing his front teeth, shook his head. "His knights are loyal to him," he said. "I had one of my men ask a knight who nearly punched him in the face for asking."

"Which knight?"

"De Winter."

Hugh snorted softly. "De Winter and de Wolfe are thick as thieves," he said. "He'll not tell you anything. What about St. Aldwyn?"

"He *did* punch one of my men."

Hugh knew he would get nowhere with the royal knights, but he had to try. Ever since he and Magnus had indulged in their contentious discussion, Hugh had grown increasingly obsessed with not only the missing Jewel, but Magnus' role in the entire situation.

Something just seemed off to him.

It was quite possible that Magnus had no role in Daventry or the missing Jewel, but it was equally possible that something *was* going on. Magnus didn't seem the least bit inclined to look for the missing Jewel, which didn't make much sense because he was a man known for his chivalry. He was one of those fools that was kind and gentle with women, and everyone knew it. Therefore, the fact that he seemed so removed from any concern involving a missing lady simply didn't make sense.

Hugh was increasingly convinced that Magnus knew more than he let on.

Therefore, Hugh had gathered several royal soldiers, men that he paid directly to do his bidding, to follow Magnus and see what the man was up to. Unfortunately, they had been unable to find him, and, according to the soldier standing in front of Hugh now, had been out all night looking for him. That only increased Hugh's suspicion. He may be ambitious and ruthless, but he wasn't stupid. Something told him that when he found Magnus, he would find the missing Jewel.

Not that he blamed Magnus, of course. Hugh had seen the

Jewels, at least a few of them, and they were all women of uncanny beauty. He'd seen the Ruby years ago, and, as he'd told Magnus, she was the most spectacular Jewel of them all. With Longshanks using them as prizes to men he wanted to reward or men he wanted to bribe, their beauty was legendary. Perhaps Magnus and all of that softness he displayed toward women had finally been his undoing with a professional courtesan. Hugh found it rather interesting that a de Wolfe knight would actually succumb to the charms of a professional whore. It only proved one thing:

That Magnus was as mortal as the rest of them.

"So you could not find Magnus all night," he finally said, mulling over the situation. "He must come back to Westminster at some point. When he does, make sure you have men follow him. He is clever, so they must be cleverer to stay out of his sight. I suspect that if he thinks he is being followed, I will never know the truth of his activities."

"But we already know the truth, my lord," the man said. "You didn't let me tell you that we discovered where he went because one of my men saw him leaving The Pox at dawn."

Hugh looked at him in astonishment. "The Pox?" he repeated. "He spent the night at that horrible place? God's Bones, only the dregs of the earth go into that place."

The soldier shrugged. "I've been there," he said. "I like it."

Hugh eyed him. "You have only proven my point," he said. "Be that as it may, was he alone when he left The Pox?"

The soldier nodded. "He was."

"There was no woman with him?"

"Not that we saw."

Hugh sighed sharply. "But this would not be an ordinary woman," he said. "She would be the most beautiful woman in

England. Red hair and blue eyes, the face of an angel. Your man did not see anyone like that?"

The soldier shrugged. "I can ask him."

"Then ask," Hugh commanded. Then an idea occurred to him, and he stood up as his servant followed him, heading over to the windows that overlooked the bend in the Thames. The Pox was along that bend, though too far away from him to really see anything. "In fact… send your men to The Pox. Tell them to look for a woman of unearthly beauty, with red hair and blue eyes. She is a courtesan, after all. Mayhap she has gone to The Pox because it is her natural setting. A whore looking for more customers. Mayhap Magnus was a customer."

The soldier was listening carefully. "You want us to find all of the whores at The Pox and bring them to you?"

Hugh nodded. "All of the ones with red hair."

"It will be done, my lord."

As the man quit the chamber, all Hugh could do was gaze upon the bend of the River Thames and smile.

Magnus de Wolfe wasn't going to beat him in this.

Hugh would have the last laugh.

ᘓ

"WHERE HAVE YOU been?" Denys demanded quietly. "Hugh is looking for you, Magnus."

Magnus had just returned from Lonsdale, and was barely into the knights' quarters when Denys was nearly on top of him. There was concern all over the man's face.

"I went to see the Earl of Hereford and Worcester," Magnus said, eyeing Denys. "Marcellus de Shera has come back to Westminster with me."

"De Lohr's knight?"

"You know the man."

"Why did he come with you?"

Denys seemed terribly agitated, and Magnus frowned at him. "What is wrong with you, Denys?" he said. "You are as nervous as a cat."

Denys watched him move from the front door and into his own chamber, the large one off the entry. The door wasn't locked because no one in their right mind would enter Magnus' chambers without being invited, so he pushed the panel open and headed to the table that held a basin, a bucket half-filled with cold water, and other grooming devices. The first thing he did was dunk his head into the bucket, then he picked up a bar of soap to scrub his hair and face.

All the while, Denys stood there and watched him closely.

"Where did you go last night?" he finally asked.

Magnus rinsed the soap off and grabbed around for a towel before answering. "I was at The Pox," he said, wiping water from his eyes. He turned to Denys and looked the man in the eye. "Before you ask another question, I was with the lady."

"All night?"

"All night."

Denys grunted unhappily and moved to the nearest chair. "I suppose I know what that means," he said. "But I will tell you that I am surprised. I never thought you were capable of such things."

Magnus ran the towel over his head and neck slowly. "Of what things?" he said. "Denys, before this goes any further, I should tell you that the situation has changed dramatically."

"How?"

Magnus paused before answering, trying to be careful in his reply. "Because I have discovered my feelings for her," he said quietly. "I do not know if this makes the situation better or worse, but somehow… *somehow*, I am attracted to her. I've never felt this way in my life."

Denys was looking at him with horror. "Are you mad?" he said. "A woman like that is not meant for you."

Magnus couldn't look at him. "I know," he said. "But I cannot help what I feel."

Denys slumped in the chair, running a weary hand over his face. "Then hiding her wasn't to save her," he said. "It was because you wanted her for yourself?"

Magnus shook his head and tossed the towel aside. "Nay, it was to save her at first," he said. "But somehow, it turned into something else. Something that fills my heart, that makes me feel giddy when I look at her. Something that overwhelms me, and I cannot explain it any better than that."

"But what of Despenser?"

"Hugh will not take her. I'll kill him if he tries."

Denys shook his head slowly. "So you would turn her into a point of contention between you two?" he said. "Magnus, you may not like the man—hell, *I* do not like the man—but he is the king's advisor. Edward will side with him in any conflict. You know that. Do not turn this into a battle of wills, because you will lose. You will lose everything over a woman who has been passed around by lascivious old lords."

Magnus looked at him. "Do not speak that way about her," he said. "She does not deserve the life she has been given. She is as powerless in this as a leaf in the wind."

"Mayhap so, but your mother will be furious if you marry a whore."

Magnus stiffened, his jaw twitching dangerously. "I told you not to speak that way about her," he growled. "I will not tell you again."

Denys knew he had pushed him a little too far, but he'd done it out of fear. "I am sorry," he said. "I did not mean to offend, but I am terrified for you, Magnus. Genuinely terrified. You have entered into a dangerous game over a woman you just met."

"I realize that."

"Did she seduce you? Is that what happened?" Denys asked, as if there had to be an explanation to Magnus' behavior. "Because you know she was taught how to do that. It is quite possible she is manipulating you to get what she wants."

Magnus was close to striking the man. As close as he'd ever been in his life. Fighting the urge, he turned his back on Denys. "You do not know what you speak of," he said. "Delaina is a woman of grace and brilliance. She is a woman above women. I know I sound as if she has bewitched me, but that is not the case. My eyes are wide open. She is the most magnificent woman I have ever known."

Denys sighed heavily. "And you're certain she did not manipulate you into this in order to gain your help?"

"I am certain."

"But you bedded her. Did she use her courtesan tricks on you in bed?"

There was judgment in that question, and Magnus' annoyance bloomed. "I had hoped for better from you," he said. "All you see is what she was, what she was forced to be. She is a woman with a heart and soul, you know. She's better than you allow."

"I am not saying she isn't, but I do not think you are seeing this clearly, Magnus," Denys said beseechingly. "If I was in this situation, what would you tell me?"

Magnus thought seriously on that. "I would think what you are thinking," he said. "I would think that you had gone mad. But I would also listen to what you are saying. Do I not get that same courtesy from you?"

"I hear you," Denys said. "But I think you have let the woman overwhelm you with her sorrows."

"That is not true."

"She wants to be free, and she is using you for her own benefit."

Magnus was finished with the conversation at that point. Disappointed and finished. "If you cannot understand the situation any more than that, then get out," he said. "I will not discuss this any further with you."

Denys stood up, looking at Magnus with great sadness. "I am only thinking of you, my friend," he said softly. "Surely you know that. I do not want to see you ruin everything you have worked for."

"I am not ruining everything I have worked for," Magnus said steadily. "That is why I went to see Worcester. That is why I have Marcellus with me. They are going to help me, and I no longer require your services."

Denys looked at him with bewilderment. "But I am your second-in-command," he said. "I am your best friend. What do you mean they are helping you? And what do you mean that you no longer require my services?"

Magnus pointed at the door in response, and Denys took the hint. Leaving the chamber, he closed the door quietly behind him.

Magnus lifted his head, tears in his eyes. He knew Denys only had his best interests in mind, but he'd banished him for a reason. Although what Denys had said about Delaina was upsetting, there was more to his reaction than simple offense.

He needed to get rid of Denys.

Magnus was going to go to The Pox, and he didn't want Denys involved. He had decided that back at Lonsdale. He wanted the man as far removed from the situation as possible so, if he were ever confronted, he could have plausible deniability. Denys was right: this *was* a dangerous game, and Magnus needed to protect him.

Even if Denys didn't understand that.

After wiping his face one last time with the towel, Magnus began to strip off his clothes, going in search of fresh ones. He intended to dress quickly in something that wasn't as identifiable as his royal standard tunic was and head over to The Pox with Marcellus. If Despenser had men out looking for Delaina, then Magnus was going to have to be very careful from this point forward. Since Hugh was already looking for him, perhaps his men were too. The last thing he wanted to do was lead them straight to Delaina.

The situation was becoming more complex by the moment.

CHAPTER ELEVEN

S HE WAS HUNGRY.

Nay, it was more than that. She was bloody well starving because she had not eaten since the night before. She had awoken sometime after dawn to an empty bed because Magnus had departed silently at some point, but she didn't feel abandoned. For the first time in her life, she felt connected to someone—in a way she never knew possible. Magnus was a man of honor, and she knew he would never abandon her, not after he proposed marriage and swore to change her life.

She had believed every word.

Therefore, it was just a matter of when he would be returning.

Delaina rose from the bed that smelled of Magnus and proceeded to get dressed for the day. There was some cold water still in the bathtub that had yet to be removed because the serving wench never did return to bring her a pot of water she could heat over the hearth, so once again she bathed in the old bathwater. But this time it was different.

Very different.

She could smell Magnus on her body. His scent was on her

hands, her arms. Everywhere he touched, she could smell him, and there was enough to make her heart flutter. Delaina had been touched by other men in the past; that had never been a secret. But, as she had told Magnus, she'd never experienced any pleasure from it. In fact, she knew that she and Magnus were going to have several difficult conversations ahead of them when he wanted to know just how much she had been schooled in the art of sexual encounters.

Her heart sank when she thought of those conversations that she simply didn't want to have. He knew that she had been trained at a brothel, and that meant she had endured several humiliating sessions as the proprietress herself trained her on how to pleasure a man.

She thought back to the very first time she had been brought into a room with a paying customer, a man who had been willing to allow an inexperienced woman to touch him. Margit had treated the situation very casually, because this was her business. There was no emotion involved, only revenue, and she had stood back and instructed Delaina to touch the man's private parts, and then proceeded to tell her what to do to him.

That had only been the beginning. Delaina thought that had been the worst possible thing to happen, until another lesson that had a man bed her so that Margit could instruct her on how to use the muscles inside her woman's center to pleasure a man as he made love to her.

Tighten up, girl! She could hear Margit hiss at her as she straddled a man who had permission to touch her. She could still see herself riding the man as one would ride a horse, astride, while Margit instructed her on how she should do things. How it should feel. It had been cold, impersonal, and businesslike.

God, she'd wanted to die.

Those were humiliating moments in her life that she had hoped to forget. Humiliating moments that had assured her she would never have a decent husband. What man wanted a wife who had been instructed by a prostitute how to use her body to pleasure a man and even manipulate him? If Magnus truly wanted to marry her, how would he ever get past the things she'd done?

Delaina spent the morning debating that very question.

She wondered if Magnus would rescind his offer once he'd had time to think about it. Men often said things in the heat of passion that they didn't mean, so Delaina was half expecting Magnus to return to her and tell her that he hadn't meant any of it. That he had spoken before he thought about it. She was fully prepared for that disappointment, the latest in a long line of them. Even so, she still hoped he would help her find a new life.

She tried not to expect too much.

The morning deepened, and Delaina's hunger grew. There weren't any crumbs left because she had already eaten them yesterday, so she had no food and no wine, and even the fire in the hearth was starting to die down. There was no more fuel in the wood box.

As the day pushed toward noon, her hunger had the better of her, and although she had promised Magnus she would not leave the room, she felt that she had no choice unless she wanted to starve to death.

She made the decision to seek out a serving wench and order a meal.

Throwing the bolt to the chamber door and opening it was something of a harrowing experience. As soon as she stood in the open doorway, she realized that the room itself insulated her from much of the sound from the common room below. It was much louder in the corridor, with men laughing and shouting at one another. Smoke from a malfunctioning hearth seemed to fill the common room and drift up the stairwell, creating a haze in the upstairs corridor.

Delaina stood there a moment, listening to the noise down below and wondering if this was such a good idea. She was hoping to see a servant on this level, but she didn't see anyone at all. In fact, she seemed very much alone on the floor. But the room down below was anything but empty; tiptoeing over to the top of the stairwell, she peered down into the room and could see that it was crowded with people. It wasn't just men, but women as well.

And they were all having a marvelous time.

That was good news, because it meant they were all occupied. Delaina began to think that perhaps no one would notice her if she went down. There were so many people that she could easily be overlooked. At least, that was the hope.

With a deep breath for courage, she headed down the stairs.

Watching the chaos and the common room from the stairwell was one thing. But being in the center of it was another. The smoke was much heavier down here, but no one seemed to notice. They were too busy drinking and laughing and throwing the occasional punch. Delaina coughed into her hand, overcome by the smoke, but she pushed onward and tried not to sputter. When she first came to the tavern, she had been whisked in so quickly that she hadn't had the opportunity to look around, but now that she had the chance, she could see just what a terrible place it really was.

It brought filth to an entirely new level.

As she'd hoped, no one seemed to notice her. They were all too busy with their food or drink or games. There seemed to be several games going on, in fact, most of them games of chance, but other games seemed simply odd. There was one man at a table who sat there with a spoon balanced on his nose while men laughed at him and tried to force him to drop the spoon. She peered at that table curiously as she headed toward the rear of the tavern in search of someone who could bring her food.

But it wasn't an easy trip.

Even if no one was really noticing her, that didn't mean they weren't pushing her around or stepping on her feet. Every time she walked past a table or a group of men, somehow, it seemed that someone bumped into her or stepped on her. She wasn't a big woman by any means, but she felt positively invisible at the moment, which, in hindsight, was an excellent thing. She was eager to request her food and then run back to her chamber and bolt the door. Given the noise and bedlam that she'd heard from the common room for the past couple of days, she knew what this group was capable of, and she wanted to get out while she could.

No wonder all of the doors on the upper floor were reinforced.

It was a wild bunch that shouted and laughed as she finally found a serving wench who agreed to bring her some food and hot water. She also requested that someone come and retrieve the tub of cold water that was still in her chamber, and the servant agreed to send someone up to get it. Lastly, she asked for fuel for her fire and was told it would be brought forthwith. Satisfied that her requests were going to be honored, Delaina turned back for the stairwell, hoping to make it to the stairs before another clumsy fool bashed into her or stepped on her toes. She was just nearing the stairwell, and safety, when someone grabbed her from behind.

Startled, Delaina gasped as she realized two men had her by the arms. They were moving swiftly for the entry to the tavern, and she opened her mouth to scream, but someone slapped a dirty, gloved hand over her lips. Unfortunately, no one in the tavern was paying any attention, something she'd been thankful for when she came down from her chamber but now something she was sorely regretting. No one to notice her, no one to help, and, even if they had noticed her being manhandled, no one made a move to question it.

As quickly as she was grabbed, Delaina was out the door, into the daylight beyond. There were other men out here, in a group, and two other frightened-looking women. Delaina had no idea why she'd been brought outside, but she didn't care; panicked, she tried to run, but one of the men still had her by the arm. She began to kick and fight, biting the hand that held her. The man howled, and as she tried to break away, something heavy hit her across the back of the head.

Everything went black.

CHAPTER TWELVE

THE POX SEEMED to be crowded this day.

Not wanting to be seen entering through the front of the establishment, Magnus and Marcellus had come in through the rear. Since the tavern sat on a waterfront that was quite busy, the usual path to enter was through the front door. But the problem with that was that it could be easily seen by anyone who happened to be on or near the waterfront. The tavern sat on a corner, crowded on the east side by other buildings, but there was a small yard and livery to the rear, accessed off an alley.

Instead of coming in on the larger road, Magnus and Marcellus came down through Watling Street, took a side alley, and ended up in the livery. They paid the stable boy well to allow them to tether their horses as they formed a plan of action. For all Marcellus knew, they were there to collect a cousin of Magnus' who was running from her abusive husband. That was the story the earl gave him, and Marcellus, a chivalrous man, was more than willing to help. Once they collected Delaina, they would be heading out again the same way they'd come, only Magnus was going to head back to Westminster while

Marcellus, with the lady, would head back to Lonsdale House.

With that plan in mind, they headed inside.

They came in through the kitchens at the rear, entering the northern side of the common room, which was divided into four big sections. The northern section usually had tables where men could gamble, open to anyone. The eastern section was usually reserved for private affairs, for those who could pay well for the privilege. The western and southern sections were the places where most people gathered. Today, it was quite crowded.

"Some cogs must have come in," Magnus said over his shoulder to Marcellus. "It is not usually this crowded."

Marcellus had the look of a hunter. He'd been forbidden to come to The Pox by the earl and, like an obedient knight, he'd stayed away, so this kind of debauchery and filth was new to him.

And exciting.

"I've been told about this place," he said, watching a man and woman fornicate over in a corner. "I've never seen it for myself."

Magnus smiled without humor. "You have not missed much," he said. "This tavern has been here for over one hundred years, and in that time, I've heard it has always been the same—the seediest establishment on the waterfront."

"I can see that."

Magnus chuckled when he turned to see that Marcellus was watching the shameless couple. The knight appeared positively appalled. Thumping the man on the arm to get his attention, Magnus motioned him toward the stairwell.

"Come on," he said. "With me."

Marcellus tore his shocked gaze away from the couple and

trotted after Magnus, following him up a narrow flight of stairs to a second floor where it was surprisingly quiet. The smoke wasn't as heavy up here, either, but the floors leaned in a rather vertigo-inducing way. Magnus headed to the first door on the right, knocking softly on it. He did it a couple of times, announcing himself, but there was no answer. Puzzled, he put his hand on the latch simply to rattle it, but the moment he touched it, the door swung open.

The chamber was empty.

Magnus stepped in, looking around the room with bewilderment. "Delaina?" he called out. "Where are you?"

There was no reply. Magnus quickly looked around, noting that her satchels were still there, and so was her coin. Everything was there, only Delaina wasn't.

"Wait here," he told Marcellus. "It is possible that she's gone to the privy, though I cannot imagine why she would leave this chamber for that hellish hole in the rear yard. I'll be back."

Marcellus nodded. "What if she returns while you are away and panics when she sees me?"

Magnus scratched his head. "Mention my name immediately," he said. "Tell her I have brought you. Hopefully that will alleviate any terror on her part, but if it does not, I will be back very shortly."

With that, he bolted out of the chamber and descended the stairs far too quickly. He couldn't imagine that they'd passed her somehow when they entered the establishment, but there were a lot of people. It was possible that they'd simply missed each other.

But he was going to give her an earful for leaving her chamber when he found her.

He charged out into the livery yard, where there were two

privies—both of them stinking to high heaven—and threw the doors open on both of them. One was occupied by a man who didn't take kindly to the exposure, while the other one was empty.

At that point, Magnus was trying not to panic. Struggling to look at it from a methodical standpoint, he began to search every inch of the livery and yard. Every barrel, every stall. He called Delaina's name a few times but received no answer. When no stone was left unturned, he headed into the tavern and went straight into the kitchen. She wasn't anywhere in the kitchen, and when the servants and tavernkeep looked oddly at the strange man in their domain, he explained that he was missing the lady that had been lodged in the room at the top of the stairs. At that point, they began to show more interest.

In fact, one of the serving wenches recalled that the very lady in question had come down from her chamber to order food not a half-hour earlier, which explained why her door was unlocked. The meat that had been boiling wasn't ready for consumption yet, which was why the servant was still down in the kitchen, still waiting for the meat. Magnus understood all of that, but he interrogated the woman as to when, and where, she last saw Delaina, and the woman could only tell him that she had been heading back toward the stairs.

But that was when something odd happened.

More serving women entered the kitchens, telling the tale of some men abducting women and taking them from the front door. It seemed that two of their servants were missing, women named Alyce and Bibi, evidently taken by these men. Patrons had seen it happen.

That had the tavernkeep moving, calling forth the armed men he'd hired for security at The Pox, men who would keep the stealing and murders to a minimum, but those men hadn't seen anyone abducted because they'd been in the eastern room watching a game of dice that was becoming heated. Abductions weren't something they normally worried over, but it became clear as the tavernkeep spoke to his servants that something was amiss. Women were missing.

Something told Magnus that Delaina was one of them.

After an hour of searching The Pox from top to bottom, he was certain of it. He collected her money and possessions, making sure to wipe the room of any evidence of her should anyone else come looking, and left.

But he couldn't shake the ghosts of Delaina that followed him.

CHAPTER THIRTEEN

S HE COULD HEAR voices.

Delaina wasn't certain how long she had been hearing them. They were muffled at first, only to disappear. Darkness fell again. Then the voices came back, louder than before, and someone was putting something cold and wet against the back of her head. It stung. The light and brightness of the world exploded around her, and she was awake, having no idea where she was or who was talking around her. In a panic, she struggled to sit up.

"Easy, lady."

Someone was holding on to her, keeping her in a supine position. She wasn't on the floor, because whatever lay beneath her was soft. Delaina stopped struggling, but her head was throbbing. Wincing, she opened her eyes to the chamber around her.

People were standing over her, looking down on her. Blinking, she tried to orient herself. There were several men around her that she didn't recognize.

But one she did.

Hugh Despenser was looking down at her with concern.

"Lady Delaina?" he said. "Can you hear me?"

Delaina blinked again, putting a shaking hand to her head. "I hear you," she said. "Where am I?"

"How do you feel?"

"Terrible."

He held up two fingers. "How many fingers am I holding up?"

She blinked, looking at the fat digits. "Two."

Hugh smiled with relief. "Saints be praised," he said. Then he looked off into the chamber, fixing on whoever was there. "You fools could have hurt her severely. Be grateful that you did not damage something, because I would have taken it out on your hide."

"She was fighting, my lord," a man said. "She was causing a ruckus, and we had to stop her."

"You did not have to hit her with the hilt of a sword."

"Would you prefer she attract attention, my lord?" the man said. "I thought we were trying to be discreet."

Hugh grunted unhappily, waving his hand at the men. "Get out," he said. "And take the other women you brought with you. I have no need of them."

"Do we return them to The Pox?"

"Take them back and leave them," he said. "Give them a coin and tell them not to mention they were brought to Westminster. Is that clear?"

"It is, my lord."

Delaina could hear the door open and close as the men departed the chamber. Hugh returned his focus to her. When their eyes met, he smiled.

It was a frightening sight.

"I am glad you are not badly injured, though you should

remain still," he said. "It has been a few years since we last saw one another. Do you remember me?"

Delaina still had her hand on her head. "I do," she said. "Despenser the Elder."

Hugh nodded. "That is correct," he said. "I am sorry to hear about Daventry. He was well liked."

Delaina didn't know what to say to that. She was feeling groggy and nauseated, so she simply closed her eyes. It was then that she realized someone was either holding her head or had an arm behind her. She could feel fingers and something fleshy supporting her neck. Opening her eyes, she craned her neck back a little to see that a man in mail and a royal tunic was behind her, supporting her.

Instinctively, she recoiled.

"Stay still, my lady," the man said. "I swear you will not be harmed. Everything will be well, I promise."

Delaina thought she recognized the voice. She'd heard it before. With a burst of strength, she sat up, recoiling from whomever was supporting her only to see that it was another face she recognized.

Her confusion grew.

"Sir Denys?"

Denys had been kneeling next to the couch where Delaina was lying. In fact, he hadn't left her since he'd seen a few of Hugh's men, royal soldiers whom Hugh paid personally, bringing three women onto the grounds of Westminster. They were carrying one of them, and given the brilliant and distinctive hair color, he recognized Delaina right away. He had no idea how they had managed to get their hands on her, but Magnus was nowhere to be seen, and his concern, and perhaps even fear, consumed him.

Taking Loring St. Aldwyn with him, Denys and his big weapon had intercepted the men at sword-point, demanding they give the lady over to him, but they would not. He threatened, and they refused. An odd standoff in the ward of Westminster went on for several minutes until Hugh himself had been notified of the issue. It was his personal appearance that broke up the standoff, but only after the men agreed to turn Delaina over to Denys.

He'd carried her into Hugh's apartments personally.

He'd also tended her personally, for she had a walnut-sized lump on the back of her head. He was as confused as she was, to be truthful, because he had no idea what had happened and was trying desperately to remain neutral so that he would be allowed to remain with Delaina. Loring, however, had been sent away, but not before Denys muttered to him:

Find Magnus in London.

No one seemed to know what was going on.

But Hugh knew. He knew very well what was going on, even if no one else in the chamber did. As the moist river breeze filtered in through his windows, he faced Delaina as she sat up on one of his fine couches, gripping the sides to steady herself. He had one of his servants pull up a cushioned chair so he could sit as he addressed her. He moved his appraising gaze over her.

"It has been some time since I last saw you," he said. "I was right. Like a fine wine, you've only grown more beautiful with age."

Delaina heard him, but she was more interested in why Denys was there and why she was there. She looked around the room, as much as her woozy head would allow, but there was no Magnus.

Then it began to come back to her.

Hugh Despenser knows of Daventry's death, and he further knows that you, the Ruby, were in Daventry's possession. He has asked me to bring you to him, but I will not do it.

Magnus wasn't here, but Hugh was here. Denys was here.

Did Denys bring her to Hugh?

She was more confused than ever.

"What am I doing here?" she said, her voice quavering. "Why did you bring me here?"

Hugh didn't seem moved by her obvious fear. "You are a Jewel, my dear," he said. "Jewels must be protected."

"That does not explain why I am here."

Hugh sat back in his chair. "You are very valuable, Lady Delaina," he said plainly. "You are valuable to me and to the king. We simply could not let you hide away. Your role in the kingdom is an important one."

He made it sound much more than it was, as if she was part of something grand. But Delaina knew the truth. She knew what her life really was.

"I am no one of importance," she said. "If I hide away, as you say, you can simply find another young woman to replace me."

Hugh held up a finger. "Untrue," he said. "Much time and money has been spent on you, making you who you are today. You have been trained in the art of seduction and love. You have been educated in all the noble subjects, a woman above all women. You are a courtesan, and a finer one has never lived. When Daventry died, that left you without a lord, and you are too valuable not to utilize. Like the greatest treasure, you must be given only to the worthiest man."

That was exactly what she didn't want. Delaina's head was

clearing a little more with his praiseful explanation, and it was a struggle not to become physically ill. Here she was, back where she didn't want to be, back in the royal fold to be used for royal purposes. That had been her life for years. A life she had run from. Just when she thought she might actually break free, with a possible future with a man she actually wanted, something terrible had happened.

She hadn't broken free at all.

She was worse off than she was before.

Without anything to say to Hugh, nothing by way of argument, she simply hung her head. It was aching, and she was feeling sick, so she couldn't stop the tears that were forming. It was all such a bloody nightmare. Every hope and dream she had given thought to since Daventry's death was finished.

She was finished.

"I would not worry, Lady Delaina," Hugh said, not oblivious to her upset. "I have a fine lord in mind for you. He is a powerful man and would treat you well. You are quite valuable, my lady, and no man will mistreat something of value. Aren't you grateful?"

Delaina refused to answer.

Hugh frowned. "Well?" he demanded. "What do you have to say to all of this? You will be taken care of. Does that not please you?"

Those words weren't helping her. He was trying to bully her. She put a hand to her face, wiping away the tears that were falling faster now. When Hugh realized she wasn't going to reply to him, he grew annoyed. In his mind, she was doing something important, something she was suited for. He couldn't understand why she didn't see it the same way.

But she didn't.

Hugh wasn't the only one who realized that. Denys did, too. He'd been watching the exchange carefully, seeing that it was only going to get worse, especially when Magnus arrived. He'd sent Loring for his friend and knew it was only a matter of time before Magnus made an appearance. Perhaps he didn't agree with Magnus' affection toward a courtesan, but that didn't mean he wasn't unsympathetic to what Magnus was feeling. As Denys has told him, he was surrounded by brothers who were in love with their wives. He knew the extent that a man in love would go to in order to protect the woman he loved, and he didn't want to see Magnus in a volatile situation with Hugh.

As he'd told Magnus, Hugh would win.

And that gave Denys an idea.

God help him, he hoped it would work.

"My lord," he said, turning to Hugh. "May I have a word with you, please?"

Irritated with Delaina as she sat on the couch and silently wept, Hugh gave a dramatic shrug and rose from the chair. "What is it, de Winter?"

Denys pointed to the adjoining chamber. "Privately, please, my lord."

Hugh wasn't inclined to go, but a pleading look from Denys sent him stomping over to the chamber, followed by Denys, who pushed him further inside and shut the door. Denys turned to speak to Hugh, but the man threw a silencing hand in his face.

"I do not know what you have to say to me, but know this," he said. "I am well aware that your commander has been lying to me. I know Magnus is behind all of this."

Denys cocked his head curiously. "My lord?"

"Do not play innocent with me, de Winter," Hugh said.

"Lies do not become you."

"How have I lied to you, my lord?"

Hugh wagged a finger at him. "You haven't yet, but I suspect you are about to," he said. "You are about to tell me that Magnus de Wolfe had nothing to do with the lady's disappearance from Haydon Square."

Denys frowned. "I was not going to say that, my lord."

Hugh cocked an eyebrow. "Weren't you?" he said. "I happen to know that Magnus was seen at The Pox, precisely where we found Lady Delaina. Will you deny this?"

Denys thought carefully on his answer. He wasn't aware that Magnus had been seen at The Pox, although it would explain why Delaina had been located there. Clearly, Magnus had been followed. It was also possible that Denys had been seen there himself, so he didn't want to engage in a lie that could very well remove all trust from this conversation. He had to *build* the trust.

He had to do what he thought Magnus would want.

He'd told Magnus not to engage in a dangerous game with Despenser, but here he was, preparing to engage in an equally and potentially friendship-ending game because he knew, at this very moment, Magnus was probably already on his way to Westminster. He knew there was going to be an explosion. He knew that he could prevent such an explosion with a bit of manipulation, but it was going to cost Magnus. If the man really wanted Delaina, if he was truly attracted to her, then this would be a defining moment.

Denys had to do what he thought was right to save Magnus.

"I will not deny it, for it is true, my lord," he said. "In fact, I want to make a suggestion that might be more attractive than offering Lady Delaina to a prized warlord. Will you listen?"

Hugh frowned. "What suggestion?"

"That you offer her to Magnus instead."

Hugh rolled his eyes. "God's bloody Bones," he muttered. "What for?"

Denys regarded him a moment. "Because he has never been under your command," he said. "Imagine if Magnus de Wolfe would obey every order? Imagine if you had a knight of that power who was sworn to do anything you wished? That woman in there can accomplish that."

Hugh's irritation very quickly turned to interest. "What's this you say?" he said. "What are you talking about, de Winter?"

"Interested?"

Hugh stared at him a moment. "In de Wolfe?" he said. "The man is beyond reproach. No amount of bribery could force him to my will."

"He has feelings for Lady Delaina. Why do you think he refused to bring her to you?"

Hugh's jaw dropped. "Then he *did* know her whereabouts!" he hissed. "I suspected but did not know for certain. He knew all along!"

"He did," Denys said. "So did I. But I am not in love with her—Magnus is."

Hugh's eyes widened. "He's in love with –?"

"Offer him Delaina in exchange for his fealty," Denys said, cutting him off. "Magnus shall have what he wants, and you shall have Magnus. Isn't that better than turning her over to a warlord who could eventually betray you? My lord… Magnus is an honorable man. If he gives you his word that he will serve your needs, then he will."

Hugh was overwhelmed with the possibilities. He'd been so infuriated by this situation, but now that Denys had presented him a positive solution, he was astounded. Turning away, he mulled over the possibilities.

"And you believe he will serve me if I turn the lady over to him?" he said. "Without question?"

Denys nodded. "Without question," he said. "You cannot gain his loyalty any other way. But she will accomplish this."

Hugh turned to him. "Why are you telling me this, de Winter?" he said. "You are the same as de Wolfe is. You are a man of honor, sworn to the king. Now you betray your friend to me?"

Denys shook his head. "I am keeping him alive," he said, trying not to let his emotions show. "Right now, he is on his way to Westminster, and he is coming to kill you for abducting Lady Delaina. I am doing this to prevent bloodshed. In the end, he may die and you may die, and the lady's fate may be in question, but the point is that there will be a good deal of unnecessary death and pain if you do not give him Lady Delaina."

Hugh knew that was true. He'd seen Magnus de Wolfe in a battle before, and the man was positively unstoppable with that massive ax he used, so instead of railing against de Winter's advice, he took it for what it was—something meant to keep the peace. If Magnus truly wanted Lady Delaina, Hugh and his soldiers wouldn't be able to stop him. It would be chaos.

And Hugh didn't particularly want to die today.

But he did see the wisdom in negotiations.

"I understand," he finally said. "I am to give him the lady in exchange for his loyalty. To me."

Denys nodded slowly. "Truth be told, de Wolfe loyalty is worth more than any warlord you have been considering for Lady Delaina, is it not?"

He had a point. In fact, Hugh thought this might be a better bargain than the loyalty of any warlord he had in mind, so he paced thoughtfully back to Denys, hands behind his back as he assumed a pensive stance.

"You are sure he is coming back to Westminster as we speak?"

"I am, my lord."

"Then meet him at the gate," he said. "Bring him to me and I will make the offer."

Denys struggled not to show his relief, because along with it was the guilt he felt for making such a suggestion. But it was only to protect Magnus. He hoped his friend would realize that before the man's hands closed around his neck.

"I will, my lord," he said. "But first… first, let me speak with Lady Delaina."

"Why?"

"Because she will take the news better from me than from you."

"What news?"

"That she is to bring a de Wolfe knight to his knees."

Hugh's brow furrowed. "Is that what you think I am going to do?"

"Isn't it?"

Hugh didn't reply immediately. He looked at Denys, inspecting him for a moment. "I think that you should reexamine that statement," he said quietly. "'Tis not I who made the suggestion to give de Wolfe his lady in exchange for his loyalty. It was you."

With that, he headed into the adjoining chamber where Delaina and the others await, leaving Denys to stew in a sea of guilt.

CHAPTER FOURTEEN

MAGNUS HAD JUST left the home of Simon Cooper, one of two sheriffs for the city of London. The position was simply a domestic peacekeeping one, meaning the sheriffs didn't get involved in anything regarding the Crown, warlords, or military circumstances. They were there purely to keep the peace between the citizens.

Including abductions.

Magnus and Marcellus had spent an hour at Cooper's home explaining the situation, and Cooper was prepared to send men out into the city to search. When he'd first been told the abduction happened at The Pox, he tried to brush Magnus off because The Pox was a place that even the sheriffs didn't bother with. The establishment was so lawless that there was no point. But Magnus assured him that this was a serious matter, indeed, involving a woman under the king's wardship—not exactly a lie, as the king had originally formed the Seven Jewels of London, but it served to underscore to Cooper that this was an incident to be taken seriously.

Therefore, the sheriff promised to prevent all of the cogs that were currently along the banks of the Thames from leaving so they couldn't spirit the lady out by water, and he further promised to secure all of the city gates in case they tried to take her out of the city. Since Magnus couldn't be in several different places at once, he had to trust Cooper in the matter.

But that didn't mean he wasn't going to remain personally involved.

He and Marcellus set out for every gate in the city to question the sentries, something that was going to take them a good deal of time, but it was necessary. There were seven main gates in London, leading in and out of the city, and also several posterns that were meant for pedestrians only. Cooper had sent messengers to all of the gates while Magnus was still there, so they knew the word went out. But Magnus wanted to see these gates for himself.

All of the London city gates were enormous in size, built on top of the original Roman gates that had allowed access to the city a millennium before. It was broad daylight when Magnus and Marcellus set out for the gates, and there were still people coming in and out, conducting their business. Magnus started with the gates nearest Cooper's home, interrogating those sentries and making sure that no one had seen men leave through the gate with a screaming woman in their arms. But no one had seen anything like that. They hadn't even seen anybody matching Delaina's description. Discouraged with the answers he received at one gate, Magnus simply moved to the next.

At some point, he told Marcellus to return to Lonsdale House and inform de Lohr that the lady in question had been abducted and that Magnus was doing everything he could to locate her. Truth be told, Magnus was relieved to send Marcellus away. The man was very nice and clearly very capable, but Magnus didn't know him very well. This was something he needed to do, and he needed to do it alone, without someone who had yet to earn his trust.

For Magnus, this was personal.

He had managed to visit three gates and received the same information from all three—that no one had seen anyone matching Delaina's description—and was on his way to visit the fourth gate when he caught sight of one of his knights heading directly for him.

Loring was plowing his way through the London crowd.

"My lord!" he called, reining his warhorse to a halt and leaping off. "I've been sent to find you!"

"And so you have," Magnus said, eyeing the man with interest. "But how? London is a big city, and quite busy this time of day."

Loring shrugged. "Because I went to The Pox and they told me you had run off in search of a lady who had been abducted," he said. "Lady Delaina?"

"Who told you that?"

"Denys," he said. Then he pointed to the gate several dozen yards behind Magnus. "I assumed you would check the gates to see if she had left the city."

Magnus glanced at the big gate. "Excellent reasoning, Loring," he said, impatient to get on with his search. "You've found me. What do you want?"

"Denys sent me," Loring said, lowering his voice even though there was no one around to hear the conversation. "He told me to tell you that Despenser's men took the lady from The Pox. They took her back to Westminster."

Magnus' heart leapt into his throat. "*He* took her?" he said, outraged. "Is she still at Westminster?"

Loring nodded. "As far as I know," he said, handing the

reins of his horse over to Magnus. "You had better return swiftly. It has taken me a while to find you, so there is no knowing what has gone on."

Magnus didn't question him. He leapt onto the horse and took off at a gallop.

೮౩

WHEN DENYS WENT back into the adjoining chamber where Delaina and a few others had been, he walked into a room devoid of everyone but Delaina. They'd all departed, and he looked around curiously, wondering why they'd left the lady alone. But then it occurred to him—they were giving him privacy to convince her that her future was best served with Magnus.

At the cost of Magnus' soul.

Denys was surprised that Hugh had actually granted him the request to speak with her personally. Delaina was still sitting on the couch where he'd left her, holding a cold compress to the back of her head. When she saw him coming, she sat up a bit straighter.

There was anxiety on her face.

"Why did they all leave?" she asked. "Despenser told me to stay here."

Denys went to stand over her, fists on his hips. "How are you feeling?"

She sighed. "My head aches," she said. "But not too terribly, considering."

"Do you feel well enough to have a conversation?"

"What about?"

Denys eyed her a moment before going to collect the same chair that Hugh had been sitting in when Delaina regained consciousness. He sat down on the silk cushion, leaning forward with his elbows resting on his knees. He looked at his hands for a few moments, contemplating the answer, before lifting his head to her.

"Magnus."

She appeared a little less woozy and a little more serious with the mention of the name. "What about Sir Magnus?"

"Do you have feelings for him?"

She blinked, surprised by the question. "You will forgive me, Sir Denys, but that is none of your affair."

"He told me that he has feelings for you," he said. "If you do not have feelings for him, then this conversation will go a different way."

She lowered the compress from the back of her head, looking into the face of the man who had once called her stupid. "What is this about?" she asked seriously. "Why must you know if I have feelings for Sir Magnus?"

"Why can't you answer it?"

"Because it is none of your business."

His jaw began to twitch. He didn't like that she was being evasive with him. "Clearly, you do not understand how serious this situation is," he said, growling. "If you did, then you would tell me everything I need to know and cease with this foolish defensiveness. I know that Magnus is in love with you, or thinks he is in love with you, so if you do not reciprocate those feelings, you had better tell me now, or I swear to you that I will turn you over to Despenser and walk away."

She stiffened. "You have no reason to—"

"Tell me now or I walk."

Delaina was beginning to grow upset. Angry and upset. "If I tell you that I do, what difference does that make?"

"A great deal of difference," he said. "Have you told Magnus?"

"I have."

Denys' jaw flexed. "Tell me that you did not tell him what he wanted to hear just so he would do as you asked," he rumbled. "Tell me you did not use your whore's tricks on him to suit your own purpose. Make it perfectly clear to me that you did not manipulate him."

He had insulted her and they both knew it, but he wasn't backing down. Delaina struggled not to become enraged at him.

"I did not do anything to suit my own purpose," she said, her voice trembling with anger. "And Sir Magnus did not do anything to manipulate me, either. What are you trying to say, Sir Denys? What is the matter?"

Denys was grinding his teeth. "I want to tell you a story, my lady," he said. "This is a story of the fall of a great knight. You see, he was from one of the greatest families in England. He had everything—breeding, training—and he was the grandson of a king. He had a prestigious position that he had worked very hard for. He was well on his way to making a name for himself, certainly well on his way to becoming a powerful warlord. Mayhap even an earl, with the right marriage. But instead, he met a courtesan and was willing to throw everything away because she shed a few tears and swayed his emotions. This woman was happy to take him out by the knees, having no regard for what he'd worked so hard for, just so she could bend him to her will. Does any of this sound familiar to you?"

It did. God help her, it did. Delaina went from anger to tears, struggling not to show how much he'd upset her.

But nothing he said wasn't true.

"I did not sway him," she whispered tightly. "I care very

much what he has worked hard for. I have told him so."

Denys wouldn't let up. "That is *not* true," he said. "You are not concerned for him. You are only concerned for yourself."

Delaina glared at him, but she had no real argument for him because, clearly, it was all true. "I never meant for him to lose his position," she said. "I would never want that for him, not ever."

Denys threw up his hands in frustration. "But that is what is happening," he said. Then he jabbed a finger at the closed door, in the general direction of Westminster's north gatehouse. "He is on his way to Westminster at this very moment to save you from Despenser, who wants to turn you into a whore for yet another warlord. Magnus is coming to try to save you from that, and the situation is about to veer out of control. It's about to explode in a bloodbath all because of you. Do you understand that?"

Delaina was beginning to tremble all over. "I did not ask for this."

Denys wasn't finished with her. "Nay, you did not," he said. "But what did you expect would happen when you seduced Magnus de Wolfe? The man is as loyal as a dog and as fierce as a lion. Somehow, you managed to convince him that he is in love with you, but we both know that is not true. You bewitched him, and now the only way to save him is to make him subservient to Despenser, a man he greatly opposes."

Tears were welling in Delaina's eyes. "What do you mean by subservient?"

Denys sighed sharply, sitting back in his chair and eyeing the woman. He was feeling so much rage and disgust that he could hardly control it.

"Despenser wants to use you as a prize to bribe some warlord for his loyalty," he said. "I have convinced him to give you over to Magnus in exchange for his fealty. Magnus will do it to save you. He gets you, you get him, and everything is fine, except Magnus has to surrender his honor to Despenser in order to do it. But you will be safe. Isn't that all that matters? You wanted to be safe, after all."

Delaina blinked, and the tears spattered. She hung her head, unable to look at the contempt in Denys' eyes. She was causing Magnus' downfall, unintentional as it was. She'd known the man just a couple of days, but in those two days, the magic of a lifetime had happened. She had experienced things she had never experienced before, with a wonderful man.

A man who was far too fine for her.

Delaina had known that from the start.

"I do not want him to surrender his honor." She wept softly. "I am not worth it. I know I am not worth it."

Denys couldn't stand looking at her cry because he was convinced it was all an act for sympathy. Therefore, he stood up and turned his back on her so he wouldn't have to look at her.

"Nay, you are not," he agreed cruelly. "Magnus de Wolfe is my friend, my lady. He is the best friend I have ever had. There is no one like him in the world, for if you searched your entire life for such a fine and noble man, you would not come up with anyone close. And he is losing all of this because of you."

Delaina's head came up, and she looked at Denys' rigid back. "You love him," she said, sniffling. "I can see that."

Denys turned to look at her then. "I had three brothers," he said. "I lost my youngest brother ten years ago. The finest young knight you have ever seen was cut down in a Scots ambush. My family still has not recovered from that. I do not want to see another fine knight cut down, this time because of a woman. He may as well be dead with what you are going to do to him. If I can prevent it, I will. You do not matter to me, my lady. But Magnus does."

Delaina could see in his eyes that he meant every word. This went beyond anger at the situation. It even went beyond anger toward her. There was something deep and emotional in Denys' expression that suggested he really thought that he was saving Magnus.

There was also a message there.

He was trying to force her into a decision, as if she had some semblance of control in all of this. Perhaps if she rejected Magnus and told him she was not fond of him, all of this would go away. Perhaps if she told him she didn't need or want his help, the wheels that were in motion would come to a screeching halt. Denys had been right about one thing—she was only concerned for herself. She had only been concerned for herself since the very beginning of all of this, when Magnus first told her that Daventry was dead. All she could think about at that point was freedom, of escaping the life she had known for so many years. Magnus, and Denys to a certain degree, had both stepped in to help her, only Magnus had gone a step further. He had assumed her burden.

She had allowed that to happen.

It was wrong.

"Then what do you want me to do?" she pleaded softly. "Tell me what you would have me do, and I will do it. I do not want to see Magnus destroyed any more than you do."

Denys looked at her, his expression skeptical. "I am not sure this can be undone."

"But if it could, what should I do?"

He lifted his eyebrows. "If it were me, I would go away," he said. "You tried that before, and I stopped you. I called you stupid and then took you to The Pox, but I swear that if I had known the situation was going to come to this, I would have let you run. I would let you run away and disappear, for as long as Magnus knows where you are, even if you belong to someone else, he will not give you up. You will only cause disaster and heartache for him."

She stood up from the couch, a bit unsteadily. "But how can I run away now?" she said. "I am a prisoner here."

Denys looked around the chamber, to the windows, the doors. There were three of them. He pointed to the one to his left, off in a shadowed corner.

"Do you see that door?" he asked.

Delaina looked at it. "The small one?"

"It is a servants' door."

"What about it?"

Denys drew in a long, pensive breath and turned away from her again. "That leads to a servant stairwell," he said. "At the bottom, there is a corridor that leads to a larger corridor that skirts the entire north side of the palace. It is mostly used by the servants, so no one will notice you. If you want to leave through that door, I will not stop you."

Delaina looked at the door, feeling the reality of the situation weighing heavily upon her. The actuality of her fleeing and leaving Magnus, leaving this place, was upon her, and she didn't know what to do.

"And go where?" she said. "Where am I to go, Sir Denys? My coin is back at The Pox. I have nothing but the clothes on my back. If I run, Despenser will only find me again. Or someone will. Mayhap Magnus will find me again. What will I tell him?"

Denys thought on that for a moment. Then he reached into the purse on his belt and dug around in it, pulling forth several coins. He turned to her again, closing the distance between them. Reaching out, he took one of her hands and pressed the coins into her palm.

"There is only one place you can go that you can never be taken from," he said, looking her in the eye. "The corridor I speak of will take you to the abbey. Go there, give them this coin, and ask for sanctuary. Tell them that your family is dead and that you are in grave danger from men trying to kill you. Tell them you wish to become a Beguine and serve God."

The cloister. There it was. Delaina had once spoken of it as being her first and only option, something that she'd talked herself out of, most especially when Magnus came around. But here she was, back at the cloister again. But Denys had given her an idea—she didn't want to be a nun and she was too old to be a postulate, so a Beguine was her only option. She didn't know why she hadn't thought of it before. A Beguine was a widow who served with the nuns but could also do other charitable work. Sometimes they didn't even live at the cloisters— sometimes they had their own farms or homes because they weren't sworn to God. Perhaps that was the future for her.

Perhaps God was showing her the way this time.

For an adult life filled with sin with men not her husband, it was time for penitence.

The tears were back as she realized that, in her new beginning, it would be the end of her and Magnus. The end of those new, fragile, and exciting dreams. But she nodded curtly, once, and headed for the door.

She paused when she reached the panel.

"What will you tell Despenser?" she asked hoarsely. "He will be angry that I escaped. You are risking much, de Winter."

Denys shook his head. "I will go into the other chamber now and tell him that I have left you to rest," he said. "He will not bother you because he is waiting for Magnus to show himself, so he is already distracted. This will give you time to get to the abbey and to safety. But hurry—there is no time to waste."

Delaina lifted the latch on the door, but she paused again. "Will you do something for me?"

"What is it?"

She swallowed hard. "When the time is right, will you tell Magnus… Tell him that I am sorry," she said. "I could not let him surrender his entire career for me. But I love him for being so willing to do it."

Denys simply nodded, and Delaina didn't waste any time. She darted through the door then shut it behind her as she slipped down the stairwell and to the corridor below.

Denys swore he could hear her sobs as she fled, and the hard heart he'd shown in the face of her situation turned into a heavy one at the sound of her sorrow. He wasn't cruel by nature. But he was determined to protect Magnus, even if it meant Delaina's misery.

With a sigh, he followed.

CHAPTER FIFTEEN

MAGNUS HAD NO obstacles entering Westminster.

The sentries at the north gatehouse let him in without question and he charged through, straight through the ward and to the royal apartments where Despenser had his lair. He saw some of his knights at the gatehouse as he passed through, and as he dismounted St. Aldwyn's horse, those knights were gravitating in his direction. When he unsheathed his sword, they came at a run.

Something was amiss, and they swarmed to support their lord commander.

Magnus entered the royal apartments with his weapon drawn. Because of this, the knights also had their weapons drawn. All of them charged toward Despenser's solar where he conducted all of his business, but that solar was near other official offices as well. No one but Magnus knew where they were going until they got there.

Hugh Despenser's guards were waiting to greet them.

Magnus didn't ask questions. He began swinging that big sword, and the royal knights joined in. He missed his grandfather's ax, the one he always took into battle, but that was back in his room at the knights' quarters, and he hadn't stopped to get it. Suddenly, there was a swordfight at Hugh's door, and men were shouting as the sound of metal on metal echoed through the building. Servants were running and screaming. More soldiers were summoned, but so were more knights. It began to turn into chaos until Hugh suddenly appeared and began to shout.

"Magnus!" he bellowed. "Cease your fighting! If you want to see her alive, you will cease immediately!"

No one knew what he was talking about except Magnus, and his sword came to an instant halt.

"Where is she?" he bellowed.

Hugh was not pleased with the battle right outside his door. Four of his men were already badly wounded, and he quickly gestured to some of his courtiers to remove the casualties.

All the while, he kept his gaze locked with Magnus.

"Send your knights away," Hugh said. "Send them away now and we will speak."

Magnus was twitching with anger, with the rush of battle. It was difficult for him to stop that momentum, but he did. He had to. Hugh had what he wanted, and Magnus was bound to obey while that was the situation.

But it wasn't going to be for long.

With a mere look to his knights, he sent them away, but as he did so, he noticed a familiar figure coming up the stairwell.

"Magnus!" Denys gasped as he took the top step. "What in the hell is going on?"

Magnus was still armed, still ready to do battle. "Where have you been?" he said. "Where is Delaina?"

Denys caught up to him, making sure the royal knights were herded back down the stairs before he answered.

"Put your sword away," he said quietly. "Despenser has her, and you are not going to get her through force. Put it *away*, Magnus."

Magnus didn't want to. In fact, Denys had to force him to sheathe his weapon. When he did that, the three soldiers that were left uninjured in defense of Despenser also put their weapons aside, and Hugh sent them away. They stumbled back down the corridor, leaving it empty, with blood on the floor.

It was eerily silent now with Magnus and Denys facing Hugh.

After a moment, Hugh sighed heavily.

"Get in here, Magnus," he commanded quietly. "Cause no more trouble and this should go smoothly, but get in here and be silent. I have something to say to you."

Magnus didn't hesitate. He marched into the chamber, a chamber he'd been in before too many times to count. It was Despenser's main solar, furnished for an emperor, that overlooked the Thames. When Denys tried to follow, Magnus shoved the man aside so hard that Denys near tripped. He caught himself on the wall as Magnus charged into the chamber, but Hugh waved him in.

"Denys," he said. "You will come as well. I may need your strength if Magnus will not listen to reason."

Denys pushed himself off the wall and followed Magnus' path into Despenser's solar, making very sure to stay at least a sword's length away from Magnus. He was quite certain this conversation wasn't going to go very well, and given he'd just come from Westminster Abbey, where he'd personally witnessed Delaina go inside, he was now about to enact the second part of his plan to save Magnus from himself. And save him from Hugh.

Waiting for the right moment to spill his revelations, Denys stood aside as Hugh faced Magnus.

For a moment, Hugh simply looked at the enormous de Wolfe knight. The man could break him in two pieces with his bare hands, and Hugh was well aware of that. Although his personal guards weren't in the solar, he remained several feet away from Magnus should the man charge. He was certain he could make it to the door before Magnus could overwhelm him, but he made sure to maintain that distance between them.

Just in case.

"Now," Hugh said. "I assume that bloodshed outside was because of Lady Delaina? It was completely unnecessary, Magnus."

Magnus watched Hugh with the intensity of a cat tracking a mouse. "Where is she?"

"Safe," Hugh said. "She will remain safe while you and I have a discussion about her future."

Magnus' jaw flexed angrily. "Her future is with me," he said. "I want her."

Hugh nodded. "I know," he said. "And you shall have her."

The answer threw Magnus off. He had been expecting to go head to head with Hugh, so the agreeable answer confused him.

"Then bring her to me," he said, wondering if Hugh was trying to trick him somehow. "I want her now."

"She will be here with you as soon as you and I agree to terms," Hugh said firmly. "Did you really think I would turn her over to you with no compensation?"

Magnus' brow furrowed. "What compensation?" he said. "You want money for her?"

"I want something more valuable than money."

"Then what? Be plain."

"I want your loyalty."

At first, Magnus thought he hadn't heard correctly. Then he began to realize what Hugh meant, and his features began to tighten up again.

"Let me see if I understand this correctly," he said through clenched teeth. "You will give me Lady Delaina, but only if I swear fealty to you?"

Hugh shook his head. "I do not want your fealty," he said. "It belongs to Edward. What I want is for you to obey my commands. If I tell you to do something, you will do it. I want your oath that the next time I order you to bring a woman to me, or abduct an unruly lord or even his wife, that you will do my bidding without question. I want your promise that you will do whatever I ask of you without question. If you swear this to me, I will bring you the lady, for I know you are a man of your word. Do you understand me?"

Magnus did. God help him, he did. He never thought he would be in a position like this, not ever, and the idea of becoming one of Hugh's puppets turned his stomach. He felt physically ill. But the price for returning Delaina to him was his promise to Hugh.

He understood that all too clearly.

"I do," he said, still grinding his teeth. "You want my assurance that I will obey every command you issue."

"That is correct."

"And you will return Delaina to me."

"I will."

"She will be mine forever."

"That is my promise to you."

Magnus wasn't sure that he could refuse this, in any case. If he wanted Delaina, he had to promise a horrible, immoral man that he would do anything he asked. He'd heard of other men in such positions, men who had to give up something in order to get what they wanted, but in this case it was a human cost. Truth be told, there was no question he would pay the price. Delaina was worth all that to him and more.

What was honor without the woman he wanted?

As he opened his mouth to agree to the terms, Denys spoke up.

"My lord," he said, addressing Hugh. "Before Magnus agrees, I think you should know that the lady is no longer in your apartments upstairs."

Hugh looked at him, bewildered by this statement. "Of course she is there," he said. "I left her there. I left her with you."

Magnus looked at Denys, his nostrils flaring. "*You?*" he said. "Damnation, Denys, were you involved in this… this abduction?"

Denys shook his head quickly. "I was not," he said. "But I saw them bringing her into Westminster and took her from Despenser's men. I thought you would want me to make sure she was protected against his dogs."

Magnus was still shaking with rage, but he understood. "Of course I would," he said. "But if she is not here, where is she?"

"Yes, Denys." Hugh was suddenly quite irate. "*Where* is she? What did you do with her?"

Denys looked straight at Hugh. "I took her somewhere you can never again claim her or use her," he said. "When you left me to speak with her, she was able to slip from the chamber and run. I followed her to Westminster Abbey. She has asked for sanctuary from the priests. Not even you can break the sanctity of the abbey, Despenser. She is out of your reach."

Hugh's face turned red. "She did *what*?" he shouted. "She has gone to the abbey?"

Denys nodded. "You can no longer threaten to use her as a prize for a warlord you would like to reward," he said, contempt in his voice. He turned to Magnus. "And you cannot marry her. She told me to tell you that she has no desire to destroy your career, Magnus, but she loves you for being willing to do it. She intends to become a Beguine."

Magnus stared at Denys as if the man had lost his mind. "My… God," he breathed. "After everything we discussed, she… she *has* joined the cloister, after all. But she told me she had no intention of doing so."

"When Hugh captured her, she changed her mind."

Magnus wasn't understanding any of it. "But how would she know my career was on the path to ruin?" he said, baffled. "Did she know of Hugh's offer to return her to me in exchange for my loyalty?"

"She did."

"How?"

"I told her."

"And you told me to make this offer to Magnus." Hugh leapt into the conversation, seething with rage. "You told me to offer Magnus the lady in return for his loyalty. Why did you do that?"

Denys was facing off against two men he'd manipulated, but he didn't care. The situation had ended the way he'd hoped— Hugh without Magnus and Magnus without Delaina. He began to feel some rage of his own as he glared at both of them.

"Because a man like you isn't worthy to lick Magnus de Wolfe's boots," he growled, posturing angrily. "You are a parasite, Despenser. We all know it. You are the most hated man in England, and for someone like you to have the loyalty of an elite knight like Magnus de Wolfe is a travesty. You're absolutely right that I told you to offer the lady to Magnus in exchange for his fealty because I knew I could stop him before he accepted. But I had to get rid of the lady first. She is the common factor in all of this. With her removed, Magnus does not belong to you, and you have no hold over him. Now do you understand my actions, you pathetic fool?"

Not only did Hugh understand, but so did Magnus. He could see that Denys had put himself at great risk to save his honor. God help him, that was the only thing he could see at the moment. He also knew he needed to get Denys out of there before Hugh did something drastic. Hugh had lost out on not only one of the Seven Jewels of London, but he'd lost the ability to command Magnus.

Nay, the day wasn't going well for him at all.

"With me," Magnus said, going over to Denys and grabbing the man around the neck. "You are coming with me now."

Denys was still tensed up, still ready to do battle with Hugh, but now Magnus was dragging him out the door. When Hugh realized he'd lost everything, he began to shout to his courtiers, screaming for them as Magnus pulled Denys out of the solar. He pulled him through the puddles of blood on the floor in the corridor, and bloody footprints followed them out of the royal apartments until they were outside on the dirt path. Then, and only then, did Magnus release Denys.

The two of them faced each other in the busy ward.

"Now," Magnus rumbled. "You are going to tell me what you've done. Make it abundantly clear to me that you did not betray me in any fashion."

Denys' eyes widened. "Betray you?" he said, aghast. "I was

trying to save you!"

"From whom? From Hugh?"

"From yourself," Denys nearly shouted. "Magnus, you are the lord commander of Edward's knights. You are answerable only to the king. You have worked hard to achieve this. But a beautiful woman entered your midst, and you've been behaving like an addle-brained squire ever since you laid eyes upon her. I cannot watch you ruin yourself!"

Magnus listened to Denys' tirade with both anger and compassion, an unusual combination. But Denys' behavior warranted both. Magnus could see that Denys was trying to do him a favor, or so he thought. That noble, stupid fool was genuinely trying to save him. He wasn't sure he could become angry at that, but Denys had managed to make a mess out of things.

Maybe.

Magnus held up a quelling hand.

"I appreciate that you are trying to protect me, Denys," he said, trying to compose himself. "I truly do. But I am going to ask you again. Did you have anything to do with Delaina's abduction from The Pox?"

Denys shook his head with great frustration. "Of course not," he said. "One of Hugh's men saw you leaving The Pox, and since you'd refused to bring Lady Delaina to Hugh, it was pure speculation on Hugh's part that you were hiding her. He sent men to The Pox to grab any redheaded woman they could find. And they found her."

Magnus understood. With a heavy sigh, he shook his head in disgust. "So he brought her here," he said. "And you saw them bring her in?"

"I did."

"But you told Hugh to promise her to me in exchange for my loyalty."

Denys nodded emphatically. "Absolutely," he said. "Hugh was going to give her to some warlord, and I knew you would get yourself killed trying to get her back. Therefore, I told him to give her to you in exchange for your loyalty because I knew you would do it. You would have the lady, you would be alive, but at the cost of your honor. Am I wrong in any of this, Magnus? I knew the moment you came back to the knights' quarters earlier that you were completely infatuated with the lady, and infatuated men often do foolish things in the name of that obsession."

"I think you are judging me harshly."

"There are four soldiers you cut down in front of Hugh's door that would disagree with that."

Magnus eyed Denys. They'd been best friends for years, and he knew that Denys was extremely loyal. He appreciated that tremendously. But he could also see that a line had been crossed.

"Denys," he said, trying to ease the situation. "You are my dearest friend, and I love you for it. But you cannot make personal decisions for me. They are my decisions to make and, if necessary, my mistakes to make. Do you understand that?"

Denys was starting to calm down, but not much. "I was not making any decisions for you," he said. "I was trying to save you and your career."

"And I understand that," Magnus said. "You have gone above and beyond. But I can make my own decisions, especially where it pertains to Delaina."

Denys rolled his eyes. "You just met her, Magnus," he said. "And, suddenly, you cannot live without her?"

"I love her."

Denys hung his head. "How can you even know that after knowing the woman for a couple of days?" he said. "How is that even possible?"

"I do not know, but it has happened."

Denys continued to look at the ground, mulling over the situation. He finally snorted. "I will tell you what I told the lady," he said. "I lost my youngest brother ten years ago."

"What does Dallan have to do with this?"

As Denys continued, he was close to tears. "He had the makings of the most magnificent de Winter knight who ever lived," he said. "He never had the chance to reach his potential, and there was nothing I could do to help him. I see the same greatness in you—you are well on your way to reaching your potential, yet you are suddenly willing to throw it all away for a woman. Not just any woman, but a courtesan. How is that fair to men like Dallan who never even had half the chances that you have had?"

Magnus was watching him carefully. "Then you are doing this for Dallan?"

Denys shook his head. "I am doing this for you," he said. "I could not help my brother. But I can help you. Whether or not you want me to."

There were now tears in his eyes. It was the most heartbreaking thing Magnus had ever heard, and it took most of the fight right out of him—but not all of it. Denys had to understand that in this situation, he had no control, no matter how hard he tried to hold on to it.

Magnus took a few steps, closing the gap between them. "You are the most devoted friend and brother that anyone could ask for," he said quietly. "I understand why you did what you did, and you did indeed save my honor from Hugh's immoral intentions. I am touched and honored that you would put yourself in harm's way in order to save me. But in this case, you must let me make my own decisions, Denys. I am not an addle-brained squire, and I was not bewitched. Sometimes, you meet a woman and you just know she is the one you are meant to be with. It does not matter that I've known her two days or two years. Mayhap I have achieved much in my life. Mayhap I am meant to achieve more. But I would surrender it all for a few brief moments with a woman who touches my soul like no one else ever has. If you have ever been in love, you would understand that."

Denys was listening with sorrow. Part of him could understand, but part of him didn't *want* to understand. "I have never loved a woman," he said honestly. "Therefore, I cannot attest to the willingness to relinquish everything I have worked for."

Magnus smiled faintly. "You will," he said. "I have every confidence that someday, you will meet a woman who shines upon you like nothing you have ever experienced before. But I have met the one who shines upon me, and I cannot go another moment without feeling the warmth of her smile. Will you please show me where she went?"

Denys had no choice. He knew that. They had come to the end of their conversation, and there was nothing more to say. Nothing more to do. With an unhappy grunt, he hung his head again.

"I am so angry with her," he finally said. "I am angry that she did this to you. I am angry that she has ruined your life."

Magnus' smile never left his lips. "She has not ruined my life," he said. "She has shown me a glimpse of a future I never thought I would have. Life does not end here at Westminster,

Denys. It goes on to bigger and better things."

Denys lifted his head and looked at him. "I said some terrible things to her," he admitted. "I told her that she was ruining everything you had worked for. I chased her into the cloister, Magnus, and I am sorry for that. But I knew of no other way to save you from getting yourself killed when you confronted Hugh."

Magnus' smile faded. "I understand that," he said. "But I am going to talk to her and convince her that marriage to me is better than the cloister. At least, I hope it is."

Denys knew there was no discouraging him, and, in truth, he knew it wasn't his right. Magnus had made himself clear, and if there was any hope of salvaging the friendship, Denys had to let Magnus do what he wanted to do.

Even if that involved marrying a courtesan.

He gave up the fight.

"She went in through the entrance to the cloister," he finally said. "They cannot keep her there, you know. They will have to send her to St. Blitha's, where the nuns of that order reside."

Magnus was well aware that Westminster was only for monks. St. Blitha's, the largest convent in London, was where the women were housed.

"Then I shall talk her out of committing herself," he said. "Show me where you last saw her."

Knowing he had no choice, Denys did.

CHAPTER SIXTEEN

S HE WAS SITTING in a corridor outside of a big chamber that
was referred to as the refectory.

It was cold and becoming dark as the sun set, casting shadows on the walls as the last vestiges of the day began to wane. Delaina sat on a wooden bench, watching the colors on the wall across from her. Ancient walls that had seen the history of England pass by them. She was to be one minor speck in the history of those walls.

A little speck that had quickly come and would be quickly gone.

She had been in tears when she first arrived at the side door of Westminster Abbey. The door led to the cloisters, so rather than go into the sanctuary and hunt for a priest, she'd gone straight to the door that led into the inner sanctum. This was where the priests conducted their business, so she figured it would be the best place to make contact.

She hadn't been wrong. As soon as she rang the bell, a young priest appeared. At first, he had been wary of her presence, and, unfortunately, she was weeping, so it was difficult to communicate. He soon understood what she wanted and tried to send her away, but she wouldn't go. Her weeping, and begging, had finally forced him to open the door to admit her, because he didn't know what else to do, especially when she insisted that she was in danger. The fact that he was young and possibly inexperienced made him more pliable.

And, hopefully, he wouldn't get in too much trouble for it.

The priest had brought her inside the door and wouldn't let her go any further. He told her to take a seat on the bench where she currently sat. That had been some time ago. Or perhaps it had even been days. Delaina was upset, and emotional, and time seemed to have no meaning. It was passing, and she couldn't even grasp how fast or how slow. All she knew was that she felt as if she was sitting in limbo, waiting for the next phase of her life to begin.

The dark, shadowed corridor spoke of the emptiness she was about to face.

The past few days had seen the greatest heights she had lived in her adult life, along with the greatest lows. The greatest height, of course, had been Magnus. She couldn't go even a few moments without thinking of him, without wondering where he was or how he was.

And wondering if her departure had prevented a disaster.

As Denys told her, Magnus had been heading for Westminster and for Hugh, and the results of that could have been catastrophic. Here she was, in perhaps one of the greatest cathedrals known to man, and she found herself praying for Magnus' safety. She had never been much of a praying woman, but at this moment she found that she very much wanted God to hear her plea. This wasn't about her and her impending future. This was about praying that Magnus lived to see another day.

She couldn't live with herself if the outcome was otherwise.

But along with the prayers came the daydreams for the life that could have been. She had been so reluctant to allow herself the luxury of indulging in the fantasy of a life where she had a husband and children. Not just any husband, but a handsome and powerful husband who was as mad about her as she was about him. Though she had only known Magnus a few short days, in those days she felt as if she had lived a lifetime. She knew that she could love him if she didn't already. He was wise and honorable, something so rare in her world. To think she nearly had that for a lifetime was something she would probably never overcome.

But Denys had been right about all of it. He had been right about her jeopardizing Magnus' career. He had been absolutely right, though she had never intentionally intended to harm him. But the fact remained that she was a courtesan, and that meant that she was nothing more than a well-dressed whore. Even she knew that. She'd never had any illusions about her position in life, but she rather understood the reality of it. Being one of the Seven Jewels of London was not a place of honor.

It was a place of ruin.

As Delaina sat there and forced herself to accept what the future would bring her, there was a knock at the side door. Startled by the sharp sound in halls of silence, she found herself turning to the door instinctively. It was an ancient door, carved from oak and reinforced with iron bars. It had been at Westminster for more than one hundred years, probably taken from the old Saxon church that Westminster was built upon. It represented a barrier between the holy realm inside the walls and the corrupt outside world, but someone was banging on that barrier.

And they sounded quite insistent.

The banging continued. Delaina had no intention of opening the door, and eventually, the same young priest who had opened it for her scurried back down the corridor, brushed past her, and went to the door. There was a tiny peephole near the top of the door and he slid it open to see who was causing such a racket.

"Who comes?" he demanded in a high-pitched voice.

"Open the door," came the throaty response.

"Tell me your business, quickly," the priest said.

"You have a woman here," the voice said. "She is my wife. Open the door."

The priest looked at Delaina, confusion on his face. Perhaps there was even some outrage. Delaina jumped up and rushed to the door, pushing the priest aside and peering out to see Magnus and Denys standing there in the dim light.

"Magnus!" she gasped. Then she looked at Denys accusingly. "You told him I was here? Why did you tell him?"

"Open the door, Delaina," Magnus pleaded softly. "I simply want to talk to you, I swear it. Nothing more."

Delaina looked him over, feeling longing fill her soul as she did. There was a pull between them that had always been there, but never more prevalent than it was now.

"Are you well?" she asked. "You are uninjured?"

Magnus nodded. "Of course I am uninjured," he said. "Are you uninjured?"

"I am."

"Good. Now, open the door, love. Please."

Love. He called her his love in a tone she'd never heard before, not when it pertained to her. There was warmth there, and feeling, something that made her feel embraced by the mere sound of his voice. It would be so easy to throw open the door and rush into his arms, but she knew she couldn't do that.

For his sake, she had to remain strong.

"There is no need, Magnus," she said, feeling the lump in her throat. "Say what you must, but know that my mind is made up."

Magnus drew in a long, slow breath. He looked away from her long enough to glance at Denys, who took the hint and wandered away. Alone at the ancient door, Magnus could only see Delaina's eyes, but it was enough.

For now.

"You made up your mind without hearing from me," he said softly. "You and Denys made up your mind. He did it to protect me, and I understand that, but he did not have my permission to make your decision for you. That is your right and yours alone. Whatever he said to you about the fact that you are ruining my career is not true."

Delaina was trying hard not to tear up. "It is true that Hugh Despenser was going to use me for his own gain," she said. "He was going to use me to force you into obedience. I could not let him do that to you."

Magnus smiled faintly. "That kind of thing happens all of the time," he said. "It is not critical. It is not as if I would actually obey Hugh. But to keep you safe, I would promise whatever I had to."

Delaina shook her head. "It is not right," she said. "Hugh was going to use me as barter. Yet again, I was going to be used as a bribe, this time for someone I genuinely care about. That is no way to start a relationship, Magnus. We would be building a foundation on something unpleasant."

"You are too concerned with something that does not matter," he said. "I would obey Hugh if I felt strongly enough about it."

"Then you would not keep your word to him?"

"I did not mean it that way."

Again, she shook her head. "Already, you are willing to compromise your integrity," she said. "And I would be the cause. Don't you see, Magnus? I am damaging your honor."

"You are doing no such thing. If I thought so, I would not be here."

It was clear to Delaina that Magnus wasn't going to back down. But, then again, neither was she. Heavily, she sighed and closed the little peephole. After throwing the bolt on the door, which was quite heavy, she pulled the panel open.

Magnus stood about two feet away, hanging his head until she opened it. God, he looked so good to her. All she wanted to do was throw herself in his arms, but she refrained. She knew that if he touched her, all would be lost. He would be lost; his honor would be lost. Everything would be lost.

She simply couldn't do that to him.

Or herself.

"Magnus," she said quietly. "I want you to listen to me, and listen carefully. Can you do that?"

"I will always listen to you carefully."

"Good," she said, taking a deep breath for courage. "My entire adult life, men have used me as a pawn. The moment my father came to collect me to pay off a debt, I have been used and used again. I have been a possession and nothing more. But I am a woman of heart and bone and feeling, and I will not be used any longer. The truth is that I am damaged property. I am of no value to anyone."

Magnus put up a hand to silence her. "Delaina, that's not—"

She cut him off before he could finish. "You said you would listen to me carefully," she said. "You are not listening. I am speaking now. Not you."

He nodded quickly, understanding her point. When she was certain he was not going to interrupt her, she continued.

"It is true that I am damaged," she said softly. "It happened well before I knew you. An old, careless lord took what was most valuable to me, and since that time, I have become something I never wanted to be. I have been dressed in the finest jewels and I have worn the finest silks. I have supped on the best food in the world and I have drunk the finest wines. I have lived a life that few women live, but it came with a cost. That has never been more evident than it is right now, at this moment. That cost, ultimately, is you. You are the man I should have married at the first, but I did not. You are the man I have always wanted to have, but I cannot. I look into your eyes and see strong sons and beautiful daughters, but it is only a dream. You must accept, above all else, that we were simply never meant to be."

Magnus didn't say anything. He gazed steadily into her eyes, waiting for her to continue, but she didn't.

"May I speak now?" he asked.

Delaina nodded.

"Thank you," he said. "While I understand your point, and you have valid points, none of that matters to me. I know what you were. I know you were used by men. But I do not care. I have told you this. I know that Denys convinced you that you would be the ruin of me, but it is simply not true. Where there is trust, and hopefully love, there is the unerring ability to manage any problems that may arise. I have already told you what we will do—we will give you a new name, a new past, and you will become my wife. We will go north, to Berwick, and we will have a happy life together where no one will know of your past. Don't you understand? None of this matters."

He was starting to beg. She could hear it in his tone, and it broke her heart.

"Magnus, please," she murmured. "You are not thinking clearly. You are consumed with the same thing that has consumed me—the chance to be with someone who can bring joy into your life. The idea of a courtship that will see us come to know and love one another. I have no doubt that we could love one another. Mayhap I already love you now, which is why I must again refuse to go with you. I cannot let you marry a woman who would shame your entire family if her secret were ever known."

His jaw flexed. "No one will ever know."

"Oh?" she said. "Can you promise that? Can you promise that the next time your father speaks to the king or to Despenser, that they will not tell tales of the courtesan you were so desperate for that you were willing to destroy your entire career for her? A courtesan who, not strangely, looks exactly like your wife? You act as if we are the only ones in the world who know of my past, but that is simply not true. You know I am right."

Magnus sighed sharply and looked away. "I do not care," he said. "I do not care if my family finds out, eventually. By that time, they will know you and love you."

Delaina could see that there was no swaying him. The truth wasn't working.

Perhaps a lie would.

"Did you ever stop to think that I've had time to reconsider all of this?" she said, hoping she wouldn't burst into tears before she did what needed to be done. "I have, you know. I simply do not wish to be married, not to you, not to anyone. I do not want to become another man's mistress, either, so the best choice for me is right here, with the church. This is where I want to be."

He looked at her then. "That is not true and you know it," he said. "Delaina, I am pleading with you. Come with me now and let us be married. I will give you everything, including my heart. I have never said that to anyone before. Will you step on it in your quest to be noble?"

The tears were starting to come, and she couldn't stop them. Better to end this now while she still had the strength to do it. The hand that gripped the door was trembling as she drank in one last look at Magnus before he was out of her sight forever.

She had no choice.

"I will," she said, barely able to get the words out. "I will step on it and smash it. Go back to the king, Magnus. Forget you ever knew me."

With that, she shut the door and threw the bolt, then leaned against the door with her hand over her mouth as the sobs began to come.

Magnus pounded on the door, begging her to open it, but she stood there and wept, wondering how long she could hold out against his pleas.

As it turned out, she had to hold out all night. Magnus stood at the door and pounded for the rest of the night, begging her to open it until he lost his voice completely.

By morning, however, he was gone.

And with him went the last vestiges of her heart.

It was done.

CHAPTER SEVENTEEN

Seven Months Later
Year of our Lord 1311
Westminster Palace

"A MISSIVE HAS come for you, Denys."

Denys was sitting in the small solar utilized by the lord commander of the king's knights. Many captains had used this room in years past, and the table they used for dispatches and other administrative duties was pockmarked with the ends of a thousand quills. It was a big table, sanded down over the years to make the surface smoother, but it was a working table and it had seen many years of service.

Denys had been looking over a dispatch from Lancashire that told of several armies standing at the ready against Edward, including the entire de Wolfe empire to the north. The past several months had seen the king at odds with his cousin, the Earl of Lancaster, and the earl was supported by many warlords all over England. This included the Earls of Warwick, Gloucester, Arundel, and several other powerful warlords. The most powerful of the bunch was the Earl of Hereford and Worcester,

Morgen de Lohr, and Scott de Wolfe, Earl of Warenton. With those two siding with Lancaster, the situation was dire, indeed.

It was becoming more and more unsteady by the day.

That sense of unsteadiness included the loss of Magnus. After Delaina rejected him, he had fled north to Berwick and his father's property of Berwick Castle. He had left with only a few words to Edward, resigning his post the very same day Delaina sent him away. He didn't even think about it. He simply told Edward he was resigning and left. It had been Denys who explained the circumstances to Edward, who was shockingly sympathetic. So sympathetic, in fact, that he had a rather heated discussion with Hugh about the situation. Admonished for trying to manipulate Magnus, Hugh had licked his wounds for several weeks after that.

As it turned out, Edward blamed Hugh for losing the best lord commander he had ever had.

That was a small victory as far as Denys was concerned, and he'd even sent word to Magnus about the situation, but he never received a reply. In Magnus' absence, Denys had assumed the position of captain of the king's knights because only Magnus had been appointed lord commander. Edward did not grant Denys that title. In fact, he told Denys that Magnus would have his former position returned to him whenever he wanted it, so Denys was under the impression that his command was only temporary.

Frankly, it didn't bother him all that much.

Denys knew what had driven Magnus out of London, and, truth be told, he'd had a hand in it. He knew he was responsible in large part for what happened, but he was still under the belief that it had been necessary to save Magnus' career. He wasn't exactly sure how Magnus felt about him at this point, and he missed his best friend, but he hoped that someday Magnus would understand that Denys really had believed he was acting in his friend's best interest. He hoped that, someday, Magnus would return to London and assume his position. Until then, Denys was an excellent replacement.

He spent the first couple of months of Magnus' absence sending missives north to Berwick, informing Magnus of what was happening in London, but again, he never received a reply. He had been forced to accept the obvious sign that Magnus didn't want to communicate with him at that time, so he threw himself into his new duties as captain of the king's knights. From watching Magnus handle that position, he knew that it was a lot of work, but he was content with it. When the warlords started distancing themselves from Edward and siding with Lancaster, he wasn't so happy with those politics. His own family, the House of de Winter, remained loyal to Edward because that was what the House of de Winter did. No matter who was on the throne, they were loyal to that person. In this case, it was a king who was driving wedges of division between himself and his very own barons.

Denys saw all of it firsthand.

"Denys? Did you hear me?"

He had, but he had been lost to his own thoughts. He looked up to see Loring standing in the doorway.

"What did you say?" Denys said, rubbing his eyes. "A missive?"

"Aye," Loring said. "Actually, it's to Magnus, but he is not here, so I thought you should have it."

Denys looked at him in surprise. "Who is it from?"

Loring's response was to put it in front of Denys. He looked at it curiously, picking it up and looking at the seal.

He didn't recognize it.

"Who sent this?"

Loring shook his head. "I know one way to find out," he said. "Open it."

Denys gave him an irritated expression. "Dolt," he grumbled. "It belongs to Magnus. I will forward it to him."

"It will be weeks before he gets it. Mayhap it is something important."

That was true. Magnus was far to the north, and if the missive contained anything important, then Denys would know how quickly he should send it. Therefore, he peered at the wax seal. Then he brushed at it and looked more closely.

His expression slackened.

"Wait," he said. "I think I have seen this seal before."

Loring wasn't too interested. "Who is it?"

Denys cast him a concerned glance before carefully breaking the seal and unfolding the vellum. That expression had Loring paying more attention to the missive itself, though he couldn't read it. But he could certainly read Denys' face.

Denys turned positively ashen.

"What's wrong?" Loring asked. "What is it?"

Denys couldn't answer. He read the missive again before standing up. The missive fluttered to the tabletop.

"When did that come?" he finally said.

"Within the hour," Loring said, peering at him in concern. "Why, Denys? What is it?"

Denys was looking at the missive as it lay on the top of the cluttered table. Then he looked indecisive for a brief moment before swinging into action. He grabbed his broadsword and strapped it on, followed by a few other daggers that he tucked into his mail and body in strategic positions. All the while,

Loring was watching him with apprehension and puzzlement.

"I must go," Denys said, pushing past him. "Command is yours until I return, Lor. If anyone asks for me… tell them I have gone on an errand. I shall return as soon as I can."

Loring simply nodded as Denys rushed past him, clearly unwilling to tell him what it was all about. It didn't make any sense to him, but then again, he was a follower and not a leader. Perhaps there were things he didn't need to know.

This was one of them.

But curiosity got the better of Loring. When Denys was gone, rushing off like a madman, Loring picked up the missive that had fallen to the tabletop.

He, too, was shocked when he read it.

Then he burned it.

CHAPTER EIGHTEEN

"DELAINA? IS THOU finished yet?"

It was a sunny day, if cool, in the kitchen yard of St. Blitha's Convent on the outskirts of London. There was a yew tree in the center of it, used for everything from kindling to shade on a warm summer's day. The tree grew strong amidst a convent that had known its share of scandal and heartache during its long and sometimes shadowed history. About one hundred years earlier, it had been the center of an assassination attempt on King John, and it had taken many years before the convent was able to restore any semblance of a reputation.

These days, it was known for its charity. But it was also known for its cheeses and fine lace.

St. Blitha's had a large herd of fat goats from which to make milk for their cheeses. Goat cheese was in high demand among the elite of London, so they had a ready supply of demanding customers for cheeses made with onion, herbs, garlic, and even anchovies when they could get them from the fishmongers near the Thames. It was a soft cheese that was delicious when spread on bread or meat.

The fine lace production of the convent was small but exclusive. Much like the cheese, the lace was in high demand from merchants, as well as the wealthy, who liked to stitch it to everything from clothing to tapestries to curtains. An Irish nun had brought the skill from her homeland years ago and taught others, so now several of them made the lace with small bobbins or with needles.

Delaina was one who used small bobbins.

She heard the other woman's soft question and looked up from her pattern to see Sister Martha Margaret smiling at her. She smiled weakly in return, for these days, she truly didn't have the energy to do much more. In fact, sitting up was the equivalent of running at full speed from one side of London to the other for her. She felt as if it expended that much energy.

Normally, she spent her days lying in bed.

"I am done for the day, sister," she said. "I think I would like to rest now."

The nun scampered into the chamber and helped Delaina to stand. The first thing that became evident through her simple garments was her enormous belly. The child wasn't due for another month or two, but it wasn't an event Delaina was looking forward to. It wasn't an event any of the nuns or postulates were looking forward to, because they had all become quite fond of the mysterious Delaina, who spoke nothing of her past. Everyone assumed that she carried the child of her dead husband for, as a Beguine, that would have been the logical conclusion. The convent hadn't pried into her past, so they only knew what she told them, which was essentially nothing.

She wanted it that way.

Even as the child began to grow inside her and she steadily weakened, Delaina insisted that she had no close family to tell. She insisted that she had no close family to take the child should she perish in childbirth, which was becoming increasingly apparent as a possibility. She had been sick since she arrived at St. Blitha's, and it wasn't simply because of the child. There was something inside of her that was dying, too, something they could all see and something that grew by the day. Something in her eyes suggested there was no longer the will to live. There was something in her soul that was shriveling away, day after day.

Delaina was on borrowed time.

There was a physic who used to come to the convent every couple of weeks to attend to anyone who was too ill for the nuns to handle, and that included Delaina and her unexpected pregnancy. Since she had been ill from the beginning, the physic paid special attention to her. He wanted to bleed her, and he had a couple of times until the mother abbess stepped in and told him she didn't think it was a good idea. Instead, she fed Delaina beef broth and cheese and butter with bread, things that seemed to make her stronger even though she didn't want to become stronger. There were whispers in the dormitories that the death of Delaina's husband had sucked out her will to live. Not even the child seemed to be able to bring her out of her grief.

As the months went on and her belly grew bigger, her spirit as well as her body continued to weaken. She was now well into her seventh month of pregnancy, and the physic had all but told the mother abbess that the lady would not survive the birth. He suggested that they find a good family for the child. Since Delaina was so lovely, he even suggested that she might be able to sell the child for a good deal of money, because it would undoubtedly be a comely baby. That upset the mother abbess so much that she threw the physic out of the convent and told him not to come back.

These days, the mother abbess was searching for a competent midwife to deliver Delaina's baby. That wasn't something they normally had need for, so she had to make sure to obtain a skilled woman and not simply some fishwife who had delivered a baby or two. Daily, the mother abbess and her minions prayed for Delaina, praying she would survive the birth because they genuinely liked her. She was clever, a hard worker, and kind to everyone. Whatever her past was, it was terrible that so sweet a lady should have to suffer so. The mother abbess hoped that the delivery of the child would not add to that suffering.

Delaina knew that. She knew that the mother abbess and the other nuns worried about her, and she was touched by their concern, but she really had no concern for herself. Her only concern was for the life she carried in her, a child of the great Magnus de Wolfe, and when the time was right, she intended to summon him to collect his child. Given how her health had deteriorated, she was also convinced that she would not survive the birth and, ultimately, she wanted the baby to be with his father.

Perhaps, in some small way, she wanted Magnus to remember her every time he looked into his child's face. Perhaps he would fondly remember their brief moment of glory together and the memory of the courtesan he wanted to marry. Considering the last conversation they'd had, she hoped it wouldn't bring him pain, but the truth was that she had little choice.

Her child was meant to be with his father.

It was, after all, a de Wolfe.

These thoughts were rolling through her head as Sister Martha Margaret helped her to walk across the floor. Even walking was exhausting these days as Delaina grabbed hold of the doorjamb to steady herself. Sister Martha Margaret stopped, allowing Delaina to regain her bearings, and then they continued down the corridor, heading for Delaina's small chamber.

It was time for her to rest again.

Delaina had one of the very few private chambers at the convent. Almost everybody slept in a dormitory, but there were a few rooms reserved for the more important nuns. Since Delaina was pregnant and needed her sleep and privacy, one of the older nuns had given up her chamber so that Delaina could have it. It was a very kind gesture, one that Delaina appreciated deeply.

Having finally reached the small chamber with the small window that faced out onto the cloister, Sister Martha Margaret lowered Delaina down onto the uncomfortable cot that had been her bed for months. It was a rope bed with a mattress stuffed with grass, something no one else had, but for a pregnant lady the sisters banded together to make the mattress so Delaina had something comfortable to sleep on. It was a lovely gesture, but even the mattress couldn't make that stiff bed any more comfortable. Still, she slept on it gratefully, on a scratchy mattress that caring nuns had made for her.

It was the first time in her adult life that women had done anything nice for her.

As she lay back on it, exhausted, she put her hands on her belly to feel the baby moving. It was quite active, kicking and rolling, and she drew joy from feeling its movements. She also drew pain. It wasn't so much pain in her memory of leaving Magnus—it was the pain of knowing she could have had the life she wanted, but the cost would have been Magnus' honor.

She'd made the unselfish choice and suffered for it.

But there was more suffering to come.

About three days ago, Delaina had started bleeding again, as she had when she was first pregnant, and the sight of blood frightened her. Her ill health was worsening. She was afraid that she could very well deliver the infant any day and pass away before she'd had a chance to tell Magnus. When she awoke that morning with more blood on her sheets, she was forced into action.

Knowing her time was growing short, she'd written a missive to be delivered to Westminster Palace using a writing kit borrowed from the mother abbess. The woman had allowed it when Delaina told her that she was writing to distant family about the welfare of her child. That wasn't exactly true, however; she wrote to Magnus and told him of his impending child, her impending death, and how it was her wish that her baby should be raised as a de Wolfe. She'd used the mother abbess' seal, and a servant had taken it over to Westminster Palace. She hoped that the missive would bring Magnus to the door of St. Blitha's, but she was resolute that she would not let her feelings for the man overcome her when she saw him again. She would simply tell him that he would be notified when she gave birth so he could collect the infant, and nothing more.

At least, she hoped it was nothing more, but she genuinely had no idea how she would react once she laid eyes on him. After all these months, her feelings for him had never left. If anything, they'd only grown stronger. Those two bright, brilliant days they spent together had taken root, and the more time they spent apart, the more her mind formed a kind of fantasy when it came to Magnus. She began to imagine almost demigod-like things for him, this powerful knight who had touched her so deeply. No one had ever been as kind or as concerned as Magnus. In her eyes, that made him a saint.

Eventually, she drifted to sleep on the stiff and scratchy mattress, and it was close to vespers when Delaina was awakened by a knock on her door. She hadn't realized that she had fallen asleep, but when she looked at the window, she could see that it was nearly dark outside. Wrapped up in a woolen blanket, she tried to rise but simply couldn't. She had no strength left in her body.

"Who comes?" she called weakly.

The door creaked open, and Sister Martha Margaret peered into the chamber, bringing an oil lamp with her. When she saw that Delaina was awake, she smiled. The woman had a cherubic face with rosy cheeks, something Delaina always found comforting.

"Thee has a visitor," she said softly. "The mother abbess has sent me to fetch thee."

Delaina could feel her heart leap at the news. "A visitor?" she repeated. "A knight?"

Sister Martha Margaret nodded. "Aye," she said. "A handsome knight. He says that he has come at your summons."

Tears sprang to Delaina's eyes. Her resolve to be cordial but firm with Magnus was shattered by the fact that he had actually come after all these months. *But no,* she told herself. She couldn't lose her resolve. She was only going to tell him to come for the infant when he was born, and nothing more.

Nothing more!

With great effort, she tossed off the woolen blanket and struggled to sit up. And struggled. Sister Martha Margaret rushed to her side and pulled her into a seated position, and Delaina clung to the woman to steady herself. The nun put her arms around her, holding her firm.

"Mayhap he should come another day, when thou art

stronger," Sister Martha Margaret said softly. "I will tell him."

"Nay," Delaina said with some panic in her voice, holding tightly to the nun. "Please do not send him away. I must see him. I will go to him."

With that, she pushed the nun away. Desperately, she tried to stand up, but she was simply too weak to do it. Even when she began to weep, she still tried to stand up, but her legs would not support her. Sister Martha Margaret tried to help her, but it became apparent that she simply couldn't make it to the entry where the knight was waiting. The more Delaina tried, the more she failed, until Sister Martha Margaret finally pushed her down onto the cot.

"Rest, my child," she said softly, pulling the blanket over Delaina again. "I will fetch him. You will rest."

"But you cannot," Delaina said, clutching the woman's hand. "Men are not allowed at St. Blitha's. You cannot let him in!"

Sister Martha Margaret patted her hand. "Not to worry," she said soothingly. "The mother abbess will make an exception. Is he a brother?"

She meant to ask if he was Delaina's brother. He wasn't, but Magnus had brothers. He was *someone's* brother. She was afraid they would send him away if she didn't give the woman a proper answer.

Even if it was a lie.

"A… cousin," she said. "I do not have a brother."

Sister Martha Margaret squeezed her hand and let it go. "Then I shall return," she said. "Do not worry so."

Overcome with exhaustion and illness, all Delaina could do was nod. Sister Martha Margaret fled from the chamber, taking the oil lamp with her, as Delaina lay there and struggled to calm her racing heart. It wasn't good for her to exert herself, so she took deep breaths, trying to steady herself.

He was coming.

Magnus was coming!

The excitement was almost more than she could bear. She wished with all her heart that she could sit up and greet him, but it was impossible, so she lay there quietly, calming her racing heart, until the door creaked open again and she saw the light from the lamp. Lifting her head, she saw an enormous figure enter the tiny chamber. Sister Martha Margaret set the lamp down and backed out, quietly closing the door.

Delaina found herself looking at Denys.

"It's *you!*" she breathed in shock. Then her eyes filled with tears. "My God, Denys. Do not tell me that Magnus refused to come."

Denys immediately took a knee beside the bed, looking over a very pale and very pregnant woman. Truthfully, he was stunned. "Nay," he said, trying to ease her. "He is not at Westminster, my lady. That is why I came instead. Magnus has gone home."

That didn't help her tears much, but at least she knew Magnus hadn't refused her. "When did he go?"

"Right after you entered St. Blitha's," Denys said quietly. "He could no longer stand to remain in London, knowing you were so near and there was no way he could... be with you."

She was still sniffling. "Is he well?"

"As far as I know, very well."

"What is he doing at Berwick?"

"Commanding his father's army," Denys said. "He asked Edward if he could return to his father, and Edward agreed, but the king holds out hope that Magnus will return someday.

Meanwhile, I have command of the knights."

That explained a good deal. Delaina didn't know if she felt better or worse that Magnus was gone. "I drove him away," she murmured. "I am so very sorry that I did that, but you were right, Denys. I very nearly ruined him. Does he understand that now?"

Denys moved his gaze over a very sick young woman. He found himself becoming more distressed by the moment. "What is wrong with you?" he asked, avoiding her question. "Is something wrong with the child?"

Delaina instinctively put a hand to her big belly. "There is nothing wrong with it," she said. "But I find that I must tell you what I was going to tell Magnus. You will have to tell him for me."

Denys eyed her. "I will send for him," he said. "You must tell him yourself."

"Nay," she said. Reaching out, she grasped the knight's hand. "I will not be here when he comes."

"Why not?"

"Because I am going to die."

Denys sucked in a sharp breath, a hissing sound. "Who has told you that?" he demanded quietly. "What is the matter?"

Delaina squeezed his hand. "Be still and I will tell you," she said. "While the child grows stronger, I grow weaker. The physic said there was something wrong with my blood, he thinks. He says I will not survive the birth, so you must tell Magnus to come and collect his child. I want it very much to go with its father."

Denys' jaw went slack. He stared at her, his eyes wide in disbelief. "*What?*" he finally said. "Who is this physic who told you that you are dying?"

Delaina smiled weakly. "Can you not see how ill I am?" she said. "It is obvious that I am dying. Please, Denys… you must tell Magnus to collect his child. Will you promise me?"

Denys was clearly overwrought with what she was telling him. He ended up on his buttocks next to the bed, his big bulk sitting on the dirt floor as he looked at her, dumbfounded.

"God," he finally muttered. "This cannot be. It is not possible."

Delaina watched his features crease with grief. "I am at peace with it," she said quietly. "I have lived an adventurous life, Denys. I have lived in the finest houses. I have known luxury that few know, and, for a few short days, I knew compassion and affection and kindness that has made my life worth living. I knew Magnus. For his kindness, I am gifting him with his child. It is all I can do for him, though I wish circumstances had been different. I think I would have made a very good wife."

Denys looked at her, hearing the seeds of the argument he had with her those months ago when he told her that she meant ruin to Magnus. He'd felt guilty when he told Magnus what he'd done, guilt that was magnified when Magnus could no longer remain in London. He felt as if he'd orchestrated his friend's misery when he'd only meant to save his career. Somewhere, somehow, he'd done the wrong thing.

He didn't want to do the wrong thing twice.

"Lady Delaina, I want you to listen to me," he said, his voice low. "When I spoke to you those months ago in Hugh Despenser's chambers, I said many things I should not have."

"What do you mean?"

Denys shook his head, averting his gaze. "I should not have told you that you were going to ruin Magnus' life," he said. "I was trying to save my friend, but I ended up making him miserable. He left London because of what I did, the anguish I caused him. He wanted to marry you, and I should have let him make his own decision. I would have defended him from Hugh and anyone else who tried to harm him, but I should have let him make his decision. I should not have made it for him."

"But you were right," Delaina said. "You were so right when you said that a man like Magnus could not marry a woman like me."

"I was *not* right," he said. "Do you know what Magnus told me about you? He told me that sometimes, a man meets a woman and he just knows that she is the one he is meant to be with. He said that he would surrender it all for a few brief moments with the woman who touched his soul like no one ever has. He meant you. How can I think ill of you when you make Magnus feel like that?"

There were tears in Delaina's eyes. "He said all of that?"

"He did."

"But… but the differences in our stations…"

Denys waved her off. "He does not care about that," he said. "I should have listened to him, my lady. I should have let the man be with the woman he loves, but instead, I said terrible things to you that I had no right to say. Just because I have never loved a woman doesn't mean that Magnus isn't entitled to experience the joys of love. I took that away from him, and I should have never done that."

Delaina flicked the tear from her eye. "You did what you felt you had to do in order to save him," she murmured. "In this case, it was from me. You weren't wrong."

"Aye, I was," he stressed. "I was completely wrong. Magnus is miserable now. How do you think he is going to feel when he knows you fell ill while carrying his child and died because of it?

His misery will know no limits. It will destroy him."

Delaina thought on that for a moment. "Then mayhap you should not tell him until… after," she said. "If you tell him now, he might come to London and try to see me before… before his child comes. I could not bear it."

"Why not?" Denys said. He was still holding her hand, and he squeezed it. "Delaina, do you feel for him as he feels for you?"

She nodded weakly. "For all time," she whispered.

"You *do* know the man is in love with you… don't you?"

She smiled, more tears filling her eyes. "I was the most fortunate woman in the world, once," she said. "But surely time and grief have muddled those feelings."

Denys looked her in the eye. "Listen to me," he said with firm, quiet authority. "The Magnus I know is not that fickle. If he loved you once, I would wager to say he never lost that feeling. You said that you will love him for all time. Is it fair that two people who love one another should be separated?"

She sighed faintly. "This is the only way to—"

"It is *not* the only way," Denys said, interrupting her. "Delaina, I do not know what is happening with you at St. Blitha's, but I do not like it. They are letting you die. Let me take you away from here and summon Magnus. If you really are going to die, then wouldn't you like to have him with you? The man will never forgive himself if you do not let him see you before this birth, so please… please let me take you away. For Magnus' sake… please let me do this."

Delaina was looking at him with shock, but there was great longing in her expression. "But… why cause him such pain?" she said. "It is best for me to remain here and let him remember me as I was, not as I am."

"But you sent that missive to Magnus," he pointed out. "You must have wanted to see him if you sent the missive. Now you do not want to?"

She was being indecisive, and she knew it. "I did want to see him," she said honestly. "But now that you have come… mayhap it will cause him less pain if you deliver the message to him. What good will it do him to come to me only for me to die in his arms?"

"You are making his decision for him, as I did. That is wrong."

"I am trying to protect him, as you were."

"And I was *wrong*."

She averted her gaze, and Denys wasn't sure what more to say. He could see that she wasn't agreeable, and he didn't blame her. Not in the least. But if he could do one more thing for Magnus, he was going to try to make this right.

He had to.

"Do you remember when I spoke of my younger brother, who had been cut down by Scots?" he said.

Delaina nodded. "I remember."

Denys' memory of his youngest brother came to the forefront, the fiery blond with such arrogance, but also such compassion. His eyes began to grow moist at the remembrance, something he didn't often do because of the emotions it provoked. Even after all of these years.

"I told you that he had been killed in battle," he said quietly. "His name was Dallan. When I remember him, I see him in several different stages of his life—as a small child who used to follow me and my older brothers about, as a young boy who very much wanted to do what I did, and as a young man who had acquired a good deal of skill. Dallan was pure talent, I assure you. He was also my mother's shadow, even up until he died. It was a tremendous bond. I heard her say once that she knew Dallan would have made a fine father and a fine husband. But he never got the chance. Delaina, I do not want to see Magnus lose his chance at being a fine father and a fine husband. It would be such a terrible waste for you both, especially if you love one another."

He made a good deal of sense. Perfect sense, in fact. Delaina hadn't been willing to even consider it until his last few sentences, and then it occurred to her that he was right. Denys, who could be so persuasive, was doing his best to help her see that he'd been wrong about Magnus.

They'd both been wrong.

"I've heard men say that they only regretted the chances they did not take," she said after a moment. "I have much regretted the chance I did not take with Magnus, but I believed it was for his own good."

"It's not," Denys said. "Please believe me that it's not. Do not waste the chance to tell him what you feel. Do not let my mistake ruin what the two of you feel for one another."

Delaina could feel herself being swayed. She was moving out of the realm of a discouraging ending to her life and into the dominion of hope, where joy was attainable. She never thought she would leave St. Blitha's alive, but one small missive to Westminster was changing that opinion.

Perhaps she did indeed owe that to Magnus.

And to herself.

"Where will you take me?" she asked.

Denys was shocked that she didn't refuse him yet again, and he was already on the move, lest she change her mind. "I am not certain," he said, thinking quickly. "I do recall that back when Magnus first met you, he went to the Earl of Hereford and Worcester for help. The man said that he would help him. I am certain that has not changed."

"Worcester?" she said. "Morgen de Lohr?"

"You know him?"

"I know *of* him."

Denys let go of her hand and stood up. "He can summon the finest physic in all of London," he said, feeling a surge of hope. "He has a fine home to the west of London. I will take you there and we will summon Magnus. My lady… please? May I do this for you both?"

Delaina had another moment of indecision. "I do not want to be the earl's burden," she said. "In my current state, that is all I will be—a burden."

Denys didn't want to hear any further arguments. As Delaina lay there with a woolen blanket pulled over her, he reached down and scooped her up into his big arms.

"You will not be a burden, I swear it," he said, moving for the door. "Magnus deserves his happiness, my lady, if only momentarily. And so do you."

Delaina couldn't argue with that.

Nor could the mother abbess when Delaina told her everything.

Before the hour was out, Denys and Delaina were heading toward Lonsdale House.

CHAPTER NINETEEN

One month later
Berwick Castle

W*HOOSH!*
The ax was swinging.

Scots had managed to make their way into the village of Berwick and raid the fish market, of all things, and the garrison at Berwick Castle was on top of them. That included Magnus. Given that he was commanding his father's army at the moment alongside his youngest brother, Titus, he was the one leading the charge against the Scots, who were making a mess more than actually stealing things.

The entire village was in an uproar. Villagers were running and screaming, trying to hide from Clan Gordon, which was the usual tempest when it came to Berwick and the surrounding lands. Astride his muscled warhorse, Magnus had his grandfather's beloved ax in hand, using it as both a murder weapon and a battering ram, depending on the situation. When he saw two big Scotsmen trying to wrest something from one of the fishwives, he charged after them and took out one man while the other fled behind the cottages.

Magnus went in pursuit.

It was like a game of cat and mouse, with the Scots running and the English pursuing, but it wasn't unusual. This kind of thing had been going on for decades, and certainly in the months that Magnus had been back at Berwick. This was the fifth such raid he'd been forced to ride to, defending the prosperous village of Berwick from raiders. Not even reivers, the wild outlaws that roamed the northern lands, but clansmen who had simply crossed the border.

It made for a wild morning.

Fortunately, it was only a morning and not an entire day or days when it came to this particular raid. It had been a smaller group who infiltrated the city, and Titus had managed to capture one of the leaders. While Magnus cleaned up the city and either killed or chased out any stragglers, Patrick de Wolfe, Earl of Berwick, interrogated the man to discover that the only reason they'd gone to the fishmongers was because his people were hungry. Evidently, some kind of sickness had worked its way through their clan and many people were ill, while those who weren't ill struggled to keep up with the sick. Gathering and harvesting food, including fishing in the River Tweed, had been limited.

Magnus hadn't known any of this, of course. Once the village was cleared and he established a heavy soldier presence to make the villagers feel better, he headed back to the castle. Night had fallen by this time, and he turned his horse over to the stable servants as he continued into the keep of Berwick, a massive thing that housed the large Patrick de Wolfe family. He hadn't taken two steps inside the door when he heard someone call his name.

"Magnus?"

It was his father. Magnus turned for the solar, with the open doors and the heat and light radiating from it because of the roaring fire in the hearth. Entering the long, rectangular chamber, he removed the ax from his shoulder and carefully propped it up by the door. Wearily, he removed his helm.

"Well?" Patrick said, standing near the hearth. "What is the final tally?"

Magnus rubbed his eyes wearily. "We did not lose any men," he said. "I've got six wounded, one fairly severely. But I believe they'll live."

"Villagers?"

"We lost at least four," Magnus said. "Fishermen who tried to prevent the Scots from stealing their catch."

Patrick went to the table opposite the hearth, the one that held the wine, and poured his son a full measure. Patrick was the tallest man in the de Wolfe family, having inherited his height from some monstrous ancestor, and all but one of his sons had inherited that height. Magnus used to always feel inadequate because he was the short de Wolfe in his family, even though he was still taller than most men. But he had a bulk and a breadth that his brothers didn't have.

When Magnus fought, men ran.

That was what made him stand out, or so he thought. That and the fact that he was perhaps more Northman than Englishman simply because he looked like his mother's father's side of the family. Patrick, however, had the de Wolfe dark looks—his hair, almost black in his youth, was now streaked with gray, but the pale green eyes were just as sharp as they ever were.

So was the man the family called Atty.

"You did good work today, Magnus," Patrick said as he handed his son the cup of wine. "You are to be commended. It could have been a lot worse had you not charged into the battle with your grandfather's ax. It seems to terrify men at the mere sight."

Magnus grinned, turning to glance at the four-foot-long ax leaning against the wall. "I am named for the man who bore that weapon," he said. "Magnus the Law-Mender, the most powerful king to his people. Seeing that reminds men that the blood of the Northmen still resides in Berwick."

"Indeed, it does," Patrick said. "It resides in you. And in Markus and Cassius and Titus. They all have it to a certain degree, but you have it more than any of your brothers."

Magnus took a long drink of wine before replying. "I do," he said. "When I was young, that always made me feel different. I remember some of the lads where I fostered used to tell me that the Northmen were going to kidnap me someday and force me to fight for them."

Patrick laughed softly. "Boys of that age are always so cruel," he said. "I wonder what has become of some of those little fools."

"They grew up like their fathers," Magnus muttered. "They grew into bigger fools. Well, not all of them. The de Shera boys didn't. Nor did the de Lohr lads."

"That reminds me," Patrick said suddenly, turning for his table. "You have a missive from Morgen de Lohr."

"For me?" Magnus said, not particularly interested. "Why?"

"I would not know."

"When did it come?"

Patrick pushed missives around on his table until he came to what he was looking for. He picked it up. "Early this morning while you were off fighting Scots in the village," he said. "Did you not see the messenger?"

Magnus shook his head. "I was occupied elsewhere," he said, pointing out the obvious as he took the missive from his father. "I wonder what de Lohr wants?"

Patrick shrugged and sat back down at his table, looking over a map of the Scottish marches and the Gordon territory as Magnus broke the seal on the missive.

"Do you know what the Gordon man told me?" Patrick said. "He said their people are going hungry. That's why they raided the fish market. Damn Scots are too proud to ask for help, but they're not too proud to steal."

Magnus unfolded the missive. "Do you have any contact with the clan chief these days?"

"Nay," Patrick said. "Ever since old Angus Gordon died, the new clan chief does not wish to talk. He only wants to drive his men to war."

Magnus set his cup down and took a seat, settling down to read. "Typical."

"True," Patrick said. "But if they are truly starving, I am not opposed to helping them."

The conversation died, mostly because Patrick went back to his map and Magnus began to read the missive. They could hear the shouts of the men in the bailey outside, sealing up the castle as night approached.

Titus de Wolfe, tall and dark and handsome, entered the keep, shouting to the servants for food and drink as he entered his father's solar with all of the grace and peace of a bull charging into a church. His sword clattered to the ground and he completely missed the table where he went to set his helm. He began stripping off belts and tunics, tossing them all around, as Patrick frowned at him.

"God's Bones, Titus," he said. "Could you possibly be any louder?"

Titus grinned brightly at his father. "I could," he said. "Shall I?"

Patrick cocked an eyebrow. "Be still," he said. "I have some questions about the battle. Your brother has already given me the casualty count."

Titus looked over at Magnus, who was reading his missive. His brother seemed so engrossed in it that he snuck over and stole the cup of wine, draining the entire thing and then belching loudly and victoriously. He belched again for good measure, speaking the words *fortis in arduis*, the de Wolfe motto, as he ripped out a nice, juicy burp.

Disgusted, Patrick picked up the nearest thing he could find, which happened to be a sealed bag of sand for his missives, and threw it right at Titus. It hit his son in the chest, ending his triumphant belching.

"Why have you done such a thing, Papa?" Titus said, rubbing his chest. "Why would you hurt me so when I have just chased Scots off your doorstep?"

Patrick cast him a long, impatient look. "I told you to sit down and be still," he said. "Be more like your brother and mayhap someday you, too, shall have a royal appointment."

Titus frowned. "I am as good as Magnus ever was."

"Magnus does not burp loudly enough for the Scots to hear."

Titus curled his lip and turned to insult Magnus, but something stopped him cold.

His brother had tears running down his face.

"Magnus?" Titus said, suddenly quite serious. "What is the

matter?"

Magnus was still looking at the missive, but when he heard Titus' question, he looked up to see both his brother and father looking at him with concern. Patrick was up from his table, heading in his son's direction.

"Magnus?" he said, concerned. "What has happened? What did de Lohr say to you?"

Realizing he was now the center of attention, Magnus quickly wiped his face. "It is nothing," he said, standing up and heading straight for the door. "Papa, I will be leaving for London immediately."

"Magnus, *wait*," Patrick said. "Stop this instant. What is the matter?"

Magnus paused at the door. He stood there a moment, unable to look at his father or his brother, but he knew they were behind him, waiting for an answer.

He wasn't sure he could give them one.

"Something… unexpected," he said tightly. "Please, Papa. Let me leave."

Patrick looked at Titus, who appeared deeply concerned for his brother. In fact, it was Titus who went to Magnus and put his arms around him, directing him back into the room. The youngest de Wolfe brother had great empathy and compassion, especially when it came to his kin.

"Sit down, old man," Titus said gently. "We only want to help if we can. A man should not have to bear his troubles alone. That is why he has family."

Magnus let his brother take him to a chair and push him down to sit. Truthfully, he was so stunned that he could barely move. He could barely think. The missive in his hand was trembling. As Titus stood close by, ready to help, ready to do what Magnus needed him to do, Magnus looked at the missive again. He read through it.

He could still hardly believe it.

"I… I do not even know where to begin," he whispered. "I don't know anything at all."

Patrick, who had been watching the situation with increasing apprehension, reached out a hand toward Magnus. "May I read the missive?" he asked.

Magnus hesitated. "Not before I explain it to you, Papa," he said. "I would not make any sense to you."

"Will you please tell me?"

Magnus took a deep breath, struggling to compose himself in the wake of a violent wave of information. He felt as if he'd been rolled over and over again still. He was still rolling. He took another deep breath, trying to stop the momentum.

"I will," he said. "Only… give me a moment, please. This is not something I expected today."

Patrick remained where he was, gazing down at his son with great concern, while Titus went to the door when a servant brought the food and drink he'd asked for. He ended up slamming the door in their face, setting the food down, and then taking the wine to his brother.

"Here," he said. "Drink this."

Magnus did. He drained the entire cup with shaking hands, and when he handed it back to his brother, he broke down in tears again. For several long moments, he simply put his hands over his face and wept.

Stricken, Patrick crouched down next to him and put his big arm around his son's shoulders. But he didn't speak; he didn't ask to know why he was weeping. Not again.

Magnus would tell him when he was ready.

It took about a half-hour before he was ready.

Titus had poured him more wine, and Patrick had nearly forced it down his throat. When he had two and a half cups of good wine in his belly, Magnus finally wiped his face off and stood up, pacing the room as he struggled to regain his composure. When he felt strong enough, he faced his father and youngest brother.

"What I tell you will not leave this chamber," he said, his voice raspy. "Not ever. Not even Mother must know. Do you understand?" Patrick and Titus nodded, and Magnus continued. "Back in September of last year, Edward held a great feast for all of the warlords who had opposed him at the gathering of Parliament," he said. "Papa, you and Uncle Scott and Uncle Thomas were invited to it."

"We were," Patrick said. "But things were too unstable in the north for us to leave."

Magnus knew that, and he went on. "There were many warlords at the feast, including Lord Daventry," he said. "You remember him, Papa. The old man with a wild amount of wealth. In any case, he brought a woman with him, one of the Seven Jewels of London. Have you ever heard of them?"

Patrick's brow furrowed, and he cocked his head thoughtfully. "Aye," he said after a moment. "I think so. Aren't those the women that Longshanks used to bribe his enemies? Whores, I think."

Magnus sighed faintly at the use of that word. "Courtesans," he corrected his father softly. "These were well-educated, very bright and beautiful women. The one that Daventry brought with him was called the Ruby, but her name was Delaina de Courant. I do not know if you have heard this, Papa, but Lord Daventry died at the feast. He went to the privy and hemorrhaged all over the place, so I was tasked with quietly removing the body and sending him, and his courtesan, home."

Patrick grunted. "I had not heard he died," he said. "Sounds unpleasant at best."

"It was," Magnus said. "But it was my job to ensure he and his party returned home. As we waited for the body to be prepared, Lady Delaina and I spoke. I discovered she had nowhere to go now that Daventry was dead, and I offered to assist her in finding lodgings or a safe place, at least for the night. When she expressed concern over her safety, I offered to hide her. She was a lone woman, and I felt it was the right thing to do."

"What happened?" Patrick asked.

Magnus sighed sharply. "I assisted her," he said. "But I also fell in love with her. I will be perfectly blunt when I tell you that Delaina is a woman among women. She is everything a woman should be. She's kind and compassionate, educated and brilliant. She's witty. I've never met a woman like her in my entire life. You called her and women like her whores, and by society's standards, they are. But in Delaina's case, she had no choice in her life. She was forced into it by a greedy father and an even greedier king. She did not deserve what happened to her, and I wanted to marry her, but she refused. That is why I came north, Papa. I could not stay in London anymore and see her around every corner."

Surprisingly, Patrick didn't react. He was listening intently to a situation that had dissolved his strong son to tears. He maintained a neutral attitude, knowing now was not the time to point out that his son had fallen for a whore.

A courtesan.

It was the same thing to him.

"What is in the missive that has you so upset?" he asked softly.

Magnus looked at the missive in his hand and started to tear up again. Unable to tell his father, he extended the missive, and Patrick took it.

He read the contents.

Your lady is our guest. She has asked me to relay to you her dying condition. He has asked that you come to Lonsdale to collect your child.

We will take great care of her and the child until your arrival.

Come with all due haste.

"My God," Patrick breathed, unable to keep his composure. "She is with child?"

Magnus nodded, trying not to openly weep. "I did not know," he said. "Papa, if I had known, I would have never left London. I would have stayed… I would have forced her to marry me. I would have never left!"

Patrick patted his son on the shoulder because he was growing agitated. "I know," Patrick said. "You are an honorable man. But why is she with de Lohr?"

Magnus wiped his face. "I'm not exactly sure," he said. "But early on, I asked the earl to help me when the lady was looking for a safe haven right after Daventry's death. She may have gone to him for help when she discovered that she… she carried my child. God, I can hardly believe it even as I say it."

"And now he is sending a missive to you."

"Aye."

Patrick thought on that. "But there is something I do not

understand in all of this," he said. "You mentioned that she feared for her safety after Daventry died. Why?"

Magnus took another deep, long breath. "Because Despenser wanted to get his hands on her," he said. "She also thought his son might try to claim her as part of his father's estate, and she was afraid of the son."

"Did he try?"

"I do not know. I left only a few days after Daventry's death."

"But you said Despenser wanted her, too?"

Magnus nodded. "Of course, he was aware of Daventry's death because he wanted to use her as Longshanks had used her," he said. "He wanted to use her as a prize or a bribe for some warlord, but he ended up trying to use her against me—he knew I was fond of her, and he offered to give her to me in exchange for my loyalty. At that point, he was holding her hostage, and he knew I would do anything to secure her release. When she realized what Despenser was trying to do, she escaped and went straight to Westminster Abbey to ask for sanctuary. She did it to save my honor, and no matter what I said to her, she would not be swayed. She thought… she thought she was about to ruin my career by resigning my honor to Despenser."

Patrick stared at him. "Despenser did that to you?"

Magnus nodded, hanging his head. "It was something else I did not wish to tell you," he said. "When the lady escaped to Westminster… I left."

Patrick's jaw began to twitch. He looked at Titus, who was positively enraged, clenching and unclenching his fists.

"Let me summon the armies, Papa," Titus said. "Let me call them together and march on that bastard. Let us make this the catalyst to removing Despenser from Edward's side."

Patrick held up a hand. His attention returned to Magnus, who was still sitting there with his head hung. As angry as Patrick was with Hugh Despenser, that was not the larger issue here. Magnus was.

It was clear his son had been through quite a lot prior to his return from London, but Patrick had never dreamed of such a terrible adventure. The fact remained that Magnus had fallen in love, and the man that sat before Patrick now had a broken heart. So very broken.

Patrick felt a great deal of pity for him.

"What do you wish to do, Magnus?" he asked quietly. "Whatever you choose, know that you shall receive no argument from me. I trust you in any decision you make for yourself."

Magnus sniffled, wiping his nose as he peered up at his father. "Do you mean that?" he asked. "You do not want to tell me how stupid I am for falling in love with a courtesan?"

Patrick shook his head. "Mayhap it is not the most desirable background," he said. "But you are a seasoned, steady man. You would not do anything foolish. If you feel she is the woman you wish to marry, then I'll not fight you on it."

Somehow, Magnus had known, all along, that his father would be supportive. After all, Patrick had stolen a postulate from a convent and married her. Magnus' mother was that former postulate, and Magnus knew that his father had even had to fight for his mother.

Perhaps it was Magnus' turn to fight.

"If anyone understands that there are times when a man falls for a woman who may not be meant for him, it is you," Magnus murmured. "You married Mother, and I am sure

Poppy was greatly against it."

Poppy was what all of the de Wolfe grandchildren called Patrick's father, the greatest de Wolfe of them all. William de Wolfe had been gone for several years now, but his memory was alive, as strongly as if he was only in the next room. He was spoken of often and fondly.

Patrick snorted at Magnus' statement. "You have no idea, lad," he said. "Poppy gave me such a fight that I truly thought it would ruin my relationship with him forever. But it did not. You are right when you say that I understand what it is to fall in love with a woman you are not meant to have. Would you like me to ride to London with you?"

Magnus' eyes widened and he stood up, facing his father. "Would you?"

"Of course I would," Patrick said, seeing how much it meant to his son. "Titus can remain here with your uncle Alec in command. Berwick can do without me for now. I think you need me more. Besides… I have a few things to say to Hugh Despenser about his intentions toward you."

Magnus felt better than he had in months. Having his father's support was everything to him. "I am going to Lonsdale to marry Lady Delaina," he said. "I want to be perfectly clear, Papa."

Patrick smiled faintly. "I am well aware, lad," he said. "In fact… I think I have something for you."

He turned back to his table, only he moved beyond it to a niche in the wall where he kept a fortified, locked iron box. That was where he kept most of his valuables and coin, and he used a big iron key to open the box. After wrenching open the old lid, because it liked to stick, he fumbled around in the box until he came across what he was looking for.

Magnus was still wiping the moisture from his face and Titus was trying to force more wine down his throat when Patrick returned to them, bearing items.

Magnus looked at him curiously. "What do you have?" he asked.

Patrick held up an exquisite dagger in the Northman fashion. It was made from steel, with intricate patterns of dragons and snakes. He put it in Magnus' hand.

"This is from your grandfather and namesake," he said. "When he visited us before his death several years ago, he brought these things with him. I think he knew he would never return, and he wanted to make sure his grandsons had something of their Norse heritage. Markus received a belt, Cassius a set of tankards, but you… he had something special in mind for you, since you were named after him. He told me that this dagger is meant for your son, and that you are to tell the lad of his great-grandfather and keep the Northman alive for your children. Will you do this?"

Magnus held the dagger reverently. "Of course I will," he said. "This is a beautiful weapon."

"It is," Patrick agreed. "I'm sure it has killed many an Englishman. But he also wanted you to have this, to give to your wife."

He held out something small, and Magnus extended his hand to have a small silver ring deposited in his palm. Upon closer inspection, it was a magnificent piece of jewelry. The band was a dragon, wrapped in a circle and biting its own tail. The dragon's eye was a big moonstone, perfect and glistening and milky.

"This is beautiful, Papa," he said. "And he wanted me to have this?"

Patrick nodded. "It belonged to his wife, whom you never met," he said. "Her name was Daina, and Magnus said she was the strongest woman he'd ever known, a true queen among her people. This is not your mother's mother, however, but the woman Magnus married later in life. They had no children, as you know, so he wanted his grandsons to have these things. You will give it to your lady when you marry her."

Magnus was overcome with emotion. He could only nod before going to his father and giving him a fierce hug. Patrick hugged him tightly, so incredibly sympathetic with Magnus' plight. Patrick had indeed married a woman forbidden to him, and he didn't know what he would have done had he not been allowed to marry the lovely Lady Brighton.

He released his son, cupping his face between his two big hands as he looked him in the eye. "I understand what it is to love a woman you are not supposed to have," he said. "I am sorry you were separated from her, Magnus. I truly am. I'm sorry that you felt that you could not tell me any of this, but I'm glad that you did. If you truly want this woman, then we shall go and get her."

Magnus was feeling emotional, especially with his father's unconditional support. "The missive said she is dying, Papa," he said, his lower lip trembling. "What if it's true?"

"Would you like to take Uncle Hector with us? He is an excellent healer, as his father was."

"So is Uncle Scott."

"Uncle Hector is closer."

"If you do not think he would mind, I would."

A missive went out to Northwood Castle before the night was out, asking Hector de Norville, Patrick's brother-in-law and commander of Northwood's army, to join Patrick and Magnus on an errand of mercy in London. Northwood was deeply entwined with the de Wolfe properties, even though it was the seat of the Earl of Teviot. But Teviot's loyalty, and friendship, ran deep when it came to the House of de Wolfe. There was never any question that Hector would answer the summons.

Within two days, the three of them, plus three hundred de Wolfe soldiers, were heading for London at a full gallop.

CHAPTER TWENTY

Lonsdale House
London

THE ENTRY WAS still and dark.

That wasn't its usual state. Normally, there were children playing about, attacking anyone who entered the manse, even attacking the servants going about their duties. Poor Marcellus had endured the brunt of the lively de Lohr children, and there were many—Christopher, the eldest, also known as Christie, followed by Kurtis, twins Bingham and Blakeney, Myles, and little Tevin. The youngest child, Abigail, was still an infant and rarely out of her mother's sight, but the boys—all six of them between the ages of three and nine—ruled Lonsdale House.

But today, there was no laughter of children inside. In fact, there hadn't been in almost two months, ever since the arrival of the lovely but ill pregnant woman from St. Blitha's. Morgen's wife and mother to the gang of ruffians, Kirra St. Hever de Lohr, had chased her children outside with their nurse to keep the house quiet, and outside was where they remained. It had become their kingdom, much to the dismay of the de Lohr soldiers. Instead of fighting enemies, they were fighting off their lord's six little boys, all of whom were wily, smart, and cunning. Purses were stolen, daggers swiped, but Marcellus had been given permission to take a firmer hand with the boys, so there was some order.

But not much.

Not enough.

However, the manse was quiet, and that was all Kirra was concerned with. She had a very sickly young woman on her hands. Her husband had told her that the woman was a distant cousin, from an unfamiliar branch of the family, and Kirra was to treat her with all due care and respect. Not that Kirra wouldn't have, had she known who the young woman really was...

Because she did.

After Morgen told her about the woman, she had overheard her husband speaking to a knight, the same knight who brought the young woman to Lonsdale. Kirra hadn't meant to eavesdrop, but it was clear the young woman had something of a past, and, for some reason, Morgen was trying to cover for her. Kirra didn't know why he should do that, but it didn't matter. Her husband wanted the poor lady to be tended to, and that was exactly what Kirra did. Whatever the woman's past was made no difference. Kirra was kind to her regardless.

Kindness was something Delaina had greatly appreciated, though in the de Lohr household, she was called Lady Violet. That had been established the night Denys brought her to Lonsdale, and she went with it because that was what the Earl of Hereford and Worcester had introduced her as. The countess had been with her daily, as had a physic from London who actually seemed to believe in sunlight and good food, and treated her weakness with things like eggs and meat and broth made from boiled bones. Every so often, he'd put a powder in her boiled wine that made her feel relaxed and happy.

Since coming to Lonsdale, Delaina had felt distinctly better.

Like this morning. The house was silent when she awoke, feeling rested, but she could hear the distant sounds of children as the earl's brood played outside. In fact, they seemed closer today than they usually did, and Delaina was able to rise from the bed without pain and waddle over to the window, seeing that they were playing down by the river even though it was quite chilly on this early summer day. She could see them chasing each other with sticks, smiling when the rambunctious twins went after one another and someone began screaming. They really were great entertainment as she stood by the window and watched.

But down in her belly, something was stirring.

Though Delaina had never given birth before, she suspected the time was upon her because a dull ache had started in her back last night. This morning, it seemed to radiate around to her belly and down her thighs. It came and went, not particularly strong, but she had a feeling her child was coming very soon. She was positively enormous, something even the physic commented on, and he'd once asked her about the size of the child's father.

Big, was all Delaina had said.

For all the physic and the countess knew, Delaina's husband was away on business for the king. That was what the earl had told them, and they hadn't asked any more than that. Big didn't really cover the size of Magnus de Wolfe. He was so much more than brawn and breadth and bone. Every day, she ached for him, wondering if he'd received the missive the earl had sent him. That had been two months ago, the day she arrived, and she knew that it would take time for Magnus to receive it, far in the north as he was.

But that didn't stop her from hoping, every single day, that he would make an appearance.

If he wanted to come, of course.

After all this time, she wouldn't blame him if he didn't.

"Good morn, my lady."

The door to the chamber abruptly opened and Kirra entered, followed by servants with food and drink and water for washing. Delaina turned from the window, smiling at a woman she genuinely liked. She was blonde and lovely and cheery, but she also had a no-nonsense manner about her. When Lady Worcester gave a command, men jumped.

"Good morn," Delaina greeted her. "I was watching your children play by the river."

Kirra came over to the window and peered through it. "Good heavens," she said. "I hope no one falls in."

Delaina grinned as she watched the twins wrestling one another. "There are several soldiers with them and their nurse," she said. "Surely someone will fish them out if they fall in."

Kirra was directing the servants to set the food and water down. "One would hope so," she said. "Did I ever tell you that Christie and Kurtis and the twins built a raft once?"

Christie was what she called her eldest son, and Delaina laughed softly. "I am almost afraid to ask what happened."

Kirra cast her a sidelong glance. "You jest, but you should ask that question seriously," she said. "Somehow, they managed to lash several small logs together. I have no idea where they got them, and they would never say, but I have long suspected that one of the soldiers helped them build it. They took it down to the river, and when they saw that it floated, they jumped onto it."

Delaina was giggling, hand over her mouth. "Did they get very far?"

Kirra nodded. "Far, indeed," she said. "They made it down to the next bend, where the Wellesbourne town home is located. Thank God that someone saw them struggling down the river, along the shore, and pulled them all in and marched them home to face my wrath. I have never been so angry in my life."

Delaina couldn't stop laughing. "Did they say where they were going?"

"Aye," Kirra said, clearly agitated. "They were going to Cornwall to become pirates."

Delaina thought that was positively delightful. "Thank God that they did not make it," she said. "Coming to know them as I have, they would make excellent pirates, but Cornwall has enough of them. They would have competition."

Kirra looked up from the meal she was removing from the tray. "Oh?" she said. "You know Cornwall?"

"I was born there."

Kirra waggled her eyebrows. "Then you are far from home, my lady," she said. "Now, sit and eat. The porridge is lovely and hot."

Delaina's smile faded somewhat. "It looks delicious," she said, watching the servants filter out. When they were gone and the door shut, she made no move to eat. "My lady... may I ask you a question?"

"Of course."

Delaina rubbed her big belly. "When you gave birth to your

children, how did you know when…" She paused and started again. "*When* it was time for them to be born. How did you know?"

Kirra snorted softly. "Trust me," she said. "You will know. The pain will tell you that it is time."

"Is the pain in your belly?"

"It can be," Kirra said. "With Christie and Kurtis, it was mostly the same. Low in my belly, but with the twins, it was in my back. I always thought it was so strange that the pain was mostly in my back, but the midwife said it was because of the way the twins were situated in my womb."

"Was there pain in your legs?"

"Very much," Kirra said. Then she suddenly paused and peered strangely at Delaina. "Why are you asking? Are you having pain in your legs?"

Delaina nodded reluctantly. "Aye," she said. "Also in my back and a little in my belly, but not much at all. Do you think it might be time?"

Kirra went to her and put her hands on Delaina's belly. She stood there a moment, feeling the solid tightness of it. "Has there been any blood?"

"A little, but that has been constant."

"Nothing more? No rush of waters?"

"Nay."

Kirra removed her hands. "I would wager to say that your body is preparing itself for the birth," she said. "And remember what the physic has told you—there is no need to fear. He does not see any reason why you should not survive the birth."

"But I have been—"

Kirra cut her off, but not harshly. "The physic who saw you at St. Blitha's was not a good physic," she said. "He was a fool, my dear. Our physic is quite competent, and he will bring his wife, the midwife, when it is time. They have delivered my last three children, and I can assure you that they know what they are doing. I do not want you to worry."

This had been the running theme since Delaina's arrival at Lonsdale. Denys had brought her in at death's door and Kirra worked hard to bring her back to health. These days, she could stand up and walk, and she could even go outside to walk around the compound. There was no fainting or extreme weakness, but the bleeding had never really stopped. That was the only thing of concern, but the physic said he'd seen it before. The truth would be known once she gave birth.

Which, evidently, wasn't too far off.

"I will not worry," Delaina said, though she wasn't sure she meant it. "But when do you think it will happen?"

Kirra handed her a cup of warmed milk with nutmeg and honey. "Who's to say?" she said. "Babies can take hours or they can take days. I will summon the physic and his wife this morning so that they are here when the pains start in earnest. This is an exciting day, Violet. Your child is preparing to come into the world, and I am very excited to meet him."

Violet. Delaina always thought it was very strange to be called that. She'd never liked it. But the earl had started the illusion, and she simply continued it. However, she didn't like deceiving someone who had been so kind to her. As Kirra moved toward the door, Delaina reached out and grasped the woman's hand.

"Wait," she said softly. "I want to… I simply want to thank you for all you've done. You have been kind and generous to a woman you do not even know, and I am so grateful. Whatever happens with this birth, I want you to know that you have been an angel of mercy to me."

Kirra smiled, squeezing her hand. "There was never any question," she said. "My husband feels that you are important, and so do I. It has been an honor to know you, Violet. I hope that even after the birth, and when your husband comes for you, that we may still be friends. I would like that very much."

Delaina was struck by her words. God, how she'd hoped to hear something like that her entire adult life, but no woman at any time had ever offered her any semblance of friendship. But here it was, even if it was all based on a lie.

Gazing into Kirra's sweet face, she could feel the guilt consuming her. Kirra had been lied to about everything, and although it wasn't Delaina's place to contradict the earl, she'd never liked that he'd lied to his wife. She knew why he did it, but she still didn't think that it was kind of him.

She didn't like deceiving a woman who was the only friend she had.

"As would I," she finally said, feeling defeated and upset that she couldn't tell Kirra the truth. "I hope we are friends for a very long time."

"We shall be," Kirra assured her. "And everything will go well with the baby. You'll see."

Delaina simply nodded as Kirra let her hand go and continued to the door. But the moment she touched it, Delaina called to her.

"Will… will you be with me the entire time?" she asked. "When I give birth, I mean. I am afraid to be alone."

Kirra smiled. "Of course I will be with you," she said. "I will not leave you, not for a moment."

That gave Delaina so much comfort, but she couldn't look into that friendly face and keep lying. Something inside of her was demanding she be truthful so that the friendship, if it continued, wouldn't be based on a lie. She simply couldn't do that to Kirra.

Quietly, she closed the gap between them as Kirra stood at the door. Delaina fixed her in the eye, reaching out to take her hand again.

"When this is over and if I survive, I should like to tell you more about myself," she said timidly. "I realize that I've been quite mysterious since I arrived, but that was only to keep the gossip at bay. There is much more to tell, and I hope you will forgive me for not telling you sooner."

Kirra's blue eyes glimmered warmly. "There is no need," she said softly. "I already know everything I need to know."

"What do you know?"

"I heard my husband speaking to de Winter, the knight who brought you here," she said, watching Delaina's expression ripple with fear. "I know enough."

Delaina sucked in a shocked breath. "You do?"

Kirra nodded. Then she grasped Delaina gently by the chin, leaned forward, and whispered in her ear.

"Do not be troubled, Delaina."

With that, she quit the room and shut the door quietly behind her, leaving Delaina awash in tears of joy and relief.

She knows, and still, she wants to be my friend.

The realization fed her soul.

Somehow, it fed Kirra's, too.

❦

THE RE WERE RUMBLINGS in Manchester.

Morgen had received a dispatch from Trevor de Lara, Lord of the Trilaterals, which was north of his properties along the

Welsh marches. Trevor had three strategic castles, called the Trilaterals, and control of a section of the Welsh marches, but the specific rumblings he was relaying to Morgen had to do with the Earl of Lancaster and his opposition to the king. Since summer was coming and the de Lohrs would be heading back to their seat of Lioncross Abbey Castle, Trevor wanted to let Morgen know that rumors were suggesting that Lancaster and his supporters were preparing to move against Hugh Despenser for slights and violations they considered unacceptable.

More than likely, that meant military action.

He wasn't thrilled.

"Morgen, my love? Are you occupied?"

Morgen looked up from the missive to see Kirra entering the solar. He put the vellum down, smiling lazily at his wife as she came into the chamber, crossed the floor, and went to the windows.

She pointed. "Did you give the boys permission to play by the river?" she asked.

He stood up and went to the window, focused on what she was pointing at. "Nay," he said. "But if you look over there, to the east, you'll see Marcellus standing there. Nothing will happen to them if he is in charge."

Kirra sighed heavily. "You know I do not like them by the river," she said. "I do not need for them to take another raft downriver because they want to be pirates."

He turned to her, grinning. "I thought it was very ingenious."

"You would."

"And why not? It was very clever of them."

Kirra would not be swayed. "Blake and Bing do not know how to swim," she pointed out rather heatedly. "Did you expect

Christie and Kurtis to save them should they fall in? The Thames is treacherous. I do not like them playing at the river. At all."

Morgen conceded, as he usually did, and pulled her into his arms, kissing her. When he tried to kiss her deeply, just to assert himself, she pinched him, and he yelped into her mouth. She pushed herself out of his arms as he rubbed his buttocks where she had pinched him with her slender, but hard, fingers.

"Do you want me to tell Marcellus to bring them in?" he said. "If that is your wish, I will do so."

"I simply do not want them to drown," Kirra said. "I should think you would not want them to do it, either, but I could be wrong."

He sighed, defeated. "Sometimes I want them to float away for a few years and return to me when they are well behaved, but nay, I do not want them to drown," he said. "I will tell Marcellus not to take them to the river."

"Thank you."

"Is there anything else you wish, any desire I can fulfill?"

He was being the slightest bit facetious, but she ignored him. "There is, in fact," she said. "I also came to tell you that Lady Violet will be delivering her child soon."

His expression tightened. "Have her pains started?"

She nodded. "I think so," she said. "I have already sent a servant for the physic and his wife. I suspect we should see her child in the next few days."

"Let us pray she lives through it."

"She will," Kirra said confidently. "Will you not send word to her husband?"

He averted his gaze. "I did when she arrived," he said. "Do you not recall?"

"I recall."

"Hopefully, his arrival is imminent."

Kirra watched him as he went to sit down at his table again, picking up the dispatch he had been reading when she walked in. She went over to the table, casually, standing there until he looked up at her.

She smiled. "I hope you do not think that you married a fool," she said quietly.

He frowned. "You are the furthest thing from a fool that I have ever seen," he said. "Why do you say such a thing?"

She folded her arms and appeared thoughtful. "Let me see if I can explain it sufficiently," she said. "I suppose I will start by asking you a question."

"Ask."

"And you will answer me truthfully."

"I am always truthful with you."

She cocked an eyebrow. "Then can you explain to me why you introduced Lady Violet de Lohr to me when her name is Delaina?"

Morgen looked at her. After a moment, he shook his head, like a man who knew when his efforts had been fruitless. In truth, he wasn't particularly surprised, because Kirra was very astute. Things in her world rarely escaped her notice, including a mysterious distant de Lohr cousin who wasn't a cousin at all.

Standing up, he went to the solar door and shut it before turning to her. "Where did you hear that?"

"From you," Kirra said. "The day Denys de Winter brought her to us. I heard you speaking to him, and I heard you call her Delaina."

"I did."

"Why did you tell me her name was Violet?"

He made his way over to her. "Because it was safer that way."

"For me?"

"For her."

"But why?"

Reaching out, he took her hand and pulled her over to a leather-bound chair near the hearth. Sitting down, he pulled her onto his lap.

"I suppose I knew I would have to explain this to you at some point," he said. "Please do not think I did not tell you because I do not trust you. I do, implicitly. But servants have a way of hearing things. They talk. And this is talk that cannot get out, Kay. It is very important that it does."

She looked at him with concern. "You know that I will not repeat it," she said. "But why all of the deception?"

"Because Hugh Despenser wants that woman," he said quietly. "Magnus asked me once to help conceal her, so I am doing that."

"But why does Despenser want her?"

"Because she is a courtesan, one of the most in-demand courtesans in England. I am certain it did not escape you how lovely she is."

Kirra wasn't particularly shocked by the revelation, but so much was becoming clear to her now. "She is exquisite," she said. "She is also extremely intelligent."

"That comes from a good deal of education," he said. "The lords that have courtesans want them to be smart and entertaining."

She nodded in understanding. "I heard you speaking to Denys about Delaina and Magnus de Wolfe," she said. "I heard you speak of Magnus enough to know that he must be the baby's father. They are not married, are they?"

It was more a statement than a question, and Morgen shook his head. "Nay, they are not," he said. "But he loves her and wishes to marry her. I suppose I did not want to tell you that part of it, but the reality is this—being a courtesan, she is not accepted by noble society. To have that kind of woman in a respectable home such as ours can be… problematic."

"You mean if it were to ever get out that we gave her shelter."

He nodded. "Aye."

Kirra pondered that for a moment. She was a reasonable woman, accepting and mostly nonjudgmental. That was one of the things that Morgen loved about her. What he'd done, he'd done to protect her and his household. The less people knew of Lady Violet's true identity, the better.

"I am not entirely sure the nobility of England would shun the House of de Lohr if they knew we harbored a courtesan, but I understand your point," she said. "Particularly if Despenser is still looking for her. Is he?"

Morgen shook his head. "I have no way of knowing," he said. "I've not heard anything, and I'm certainly not going to ask."

"Then we must keep this very quiet," she said. "We will continue to call her Lady Violet. It is safer that way."

"I agree."

"Is Magnus truly coming?"

Morgen shrugged, pulling her close. "I hope so," he said. "I sent him word as soon as Denys brought the lady here, so he has had time to receive the missive and start his journey southward."

"Unless he comes in the next few days, he will more than

likely miss the birth," Kirra said. "She still believes she is going to die, Morgen. I do not know how to convince her otherwise."

Morgen rolled his eyes unhappily. "St. Blitha's has seared doom and gloom into her brain," he said. "Those nuns nearly killed her with their mistreatment. Thank God Denys had the sense to bring her here when he did."

"Thank God, indeed," Kirra agreed. "I... I feel a good deal of pity for her. She is so sad. So very sad. She wants to be friendly, and I believe she wants to smile, but it is as if something is missing in her. Something is broken that cannot be repaired. She never speaks of Magnus, but I sense that her melancholy is because of him. She misses him. God help us if Magnus refuses to come at all."

Morgen didn't want to admit that it was a distinct possibility. According to Denys, the lady had rejected Magnus. It was possible the damage was too great.

"We will know soon enough," he said quietly. "But if he does not come... what do you want to do with the lady?"

Kirra didn't hesitate. "She will stay," she said firmly. "Her son shall be raised with our children, and she shall be their tutor. As I said, she is very smart. She would teach them a great deal. Mayhap she can be my lady in waiting. I do not have any, you know."

"I noticed."

"She would be a fine one, I am sure."

"Then you will not send her away?"

"Where would I send her to, Morgen? If she had any place to go, she would not have been brought here." She shook her head. "Lady Violet stays, whatever happens. And so does her child."

He squeezed her, kissing her cheek. "Ever charitable, my

lady," he said, admiration in his tone. "God has a special place in heaven for people like you."

Kirra smiled at him, wrapping her arms around his neck, when there was a loud rap on the door. Startled, she climbed off Morgen's lap as he went to the solar door and opened it.

The housekeeper, a stout and strong woman, was standing at the door.

"My lady," she said. "You must come. Quickly."

Kirra was already on the move. "Why?" she said. "What has happened? Where are my children?"

The housekeeper shook her head. "Not the children, my lady," she said. "Lady Violet. The child is coming and her waters have broken."

Kirra rushed out into the entry, heading for the mural stairs, with Morgen and the housekeeper on her heels.

She could hear the groaning by the time she hit the second floor.

CHAPTER TWENTY-ONE

"WORD MUST HAVE reached Westminster by now," Titus said. "Surely they know a de Wolfe contingent is near London."

"Are you hoping for a welcome?" Hector de Norville glanced at his nephew, son of his wife's brother. "I have terrible news for you, Titus. Edward will not have a great feast in our honor. If anything, there would be men in these trees waiting to ambush us."

Titus cast his uncle an unhappy snarl, watching Hector snort at him. He had come with his father and brother because he'd begged and pleaded, insisting that Alec Hage was perfectly capable of commanding Berwick without him. That was true because Alec, Patrick's second-in-command, was an efficient commander, but he needed knights. With the Scots being squirrely, he needed skilled warriors to lead the men.

But Titus would not be left behind. He wanted to go to London, too.

Even after his father told him not to come. Even after his father *forbade* him to come. They'd left Berwick with no sign of Titus only to find him hours later, waiting for them down the road. After that, Patrick had no choice.

Titus had triumphed.

Surprisingly, he had also behaved himself on the southward journey, but he wasn't beyond sulking. As Hector jested at his expense, Titus spurred his warhorse forward, getting ahead of the pack. The road was heavily foliaged on either side, but they weren't far from Lonsdale House.

Patrick, astride an enormous dapple-gray horse, called up to him. "Ride ahead and tell de Lohr we are approaching," he said. "Make sure they are aware we have three hundred men with us so they do not think they are being attacked before they realize it is us."

Titus lifted a hand and waved at him, rushing on ahead.

"At least he is making himself useful," Patrick muttered, looking over at Hector, who grinned. "I blame Poppy for him, you know. He spoiled Titus until we could do nothing with him."

Hector snorted. "He did that with several of his grandchildren," he said. "My father got to Hermes and Atreus before Uncle William could, but he was worse. He encouraged them to fight each other, and then he would laugh when they beat each other bloody. There were several times when I thought Evelyn was going to bloody him herself."

Patrick started laughing at the memory. Hector's eldest sons, Hermes and Atreus, were natural-born fighters from a very early age, but mostly against each other. Hector's father, Paris de Norville, who also happened to be William de Wolfe's best friend, identified that aggression early on and often pitted the boys against one another. It was hilarious when they were young, but when they became older and stronger, those brawls turned into bloody events. Patrick's sister and their mother,

Evelyn, was not so amused.

But it made for hilarious memories.

"They outgrew it," Patrick said. "Though I will miss the days when they were around ten and nine years of age and would fight for the soldiers to bet on them."

Hector fought off a grin. "If Evelyn caught them, she took a stick to them."

"She simply does not understand a man's need to fight his brother."

"Nay, she did not."

They grinned at one another, shaking their heads at the antics of Hector's unruly sons. Then Hector jabbed a finger at Patrick. "Do not pretend that my sons were the only aggressors in the de Wolfe and de Norville stable," he said. "I can recall plenty of times when your sons would come around and there was chaos to be found. I've never seen Bridey so angry as she was when she found Magnus and Titus wrestling with Atreus and Hermes. Do you remember that?"

Patrick burst out laughing at the mention of his wife and the infamous incident. "You mean when Magnus and Titus tied Hermes to a tree and were in the process of capturing Atreus when Bridey came upon them. Magnus, do you remember that?"

Magnus, who had been riding silently since daybreak, cracked a weak smile. "I still have the scars on my backside from Mother's rage," he said. "But in my defense, Atreus and Hermes attacked us first."

"How did they do such a thing? They were half the size you were."

"Because they had a rope that they'd strung across the entry to the knight's quarters," Magnus pointed out, as if his father didn't remember. "When I walked out, they pulled it tight and tripped me. Then they jumped on top of me and tried to rob me. Had Titus not come along when he had, they would have robbed me blind."

Both Patrick and Hector laughed uproariously, and even Magnus chuckled, but he certainly wasn't in the chuckling mood. He knew that his father and uncle were keeping up a running conversation to keep his mind off what was coming, and he appreciated that, but the truth was that he was damn terrified with what he would find at the end of that road.

She has asked me to relay to you her dying condition

That passage from Morgen's missive was rolling around in his head, and he couldn't shake it. For the past four weeks, ever since he'd received the missive, he couldn't shake it. Now, he would know Delaina's fate this day. He wasn't sure he was strong enough.

But here they were and he had no choice.

He had to be strong.

God help him, he had to be.

⁊

DELAINA WAS SITTING in the great room of Lonsdale House, a rather enormous receiving chamber just off the entry that had a spectacular view of the river. There were four towering windows that faced out over the water, and at midday, the humidity from the river was trickling in.

It was going to be another warm afternoon.

Clad in a yellow garment of lightweight wool, with her spectacular hair pulled back at the nape of her neck, Delaina was focused on a piece of needlework in her hands depicting several butterflies. It was intricate and lovely, but she was particularly good with the details. It kept her mind off her life, her sorrows, and her future, or the lack thereof.

It kept her from going down the rabbit hole of anguish.

Servants were wandering in and out of the chamber, bringing wine and bread and a tray filled with fruit. Kirra sent her servants to a local market every Friday, and they always returned with pounds of freshly picked fruit. There were apples, pears, apricots, grapes, and even strawberries, which Delaina favored.

But she didn't feel like any fruit today.

She didn't feel like much of anything.

Kirra was with her children on this day because there was a seamstress who had come all the way from London to make the children some new clothes. Kirra didn't sew, and her maids mostly did the laundry but didn't sew it, except for the housekeeper. But Christie and Kurtis in particular were outgrowing everything and required new garments, so Kirra was with them upstairs in the nursery while the seamstress took measurements.

Delaina could hear the distant screaming.

Morgen was outside, somewhere, doing something with his men because Marcellus had an attack of fever and was laid up in his quarters. The physic had come and gone, assuring him that it would pass, which left Delaina mostly alone on this day.

She preferred it.

But that was until the entry to the manse opened and she could hear boots. Her time of solitude was soon to be over. The boots struck the stone floor loudly, and she could hear a servant speaking and then a low-voiced reply. She assumed that it was Morgen, even when the boots came into the reception room. She was focused on her stitching and didn't look up until someone spoke to her.

"Greetings, my lady."

Startled by the unfamiliar voice, she looked up to see a very tall, quite handsome knight with dark hair and golden eyes. And he was also quite young. He was in full regalia, dressed for battle, and he removed his helm to be polite, which revealed a crown of dark, shoulder-length hair.

She put her sewing in her lap. "Greetings," she said. "I apologize; I did not know that Lord Worcester had a visitor. Please excuse me."

She started to get up, but he stopped her. "Nay," he said. "Please do not leave. Worcester wasn't expecting us, at least not at any particular time. He sent me in here to wait for him."

"I see," Delaina said. Part of her courtly training had been to entertain, so she immediately slipped into that mode, since Kirra wasn't here. She put the sewing on a table and stood up. "Please allow me to pour you some wine. Have you been traveling long?"

The young knight watched her as she went over to the table next to him and deftly poured him a cup of wine from an undoubtedly heavy pitcher.

"It feels like years," he said. "My name is Titus, by the way."

She smiled as she handed him the cup. "I am Lady Violet," she said. Then she indicated the enormous tray of fruit and bread. "May I offer you some food? Given that it is summer, the harvests have been quite delicious."

Titus nodded. "Thank you," he said, watching her collect a small bowl and begin putting grapes and strawberries in it. "Do you live here?"

Delaina nodded. "I do," she said. "And where are you from, Sir Titus?"

"Berwick."

The bowl in Delaina's hand clattered to the tabletop. Quickly, she tried to recover it, but her hands were suddenly shaking and her heart was racing.

"Berwick," she said, half-spilled bowl in her hand as she looked him over. "Berwick Castle?"

Titus nodded. "Aye," he said. "Have you ever been there?"

She shook her head. "I have not," she said, feeling weak in the knees. "Who… who do you serve, Titus?"

"The Earl of Berwick," he said. "He happens to be my father, Patrick de Wolfe."

The room began to rock. Delaina carefully set the bowl down, facing the young knight who, upon closer inspection, had a faint resemblance to Magnus.

She could hardly breathe.

"Is your father here?" she asked breathlessly.

Titus didn't seem to notice that she'd gone pasty white. He picked up the bowl that she'd dropped, only half-filled with fruit, and began shoving strawberries in his mouth.

"Aye," he said, chewing. "He's outside speaking to my father and brother."

Oh God, Delaina thought. She gripped the table so she wouldn't fall over.

"Who is your brother?"

"Magnus."

She bolted for the entry door before Titus realized what had happened. Running blindly, Delaina rushed from the entry door and out into the ward, which was rather big. She could see a small army of soldiers pouring in through the open gates, but more importantly, she could see Morgen with his back to her as he spoke to one extremely tall knight and a shorter, broader one.

But there was no mistaking who that shorter, broader one was.

On legs that felt like jelly, Delaina took a few halting steps toward them, moving so that Morgen wasn't between her and the shorter knight any longer. It seemed as if it all happened in slow motion; one moment, she was looking at Morgen's back and the limbs of the man he was talking to, and then abruptly, she was looking at Magnus.

He had come.

Dear God… he had come!

"Magnus?" she said weakly.

Magnus' head snapped in her direction as if he'd been struck. Violently struck. She heard him groan, perhaps even calling out to God for strength, because he seemed to stagger. Even as he headed in her direction, he seemed to stagger. He couldn't seem to walk a straight line. He ripped his helm off, tossing it into the dirt as he went.

Delaina could only stand there and look at him.

"Magnus," she breathed. "Is it really you?"

He put a hand to his mouth, and she watched his eyes fill with tears. "Sweet Jesus," he whispered. "You're not dead."

She shook her head. "Nay," she said, a lump in her throat because he was falling to pieces before her very eyes. "I am very much alive."

Magnus came to an unsteady halt a few feet away from her, afraid to go any closer. "The missive," he said, hardly able to speak. "The missive I received from Worcester said you were dying."

Delaina began to realize what had made him so upset, so colossally unsteady. "I was unwell for quite some time," she said. "After I went to Westminster, they sent me to St. Blitha's Convent. It was not their fault. They simply did not know how to tend to a woman carrying a child. Their physic told me I would not survive the birth, and I believed him. Foolishly, I believed him. That was why Worcester told you that."

Tears were pouring down his cheeks and his hand was still over his mouth. "And he was wrong," he said. "You look… you look more beautiful than I remembered. Are you well?"

She nodded. "It was Denys who brought me to Worcester," she said. "It was Denys who convinced me… He convinced me that I had been wrong all along. Magnus, I do not know if this matters to you because it has been so long, but I am sorry. For refusing to marry you, for sending you away… I should not have done that. I thought I was saving you, but you did not need saving. We needed each other, but I was afraid of what would happen to you if I remained by your side. I hope you understand that I did not do it to be cruel."

He was nodding even before she finished, and his hand came away from his mouth. "I know that," he said. "You needn't apologize because I know you were doing what you believed best. I am touched and honored that you would care enough for me to do it. But you are right—we needed each other. I still need you. I have never stopped needing you, Delaina. I need you and I need our child, if you will still have me."

The tears she had managed to stave off now came full force. She couldn't help breaking down in soft sobs. "There is something you must know," she said. "Our son was born with the cord wrapped around his neck and he could not breathe. He did not survive the birth, Magnus. He was christened William, after your grandfather, and buried at St. Peter's Church, just down the road."

Magnus looked at her with sorrow that went beyond tears. He couldn't even cry for the son he'd lost. All he could do was feel grief and empathy, mostly toward Delaina and what she had been through. So much turmoil, and then a dead child on top of everything.

After a moment, he found himself looking at the house behind her, the trees, even the sky. All the while, he was processing what she had told him, dazed and overcome. But eventually, his gaze fell upon her once more.

"I thought that I was coming to Lonsdale to find you dead and a new infant that I was responsible for," he said hoarsely. "But it seems that God had another plan in store for us. He knew that I would be devastated the rest of my life over the loss of you. Though I deeply mourn the son I never met, he is in God's hands and he is safe. But you… I have been given a second chance with you, Delaina. There will be more children for us. But there will never be another you."

Delaina closed her eyes to his sweet and poignant words, tears continuing to course down her pale cheeks. "Do you not understand, Magnus?" she said. "There is no longer a child involved. You do not have to marry me. I know you came here to do the noble thing, but I am telling you that you do not have to. After everything that has happened, I do not expect it. Moreover, I have nothing to bring to this marriage. No money, no possessions. If you wish to think about this, then I under-stand."

He wiped his face, composing himself. "Let me make myself plain," he said. "I love you. I am going to marry you whether you like it or not. As for the money, I have your money. I collected it from The Pox the night I went searching for you, so

I have had it all along. I will return it to you. But you and I are going to be wed. Is that clear enough?"

Delaina was still weeping, but a smile flickered on her lips. She closed the distance between them, putting her hands on his face as he stood there and quivered.

"It is clear," she whispered. "As long as you are certain."

"I am."

"Then we must make ourselves a promise."

He wanted very badly to take her in his arms, but he simply didn't feel that he could. Not at the moment. Once he did, the conversation would be lost, and there was still much that needed to be said. But this time he wasn't going to lose control. He wasn't going to lose her.

This time, he was going to make sure she was part of him forever.

"What is the promise?" he asked, his voice raspy.

She smiled at him, finally allowing herself to feel some joy, the only joy she'd felt since the day he walked out of her life. "Worcester has told everyone that my name is Violet de Lohr," she said. "Do you remember when you and I discussed changing my name to protect your family from my past? Morgen has done that for us. He has introduced me to everyone here as his cousin. That is all anyone need know. For our children's sake and for the sake of Morgen's honor, we must promise to keep the illusion. Let it start now."

He couldn't disagree with her. The nobility of England was an unforgiving thing, and if it were well known that the mother of his children was a former courtesan, finding spouses would be difficult. It also wouldn't look good for Morgen to have housed a fugitive courtesan. Although Magnus hated that he had to do it, for so many reasons, it was necessary.

He nodded. "Violet," he murmured. "I like it. But who knows the truth?"

She shrugged. "Morgen does, clearly," she said. "His wife does. Kirra and I have grown very fond of one another. She was my strength throughout the ordeal, Magnus. I shall never forget that."

"Nor I," he said, finally bringing his trembling hands up to cup her face. The first touch of her flesh against his in so many months nearly brought him to tears again. "I shall forever be indebted to them for giving you back to me. May I tell them that?"

Delaina looked off to his left to see Patrick and Morgen standing there, beaming emotionally, as fathers would. When Morgen met her gaze, he smiled broadly and nodded as if to tell her that all was well. That this was the way the situation was supposed to end. That the passing of their baby would only make them stronger.

For certain, they had endured much in order to be together.

Strength in times of trouble.

That was the de Wolfe mantra.

Now it was hers, too.

"They already know, Magnus," Delaina said, wrapping her arms around his neck. "Trust me, my love. They already know."

And they did.

CHAPTER TWENTY-TWO

Berwick Castle
Two months later

"There once was a lady fair,

With silver bells in her hair.

I knew her to have,

A luscious kiss… it drove me mad!

But she denied me… and I was so terribly sad.

Lily, my girl,

Your flower, I will unfurl

With my cock and a bit of good luck!

Your kiss divine,

I'll make you mine,

And keep you a-bed for a fuck!"

T HE GREAT HALL of Berwick exploded in laughter and cheers as Blayth de Wolfe, Magnus' uncle, sang what was known throughout the de Wolfe, de Norville, and Hage families as the "Naughty Wedding Song." Or, at least, one of them. There were actually two, and it was expected that one of them would be sung—and sung frequently—at any wedding involving those three families.

Magnus' wedding was no exception.

What was different, however, were the missing grandparents. Jordan de Wolfe, Magnus' grandmother, had passed away a couple of years earlier, having lived well into her ninth decade. Normally, when Blayth started with his singing, she was there to stop the lewd songs, usually with sticks and switches, but these days, with no Jordan available, it fell to her daughters and the wives of her sons.

And they were out in force.

Avrielle de Wolfe, Lady Warenton, had taken the mantle happily. As the wife of the head of the House of de Wolfe, it was her duty. But Scott de Wolfe had a twin, Troy de Wolfe, and his wife Rhoswyn was a Scots lass and twice as frightening as any knight. She was the one who took great pleasure in taking a switch to the big English knights, and when Blayth saw her coming, he began to scatter. His own wife, Asmara, was a Welsh warrior lass and more than a match for Rhoswyn, but she stayed out of the way as Rhoswyn went after Blayth. In fact, Asmara encouraged her.

The entire hall was in an uproar.

"I do not understand what is happening," Delaina said, seated at the dais with Magnus. "Why is your aunt Rhoswyn chasing your uncle Blayth?"

Magnus was grinning at the antics of adults that were probably far too old to be engaging in such things, but it was tradition. No one would stand in the way of Blayth's naughty songs or the de Wolfe women in their quest to punish him.

"Because he sang a song that was lewd," he said. "Did you not hear the words?"

"Aye, but I've heard worse."

Magnus shook his head. "Not in these halls, you have not," he said. "These weddings are known for the naughty songs and the ensuing chaos. We are being honored by it."

She eyed him. "Are we?"

He laughed softly, leaning over to pull her against him. "Indeed, we are," he said. "I have been to many weddings that have been worse than this. If they did not love us, they would not bother. You are accepted, Lady de Wolfe. You are loved."

Her smile faded. "Because they think I am a de Lohr."

He didn't have an answer for that, mostly because it was the truth. He kissed her forehead, giving her a squeeze. "Sometimes we must make sacrifices," he whispered. "Lady Violet de Lohr de Wolfe is a woman of great honor and prestige."

"Until someone from London recognizes me."

"We will deal with that when, and if, it comes," he said. "Now… shall we retire for the night before this mob becomes more unruly? I do not see several of my uncles, which is a good sign. They are occupied elsewhere, so it is time for us to leave."

Delaina agreed with him, but not before she collected the dagger on the table next to her. She held it up.

"This is such a sweet gift from your grandfather," she said. "Our son will be most honored to carry it and pass it down to his children."

Magnus looked at the beautiful, detailed weapon. "He will, indeed," he said. Then he held up her hand. "And the ring? Does it fit?"

Delaina admired Queen Daina's ring as it gripped her finger. "Perfectly," she said. "I shall cherish it, always."

"Good."

He kissed her hand and pulled her out of her chair, whisking her out of the hall while the guests were still involved in Rhoswyn and Blayth's antics. It was enough of a distraction that Magnus and Delaina could slip out unnoticed. As they headed toward the keep on a dark and moonless night, they were met at the door by a familiar figure.

Magnus' uncles, Scott and Troy, were standing in the doorway.

Magnus put out a hand.

"Let me say this here and now," he said. "While I love you both, if you try to invade my marriage chamber, know that I will not tolerate such interference. Will you let us pass peacefully?"

Scott, blond and distinguished, shook his head. "We are not here to interfere, I promise," he said. "But we wished to speak with you before you disappear into the bedchamber and we do not see you again for a week."

Magnus looked at Delaina. "A week?" he said. "I suppose that could be arranged. Are you agreeable?"

She laughed softly. "Anything you wish, my love."

As they shared a joke between them, Troy spoke up.

"We wanted to tell you that Atty told us about Lady Violet's… background," he said. "He wanted us to know in case some fool from London recognized her from her former life and began to spread rumors. Be assured that he told no one but us, but we want you to know that if anyone recognizes you and seeks to cause harm, we will deal with them in a forceful manner."

"A deadly manner," Scott muttered.

Magnus looked surprised, while Delaina tried not to look too ill that Magnus' uncles knew about her. "It is in her past," Magnus stressed. "Moreover, it was not her choice. She was forced into the situation. I—"

Troy cut him off. Big, dark, frightening Troy seemed to be the most compassionate, surprisingly. "You need not explain," he said. "She is a de Wolfe now, and she is part of our pack. If you love her, then we love her. And we will defend Lady Delaina to the death against anyone who tries to identify the woman she once was. We just thought you should know."

With that, he and Scott pushed past the astonished couple, who turned to watch them go.

Shocked, Delaina turned to Magnus. "Are they always so… so *dedicated* to family?" she asked. "Even a new family member?"

Magnus turned to her, grinning. "As he said, you are one of us now," he said. "In fact… I am glad they know. I am comforted by that."

Delaina wasn't as sure as he was, but she didn't argue.

They continued into the keep and up the stairs, heading for the additional stairs that would take them to the upper reaches of the keep. They were midway down the darkened corridor when two more figures stepped out of the shadows.

Magnus and Delaina found themselves face to face with Edward de Wolfe and Thomas de Wolfe, Baron Kentmere and the Earl of Northumbria, respectively.

They stepped forward into the light.

"Greetings," Edward said. The diplomat of the family, he had a smooth, deep speaking tone. "We wanted to see you both before you retired for the night."

Magnus grinned. "So you have been waiting here, in the

shadows, like a pair of bandits ready to pounce?"

Edward grinned back. "What are we going to steal from you?" he said, but he was eyeing the dagger in Delaina's hand. "Though that dagger is quite beautiful. I have a feeling the lady would use it on me if I tried to take it."

Delaina giggled as Magnus nodded. "Or I would," he said. But he sobered quickly. "What is so important that you are lurking in the darkness?"

Thomas spoke first. "Atty told us about the lady's… secret," he said. "Do not worry; he did not tell anyone else, and he swore us to secrecy, so the information is safe. We just wanted to tell you and your wife that her past does not matter to us. She is part of us now, and that is all we are concerned with."

"That is true," Edward said. "But I spend a good deal of time in court, as you know. In fact, the new Lord Daventry, Jerome de Staverton, is trying to make his mark in Edward's court now. If anything comes up about his father's former courtesan, I will be there to shut him down."

Magnus was fixed on his uncle. "What of Despenser?" he said. "He knows that I was fond of the lady. But he also knows she was committed to St. Blitha's. If he's not yet forgotten her and goes looking for her, the truth that she has left may come out."

Edward shook his head. "Despenser has more serious things to worry about than a missing woman," he said. "I am sure she is the furthest thing from his mind these days, but even if she isn't, the point is that I simply do not want you two to worry. I will take care of anything that arises. I am glad Atty told us, but in the end, her past does not matter. You love her, and that tells me all I need to know. She is worthy of the de Wolfe name."

With that, he leaned over and kissed Delaina on the cheek

before slapping Magnus on the back and continuing down the hall. Thomas followed suit, though he was bigger and stronger and nearly bowled Magnus over when he went to congratulate him. Magnus chuckled at his uncles as they headed down the stairs and left him and Delaina standing alone in the dim corridor.

"So… your father told them all, but did not tell one that he told the other?" Delaina said, amused. "They are all sworn to secrecy, even from each other?"

Magnus snorted. "Evidently," he said. "But I am glad they know. And I think it is very touching that they should make sure we know that they do not care about your past. Truthfully, that means the world to me."

Delaina looped her arm through his as they continued their walk. "And to me," she said softly. "I suppose that proves my theory wrong."

"What theory?"

"That they only love Violet de Lohr."

Magnus kissed her hand. "Very true," he said. "Do you feel better now?"

She nodded. "It's so strange, Magnus," she said. "I have spent my entire life alone. Virtually alone. No family, no real friends. No one. And now I have more family and friends than I could have possibly imagined, all of them willing to do battle for me. It's surreal."

They reached the staircase leading to the upper floor where their bridal chamber was prepared and waiting. "It is no less than you deserve," he said quietly as he began to lead her up the steps. "I promised you a new life, my love. I meant it."

She lifted her skirt so she wouldn't trip as she took the stairs. "You did," she said. "The moment I entered the halls of

Westminster on that fateful night was the moment my life would change forever, and I did not even know it yet. But it wasn't simply you who changed it. It was Denys, Morgen, and Kirra. It was even the mother abbess and Sister Martha Margaret. It was everyone who had a part in this, people I will be forever grateful to."

Magnus glanced at her. "People who did not even know you," he said. "They simply knew it was the right thing to do. Helping you when you needed it most."

Delaina nodded. "I am sorry that Denys could not attend our wedding," she said. "Nor could Morgen and Kirra, though I understand in their case. She is newly pregnant and did not wish to travel."

They reached the landing with their chamber at the far end. "Denys is now in command of Edward's knights," he said. "He did not feel as if he could leave at this time. He is needed more at Edward's side, helping the opposition when it comes to what is happening in Edward's court and keeping an eye on Hugh, who is becoming more power-hungry by the day."

"Denys is a spy."

"He is, but he is a valuable one."

"But I will thank him someday. Even if he did call me stupid, once."

Magnus chuckled as he put his arm around her shoulders, leading her down the corridor to the chamber that awaited them. The chamber where they would begin their married life, where their children would be conceived. A chamber that represented everything Delaina had left behind and a future she very much wanted.

A future with Magnus.

A man who had made all things possible.

Delaina was finally home.

EPILOGUE

Year of Our Lord 1354
Raechester Castle, Northumberland

"T HEN MOTHER'S NAME is not Violet?" Padraig asked, his features pale with shock. "And she's *not* a de Lohr?"

Magnus wasn't unsympathetic. The story he'd just told his son and grandson was a good deal to accept when one was old and had always believed his mother to be a woman named Lady Violet de Lohr de Wolfe, from the prestigious House of de Lohr.

It was shocking, to be truthful.

"Nay, lad," Magnus said softly. "She is not a de Lohr. And you were born less than a year after the son we lost, and we named you Padraig, after my father. So, you see, it does not matter that the woman Val wants to marry has a sister with a compromised reputation. Your mother was so gravely compromised that she nearly refused to marry me, but as you can see, she relented. And we have been wildly happy all of these years. I cannot imagine my life without her. So do not punish Val for loving a woman with an unchaste sister. She is not responsible for her sister's behavior. Moreover, if he truly loves her, then things like that simply do not matter."

Padraig was pale with shock and sorrow after having just heard a story that completely upended everything he ever thought about his life.

And his mother.

"She really went through all of that?" he asked. "Mother, I mean. She was one of the Seven Jewels of London?"

Magnus nodded. "Have you heard of them?"

Padraig shrugged. "There is still a group of courtesans who call themselves that," he said. "I've heard of them, of course. Anyone who spends time in court has. But Mother was an original Jewel?"

"She was," Magnus said. "And the most beautiful Jewel in the group. When I met her and we fell in love, it was like nothing I'd ever experienced before or since. I am begging you not to take that away from Val. Men cannot help who they fall in love with. I am a prime example of that."

Padraig was still distressed over the situation, but more distressed with his mother's secret history than anything else. He turned to look at his son, who seemed quite upset by the whole story. Val gazed back at him with sorrow.

Padraig cleared his throat softly. "Papa, it is not that I wish to cause my son anguish," he said. "But—"

The door to the solar opened at that moment, revealing a lovely older woman with red hair peppered with white. She wore a simple scarf around her head and a smile on her lips. She ushered in a servant bearing a tray of wine with cups, indicating for them to be set upon the nearest table.

"I am sorry to interrupt," she said. "But the three of you have been in here a long time. I thought you might like some refreshment."

Magnus reached out a hand to her, and she came to him, taking it. He kissed her hand. "We were simply speaking on women," he said. "Val wishes to marry. It is a serious venture."

Delaina looked at her grandson with glee. "Phoebe de Wallington?"

Val nodded. "Aye."

Delaina put her hand on Magnus' shoulder. "Amag and I are delighted," she said, watching Magnus smile weakly. But she could see something in his expression that caused her to look at Padraig. "Padraig? Is this not a wonderful occasion?"

Padraig looked at his mother. His elegant, lovely, and sweet mother whom he'd always been so close to. The sun rose and set on his mother as far as he was concerned, and as he looked at her, he recalled his father's story on how they first met.

The family story had always been that they'd met through Morgen de Lohr because his mother was a de Lohr cousin, but he could see that his mother's past had been whitewashed. Made acceptable. Perhaps Rosemary de Wallington wasn't so wild, after all. Not after he'd heard the tale of the Ruby.

Padraig could see his mother and father looking at him curiously, and Val looking at him rather anxiously.

Do not punish Val for loving a woman with an unchaste sister.

As it turned out, Padraig was himself guilty of loving a woman who, in her past, had been unchaste. But not by choice. His mother had been forced into that life against her will, and it had taken a man of incredible strength and compassion to give her the life she deserved.

His father.

Suddenly, the unchaste de Wallington sister didn't seem so

bad. With love involved—and Val was clearly in love—something like that simply didn't matter.

Padraig stood up from his chair. "It *is* wonderful," he said hoarsely. As he headed for his parents, he glanced at his son. "You will get no further argument from me, Val. I hope you and Phoebe are very happy in your new life together."

Val beamed. He was so thrilled that he leapt out of his chair and shook his fists in the air. As his jubilant celebration was going on, Padraig went to his mother and took her in his arms, hugging her fiercely.

"I love you, Violet de Wolfe," he whispered in her ear. "And I love Delaina, too."

With that, he let her go and quit the chamber, but not before both Delaina and Magnus saw him wiping at his eyes. Delaina was looking at him in shock, and when she realized he was weeping, she turned her wide eyes to Magnus.

"What was that about?" she asked softly. "What did you tell him?"

Magnus nodded, pulling her into his arms. "The truth," he murmured. "It was time. It was time he learned what a remarkable, resilient woman his mother is. There is no shame there, my darling."

Delaina wasn't sure what to say to that. She had always known that, someday, her children would know the truth, but the reality of it was somewhat different. Padraig had always been a rigidly pious man, unbending in so many ways, so his acceptance of her path, without question, was indeed a poignant moment.

And a thankful one.

As Delaina and Magnus embraced, they suddenly felt another pair of arms go around them. Val was hugging them both, so incredibly happy in the direction his life was about to take. He adored his grandparents more than words could express, and when Delaina turned to him and kissed his rough cheek, he smiled broadly at her.

"I can only hope that Phoebe and I are half as happy as you and Amag," he said. "As for what Amag told us… I am proud of you, Grandmama. Next to my mother, you are the strongest woman I know, and I am proud to be your grandson."

He kissed her on the cheek and quit the chamber, undoubtedly running off to seek out Phoebe de Wallington on this most momentous occasion. Delaina and Magnus watched him practically skip out of the chamber.

"I wonder if he means it," Delaina said softly.

Magnus looked at her. "What do you mean?"

"If he is proud of me. I wonder if, after he's had time to reflect, he truly means it."

Magnus smiled knowingly at her. "He has never said anything he does not mean," he said. "Or do you require something more than just his word?"

Delaina shook her head. Val was, if nothing else, an honorable man and a great source of pride for her and Magnus. He had always been a man of truth.

But her proof was yet to come.

On the event of Val's marriage, Padraig gave his son the dagger that had been passed down from Magnus, the Law-Mender. As Magnus had hoped, generations of his descendants would carry the old Northman dagger with pride, and the following year when Phoebe gave birth to her first child, a daughter, Val already had a name selected.

Delaina de Wallington de Wolfe had a special ring to it.

❧ THE END ❦

De Wolfe Pack Generations:
WolfeHeart
WolfeStrike
WolfeSword
WolfeBlade
WolfeLord
WolfeShield
Nevermore
WolfeAx

Children of Magnus and Delaina
Padraig
Daina
Katrine
Christina
Boden
Kirk
Denys
Morgen

THE PARENTS, CHILDREN, AND GRANDCHILDREN OF DE WOLFE

(Note: Don't be intimidated by these family trees—refer to them if you need clarification on a relationship)

<u>William (deceased 1296 A.D.) and Jordan Scott de Wolfe (deceased)</u>

Total children: 10

Total grandchildren: 75+ (including 4 deceased, 7 adopted, 3 step grandchildren)

Scott (Troy's twin)—(Wife #1 Lady Athena de Norville, has issue. Wife #2 Lady Avrielle Huntley du Rennic, has issue)

With Athena

- William "Will"
- Thomas "Tor"
- Andrew (deceased)
- Beatrice (deceased)

With Avrielle

- Sophia (with Nathaniel du Rennic)
- Stephen (with Nathaniel du Rennic)
- Sorcha (with Nathaniel du Rennic)
- Jeremy
- Nathaniel

- Alexander
- Seraphina
- Jordan

Troy (Scott's twin)—(Wife #1 Lady Helene de Norville, has issue. Wife #2 Lady Rhoswyn Kerr, has issue)

With Helene

- Andreas
- Acacia (deceased)
- Arista (deceased)

With Rhoswyn

- Gareth
- Corey
- Reed
- Tavin
- Tristan
- Elsbeth
- Madeleine

Patrick—(Married to Lady Brighton de Favereux, has issue)

- Markus
- Cassius
- Magnus
- Titus
- Thora
- Kristiana

James—(Wife #1 Lady Rose Hage, has issue. Wife #2 Asmara

ferch Cader, has issue)

With Rose

- Ronan
- Isabella

With Asmara (as Blayth)

- Maddoc
- Bowen
- Caius
- Garreth (known as Garr)

Katheryn (James' twin)—(Married to Sir Alec Hage, has issue)

- Edward
- Axel
- Christoph
- Kieran
- Christian

Evelyn—(Married to Sir Hector de Norville, has issue)

- Atreus
- Hermes
- Lisbet
- Adele
- Aline
- Lesander (goes by Zander)

Baby de Wolfe—(Died same day. Christened Madeleine)

Edward—(Married to Lady Cassiopeia de Norville, has issue)

- Helene
- Phoebe
- Hestia
- Asteria
- Leonidas
- Dorian
- Dayne
- Stephan
- Pallas

Thomas—(Married to Lady Maitland "Mae" de Ryes Bowlin, has issue)

- Artus (adopted)
- Nora (adopted)
- Phin (adopted)
- Marybelle (adopted)
- Renard & Roland (adopted)
- Dyana (adopted)
- Alexander
- Cabot
- Matthew
- Wade
- Tacey
- Morgan

Penelope—(Married to Bhrodi de Shera, Earl of Coventry, hereditary King of Anglesey, has issue)

- William
- Perri
- Bowen
- Dai
- Catrin
- Morgana
- Maddock
- Anthea
- Talan

Kieran and Jemma Scott Hage

- Mary Alys (adopted)—(married, has issue)
- Baby Hage, died same day. Christened Bridget.
- Alec (married to Lady Katheryn de Wolfe, has issue)
- Christian (died in the Holy Land 1269 A.D., no issue)
- Moira (married to Sir Apollo de Norville, has issue)
- Kevin (married to Lady Annavieve de Ferrers, has issue)
- Rose (widow of Sir James de Wolfe, has issue)
- Nathaniel

Paris and Caladora Scott de Norville

- Hector (married to Lady Evelyn de Wolfe, has issue)
- Apollo (married to Lady Moira Hage, has issue)
- Helene (married to Sir Troy de Wolfe, has issue)
- Athena (married to Sir Scott de Wolfe, has issue)
- Adonis
- Cassiopeia (married to Sir Edward de Wolfe, has issue)

Holdings and Titles of the House of de Wolfe and close allies as of 1293 A.D.

Scott de Wolfe—Baron Kilham, heir to the Earldom of Warenton (Heir: William "Will" de Wolfe)

Troy de Wolfe—Lord Braemoor (Heir: Andreas de Wolfe)

Patrick de Wolfe—Earl of Berwick (Heir: Markus de Wolfe, Lord Ravensdowne.)

Blayth (James) de Wolfe—Baron Sydenham (Heir: Ronan de Wolfe)

Edward de Wolfe—Baron Kentmere (Heir: Leonidas de Wolfe)

Thomas de Wolfe—Earl of Northumbria (Heir: Alexander de Wolfe, Lord Easington)

Wark Castle (Wolfe's Eye):

Larger outpost for the Earl of Warenton. Literally sits on the border between England and Scotland.

- Titus de Wolfe (son of Patrick de Wolfe), commander

Berwick Castle (Wolfe's Teeth):

Massive border castle, strategically important, de Wolfe holding and seat of the Earl of Berwick, Patrick de Wolfe.

- Alec Hage, commander
- Edward "Eddie" Hage, commander

Castle Questing (Wolfe's Heart):

Massive fortress, seat of the Earl of Warenton, Scott de Wolfe.

- Apollo de Norville, second
- Nathaniel Hage
- Owen le Mon

Rule Water Castle (Wolfe's Lair):
The largest outpost in the de Wolfe empire, known as The Lair. At this time, commanded by Thomas "Tor" de Wolfe.

- Magnus de Wolfe, second
- Adonis de Norville, second
- Perri de Shera, son of the Earl of Coventry and Penelope de Wolfe de Shera (squire)

Monteviot Tower (Wolfe's Shield):
Smaller outpost in Scotland, strategic. Holding of Troy de Wolfe.

- Brodie de Reyne, commander

Kale Water Castle (Wolfe's Den):
Larger outpost on the England side of the border, strategic.

- Troy de Wolfe, Lord Braemoor, commander
- Troy also commands Sibbald's Hold, former home of Red Keith Kerr (his wife's father). A minor property commanded by son, Gareth de Wolfe.

Kyloe Castle (Wolfe's Howl):
Seat of the Earl of Northumbria, Thomas de Wolfe.

- Christoph Hage, second

Roxburgh Castle (Wolfe's Claw—unofficially) *
Large royal-held castle near Kelso, formerly manned by knights from Northwood, but awarded to the House of de Wolfe by royal

decree for meritorious service to the crown. Volatile location, often attacked by Scots, and is manned by both royal and de Wolfe troops.

- Blayth (James) de Wolfe, Lord Sydenham, commander
- Axel Hage, second

*Note: Because of the extreme volatile location and nature of this garrison, Blayth (James) de Wolfe was given the title Lord Sydenham and the Sydenham Barony, a small but strategic barony between Wark Castle and the town of Kelso.

Carlisle Castle (Wolfe's Fangs):

Massive and large royal-held castle, perhaps one of the largest castles in the north. Awarded to the House of de Wolfe by royal decree. Very volatile location, often attacked by Scots, and has changed hands many times in its history. The castle is manned by both royal and de Wolfe troops.

- Will de Wolfe, Lord Irthington, commander
- Hermes de Norville

Northwood Castle:

Massive border castle, very important and strategic. Belonging to the Earls of Teviot. Not part of the de Wolfe empire, but strongly allied to de Wolfe by marriage and blood. The Earl of Teviot is John Adrian de Longley, Adam de Longley's eldest son. John's mother is Cayetana Fernanda Teresita Silva y Fausto de Longley, Princess of Aragon.

- Hector de Norville, captain of the guard (also Lord Bowmont)
- Atreus de Norville, second

- Tobias de Bocage, second

Castle Canaan (Wolfe's Bite):
The Earl of Warenton's southernmost holding in Kendal, not directly related to the Scottish border but a source of additional troops if needed. Inherited the property when he married the widow of Castle Canaan.

- Stephan du Rennic, commander

Seven Gates Castle:
Seat of Edward de Wolfe's Barony—Kentmere in Kendal that adjoins brother Scott's lands at Castle Canaan.

- Isleworth House, Surrey

Hell's Guardhouse (The Hermitage):
- Andreas de Wolfe, commander
- Theodis de Velt, second

Ravenscar (fortified manse near Scarborough):
- Ronan de Wolfe
- Christian Hage

Kathryn Le Veque Novels

Medieval Romance:

De Wolfe Pack Series:
Warwolfe
The Wolfe
Nighthawk
ShadowWolfe
DarkWolfe
A Joyous de Wolfe Christmas
BlackWolfe
Serpent
A Wolfe Among Dragons
Scorpion
StormWolfe
Dark Destroyer
The Lion of the North
Walls of Babylon
The Best Is Yet To Be
BattleWolfe
Castle of Bones

De Wolfe Pack Generations:
WolfeHeart
WolfeStrike
WolfeSword
WolfeBlade
WolfeLord
WolfeShield
Nevermore
WolfeAx

The Executioner Knights:
By the Unholy Hand

The Mountain Dark
Starless
A Time of End
Winter of Solace
Lord of the Sky
Splendid Hour
The Whispering Night
Netherworld
Lord of the Shadows
Of Mortal Fury

The de Russe Legacy:
The Falls of Erith
Lord of War: Black Angel
The Iron Knight
Beast
The Dark One: Dark Knight
The White Lord of Wellesbourne
Dark Moon
Dark Steel
A de Russe Christmas Miracle
Dark Warrior

The de Lohr Dynasty:
While Angels Slept
Rise of the Defender
Steelheart
Shadowmoor
Silversword
Spectre of the Sword
Unending Love
Archangel
A Blessed de Lohr Christmas

Realm of Angels

Highland Warriors of Munro:
The Red Lion
Deep Into Darkness

The House of de Garr:
Lord of Light
Realm of Angels

Saxon Lords of Hage:
The Crusader
Kingdom Come

High Warriors of Rohan:
High Warrior

The House of Ashbourne:
Upon a Midnight Dream

The House of D'Aurilliac:
Valiant Chaos

The House of De Dere:
Of Love and Legend

St. John and de Gare Clans:
The Warrior Poet

The House of de Bretagne:
The Questing

The House of Summerlin:
The Legend

The Kingdom of Hendocia:
Kingdom by the Sea

Regency Historical Romance:
Sin Like Flynn: A Regency
Historical Romance Duet

Gothic Regency Romance:
Emma

Contemporary Romance:

**Kathlyn Trent/Marcus Burton
Series:**
Valley of the Shadow
The Eden Factor
Canyon of the Sphinx

**The American Heroes Anthology
Series:**
The Lucius Robe
Fires of Autumn
Evenshade
Sea of Dreams
Purgatory

**Other non-connected
Contemporary Romance:**
Lady of Heaven
Darkling, I Listen
In the Dreaming Hour
River's End
The Fountain

Sons of Poseidon:
The Immortal Sea

**Pirates of Britannia Series (with
Eliza Knight):**
Savage of the Sea by Eliza Knight
Leader of Titans by Kathryn Le
Veque
The Sea Devil by Eliza Knight
Sea Wolfe by Kathryn Le Veque

Note: All Kathryn's novels are designed to be read as stand-alones, although many have cross-over characters or cross-over family groups. Novels that are grouped together have related characters or family groups. You will notice that some series have the same books; that is because they are cross-overs. A hero in one book may be the secondary character in another.

There is NO reading order except by chronology, but even in that case, you can still read the books as stand-alones. No novel is connected to another by a cliff hanger, and every book has an HEA.

Series are clearly marked. All series contain the same characters or family groups except the American Heroes Series, which is an anthology with unrelated characters.

For more information, find it in **A Reader's Guide to the Medieval World of Le Veque**.

About Kathryn Le Veque

Bringing the Medieval to Romance

KATHRYN LE VEQUE is a critically acclaimed, multiple USA TODAY Bestselling author, an Indie Reader bestseller, a charter Amazon All-Star author, and a #1 bestselling, award-winning, multi-published author in Medieval Historical Romance with over 100 published novels.

Kathryn is a multiple award nominee and winner, including the winner of Uncaged Book Reviews Magazine 2017 and 2018 "Raven Award" for Favorite Medieval Romance. Kathryn is also a multiple RONE nominee (InD'Tale Magazine), holding a record for the number of nominations. In 2018, her novel WARWOLFE was the winner in the Romance category of the Book Excellence Award and in 2019, her novel A WOLFE AMONG DRAGONS won the prestigious RONE award for best pre-16th century romance.

Kathryn is considered one of the top Indie authors in the world with over 2M copies in circulation, and her novels have been translated into several languages. Kathryn recently signed with Sourcebooks Casablanca for a Medieval Fight Club series, first published in 2020.

In addition to her own published works, Kathryn is also the President/CEO of Dragonblade Publishing, a boutique publishing house specializing in Historical Romance. Dragonblade's success has seen it rise in the ranks to become Amazon's #1 e-book publisher of Historical Romance (K-Lytics report July 2020).

Kathryn loves to hear from her readers. Please find Kathryn on Facebook at Kathryn Le Veque, Author, or join her on Twitter @kathrynleveque. Sign up for Kathryn's blog at www.kathrynleveque.com for the latest news and sales.